STRANDED

STUART JAMES

First published in 2020 by Bloodhound Books

www.bloodhoundbooks.com

Print ISBN 978-1-913419-89-9

ALSO BY STUART JAMES

The House on Rectory Lane

Apartment 6

To my wife, Tara, and my beautiful children Oli and Ava.
Also, for my mum and dad.
The most incredible people in my life. Always.

PROLOGUE

I've always been taught to respect others; that's the main rule. The one I've followed all my life. I'm a gentleman. If you ask anyone for a character reference who knows me, they'd say the same. I hold doors open; I knock before entering a room.

I'm the last to sit at dinner, and the fork doesn't enter my mouth until everyone else has started to eat. The cutlery must sit right, in the correct position. I use a napkin.

I stand when someone enters a room and welcome people, friend or stranger. The latter will usually become an associate. They'll learn to trust me, and I'll do anything for anyone.

I dress impeccably, and I compliment everyone. I may comment on the style of a person's hair, their earrings, their beautiful dress, pressed shirt or elegant jacket. I'll tell them how amazing they are, how I admire what they're doing. I'll talk about their beautiful family, and I'll listen. That's another trait of mine. If someone has something to talk about, I'll give a hundred per cent concentration to what they're saying. If it's important to them, it's important to me. I make eye contact, I make the person feel special. At ease. Everyone has a voice and we're all unique in our own special way.

I never tell a rude joke, and I always laugh when someone says something funny. Of course, that's once everyone else is laughing.

I haven't laughed since the night it happened. Something snapped that night. See, I hate people who do wrong and go unpunished. It's the major flaw in life. My main bugbear. It drives me crazy, insane, psychotic. I can't control the rage as it builds inside my body. An error cannot occur without consequences.

So really there is only one way to deal with the anger.

I'm not a believer in waiting, in hearing people say that they'll get their day or karma will come to their door. I will bring that day to them.

I have to discipline the injustice.

Tonight.

It's the only way.

1

THE JOURNEY

'We're making good time.' Ben lifted the cuff of his shirtsleeve and quickly glanced at his watch.

It was just gone half four and it was getting dark. 'The flight doesn't leave for another five hours or so. It makes a change being early for once. Staying on the M25 would be a nightmare. I hate that road at the best of times. This route should be much quicker. The roads aren't great, but we can't risk the traffic building.'

He directed the remark towards his wife who was deep in concentration, her eyes flicking left and right over her Kindle screen like windscreen wipers furiously batting water from a heavy storm.

Ben glanced in the rear-view mirror, slightly adjusting it to see his daughter better. 'Milly, you excited?'

'One second.' She removed the phone from her ear. 'Yes, Dad. Although not as much as you, it would seem.' She smiled, bringing the phone back to the side of her head and tucking it under her long blonde hair.

'What's the first thing you're going to do when you get there?' Ben asked, hoping for a little conversation to dampen the boredom. 'I say we drop the bags and jump straight into the pool. You up for that?' Ben saw his daughter whispering into the phone. He turned the radio down slightly, listening to her conversation as Milly felt for the sound bar and cut the volume on the phone.

'Dad, please. What are you like?'

'Who are you talking to anyway?'

'Zac. He says hello.'

Ahh. *Zac. The on-off boyfriend who flits in and out of my daughter's life whenever he pleases. Who comes into my house, places his feet on my coffee table and leaves his jacket lying across the sofa.* 'Yeah. Hi, Zac. Gonna miss you,' Ben sniped.

Milly rolled her eyes, realising her father's sarcasm.

'Laura, straight into the pool, an early morning dip before a few hours' sleep and then lounging all day on the beach?' Ben looked towards his wife; she was oblivious to the outside world. Lost in a book trance.

'Huh?'

'Are you excited?'

Laura took a deep breath, pushed out a huge sigh and dropped the Kindle onto her lap. 'Of course I'm excited, Ben. It's been a long time coming.' She smiled at her husband, tempted to bring the Kindle back into view. She hated being interrupted while reading. 'Why don't you and Milly go for a swim while I have a glass of wine on the balcony? That sounds so much better.' They weren't arriving in Barcelona until the early hours, and the last thing on her mind was plunging into the pool.

Ben turned the radio back up. The Eagles were playing 'Hotel California'. The place they were going may not be that extravagant, Ben thought, but at least his family were together, and they were going to enjoy the holiday.

They'd reached Surrey on their way to Gatwick airport. They'd set off from north London early, giving themselves plenty of time. They'd stopped at the services just before the M25 for snacks and a quick toilet break. The roads were quiet, and the satnav was bringing them deep into the countryside. Ben hated motorways and had driven a couple of junctions before quickly coming off.

Milly was still talking to Zac; Laura had her head down. Ben opened the window to get some fresh air. The rain had started, a drizzle at first, the wiper blades kicking into action, gliding the water away, a gentle nudge as if to say, 'You're not wanted.'

And then it seemed like the sky had opened up, an uncontrollable cascade pouring from above. The rain flicked into the car, wetting the side of Ben's face. He edged his right foot forward, tapping the brakes.

'Dad, the window! I'm getting soaked,' Milly exclaimed.

'Sorry. I don't know where this weather came from. It was dry a few minutes ago. All it's done is rain lately. It won't be like this in Barcelona. How good will it be to see the sun, huh?'

Milly ended the phone call to Zac and leant forward between her mother and father. 'I'm hungry. Are there any sandwiches left?'

'I think your mother had the last ham and cheese. There's a tuna one if I'm not mistaken.' Ben looked to his left at the carrier bag in the footwell.

'Tuna-schmuna. I'll pass.' Milly placed her chin on the back of her father's shirt. 'Wow. This really is the middle of nowhere.' She looked to her left and out of the window, glancing over the fields that seemed to go on for miles. The sky was a deep grey, the clouds were thick and sweeping fast above them, the rain pelting down heavily. It was getting dark.

Ben reached forward, wiping the windscreen with the back of his hand, jabbing the brake, the car jolting slightly as he ramped up the heater and welcomed the warm air now blasting into the vehicle.

They were twenty miles from Gatwick; Ben preferred the back roads. He'd got stuck in traffic on an M-road previously, a seven and a half-hour tailback which needless to say, ruined their short break.

'You don't like Zac that much, huh?' It was more an observation from his daughter than a question. Milly braced herself for the answer. She wanted her parents to like Zac. They'd been seeing each other for a while now, and it was getting serious. Milly and Zac spoke about their future plans and moving in together. She kept that part from her father.

Ben gripped the corner of his seat, unprepared for the barrage of questions. 'It's not that I don't like him.'

'Umm.' Laura's tone was laced with sarcasm.

Ben turned his head to the left. 'Oh, you're still with us? I thought you'd fallen out miles back.'

'You'd love that,' Laura said, a pert smile on her face.

'He's just, oh, I don't know. Help me out here, Laura.'

'I like him. You can dig your own hole,' his wife instructed.

Ben took a deep breath. 'Okay. A father… Most fathers, well, fathers I know anyway–'

Laura burst out laughing. 'Go on. This will be interesting.'

'No one is ever good enough for their princess. That's all I'm saying. Plus his eyes are a little close together.'

Laura winced at her husband's remark as she placed the Kindle back on her lap, stretching her arms above her head. 'Come on, Ben. Let's face it. You'll never get used to the attention Milly gets. It's natural. I know where you're coming from–'

'Dad, look out!'

Ben slammed the brakes. A man was standing on the road, a bright neon jacket glinting in the darkness. He had a hood pulled over his head; only his thick stubble was visible. He was swinging his right arm, beckoning for the car to turn left.

Ben wound the window further down and rolled the car to

where he was standing. 'Hi. What's the problem?' The wind pounded rain against Ben's face.

'The road's shut ahead. There's a tree down. You need to take this route.' The guy's voice was deep, unfriendly. The instruction was a quick order and a *get going* type of statement.

Ben had stopped in the middle of the road. He was tapping the screen of the satnav. He waited a couple of seconds, looking in the rear-view mirror for any other vehicles. He hadn't seen one for ages. He peered to his left-hand side, looking into the distance. 'I'm sorry, but it looks like this will take us around in one big circle. Are you sure...?'

'Move!' the guy shouted.

Ben spun the steering wheel, doing as he was instructed. As he drove, the glare of the man's bright jacket disappeared out of view.

'Charming. What the hell was his problem?' Ben asked as he closed the window.

'Wouldn't you be narky out here, diverting traffic? He must be freezing, bless him.' Laura had powered her Kindle down.

Ben kept quiet, watching the road ahead, the full beams forcing light along the path in front of them. It looked like a dirt track, a mix of sprouting grass and pebbles. There were fields either side of the pathway which spread out for miles, broken only by the track ahead. Short, stumpy poles were planted on the side of the road, and barbed wire hung loosely, perhaps pushed aside by hikers wanting to explore the bleak surroundings.

Gravel crunched under the tyres. They were alone and Ben felt as though he was a pawn being drawn into a tournament he wasn't interested in playing. It seemed the stranger on the road was playing stupid games he didn't want to be a part of.

The route on the satnav rolled in one huge circle. 'Look, he's told us the wrong way to go. For Christ's sake. There's always some mishap to ruin the plans.'

Laura pushed her body forward. 'There must be another way surely?' She continually tapped the screen.

'Dad, turn back. I don't have a good feeling about this.'

Ben contemplated what his daughter had said. But there was nowhere to turn. The road was narrow. They'd struggle to pass an oncoming vehicle. The rain was still pelting down, heavy droplets of water hitting the windscreen. It was dark, and they were alone. He thought about reversing. The guy they'd encountered would just order them back. Tell them it's the route they had to take. He'd force them. *Maybe I could reverse hard; he'll see us coming and move out of the way*, Ben thought.

The satnav continued to recalculate the route. Three miles had been added to the journey.

It was one huge detour. For what? Why did he send us this way? A wind-up? His way of getting kicks? Ben began to feel uneasy. *If this really was a diverted route, where were all the other cars? Why wasn't there traffic? People standing out on the road and asking what was happening? Vehicles revving? Overheating? Tempers fraying? Shouts, panic? People realising they'd miss their flight?* Gatwick airport had thousands of visitors during any day. Why was his family the only one on the diverted road to the airport? *Maybe the satnav was indeed wrong. It happens. But something isn't right.*

Ben needed to take his mind off the situation. 'We've got the passports, right?'

Laura placed her hand on his leg. 'Yes. We have the passports.'

'Sun cream, mosquito repellent, rubber dingy?' Ben laughed. The suitcases rattled in the back as the tyres bounced into potholes. 'Christ, we'll be lucky to make it in one piece. This road is a bloody nightmare.' Ben steered the car left and right, hoping the wheels were coping.

'Slow down. There's no rush. We still have loads of time, Ben.' Laura looked ahead as Ben slowed the car. 'What's going on? There's something in front of us.'

Milly was sat up, still pushed forward between her parents. 'It's a coach. See, the guy was right. It is a diversion.' There was relief in her voice.

Ben pulled behind the coach and pressed the car horn, not expecting it to sound so loud. 'Oops.'

'Have patience, love. Maybe they're taking a leak.'

'What, all of them?' Ben asked.

'When you have to go...' Laura pointed out. 'Oh, I'm feeling excited now – a week of sun. You don't know how much I need it! We all do. I worry though, you know.'

Again, Ben wound the window down, pushing his head out to see what was happening in front. 'About what?' He wiped the water from his short black hair and closed the window.

'Leaving the house,' Laura said.

'The neighbours said they'd keep an eye out. They'll call us if anything happens,' Ben stated. He didn't want Laura's holiday marred by concerns about what was going on at home.

Laura thought for a second. 'I'd rather they didn't. What you don't know and all that.'

'All I'm saying, Laura, is there's no need to worry. Oh, for Christ's sake. What is going on?' Ben hammered his fist on the horn, holding it down for a second too long. The noise vibrated through the fields. 'That's it.'

'That's what, Ben?' Laura asked.

He opened the car door. The cold air hit him as he noticed the smell of damp grass hanging over where he stood. 'I'm going to kick some ass.'

Laura turned to her daughter, sarcastically rolling her eyes. Milly laughed, trying her best to hide it from her father.

The car door closed and Ben moved towards the coach.

A couple of minutes passed. The anticipation caused silence between the two women. Laura turned the radio off and the heater to the lowest setting. The car engine was still running. Five minutes had passed, now six.

'Where is he, Mum? He's been gone a long time.'

Laura was waiting, hoping to see her husband shaking hands with the driver, apologising for being so aggressive and wishing everyone a safe journey.

Milly said, 'He wouldn't do anything stupid. Fronting someone up, arguing with them, would he?'

'Your father? No, he's all mouth and trousers.'

They both laughed.

Another two minutes passed. Laura opened the passenger door, pushing hard against the wind. Milly followed her mother. They stood out on the country road. 'Ben? Are you okay?' Laura called. She glanced at her daughter. 'Wait there.'

'I'm coming with you.'

They moved slowly, edging towards the coach. The road was vacant behind them. There was no sign of Ben or the coach passengers. They looked into the fields to the right side, no movement, no shadows, no sign of anyone. To the left, the same. It felt like it was just the two of them out here in the middle of nowhere. Laura crept forward, twigs breaking under her trainers. She wore a light top and denim shorts. The cold hit her hard, and she wished she had worn something much warmer. Her hand reached behind, holding Milly's, guiding her.

Laura moved closer to the coach, assisted by the lights from their car. She saw the back tyres were flat, like someone had jammed a knife into them. She climbed onto the grass verge, trying to peer inside the window. It was too dark to see anything, the engine was running, and the windows were stained with condensation from the inside.

'Ben, are you okay?' Laura gripped Milly's hand. They stood, waiting, listening. Then they moved around the back of the coach to the left side. 'Where are you, Ben? This isn't funny.'

Suddenly, someone came to the door of the coach. 'Go back. Please, both of you go back.'

'Ben, you're scaring me. What's happened?'

'I beg you, don't come to the door. Please, stay there.'

Laura stopped suddenly, causing Milly to bump her head off the corner of her mum's shoulder.

'Dad, what's going on?'

Ben disappeared from the doors.

Laura turned to Milly. 'I'm going to see what's happened.'

'I am too. I'm not staying on my own.'

Laura and Milly edged towards the front of the coach. The country lane was empty, only for the coach blocking the middle of the road. There was no sign of anyone. From where they stood, it seemed like the passengers of the coach had disappeared, leaving the vehicle like a ghost ship sailing alone in the middle of the ocean. Laura spun around, watching the bleakness behind. She searched for a vehicle light, a sign of civilisation. They reached the open door of the coach. Laura stretched her foot forward, placing it on the first step, hoisting herself up with the handrail to her left. Milly waited on the road.

Laura stepped up beside the driver's seat. She saw Ben, walking slowly along the floor of the coach. He spun around.

'I told you not to come up here, Laura. Where's Milly?'

'She... she's coming behind me.' Laura looked back.

'What the heck's going on?' Milly looked along the coach and instantly realised the seriousness of the situation. People were strapped to their seats, held with thick rope; gags placed tightly around their mouths. There was a strong smell of faeces and stale urine. She looked at the people nearest to where she stood – an elderly couple, both around seventy. On the seat directly behind them sat a younger woman, strapped to the window seat. Her hair was stained with blood that was dripping onto her brown jacket, a continuous flow.

Milly screamed, panic suddenly rising through her body.

Laura was reaching out to prevent her daughter from seeing the carnage in front of them. Like passing a car accident, you see flashing blue lights, a stretcher. You drive slowly, unable to turn away, knowing you shouldn't look. But you do. You end up taking a peek and curiosity takes over. Milly looked to her left, towards the centre of the coach, seeing a woman wearing a gag, strapped tight to the aisle chair. Further back on the same side, a guy sat alone, strapped and gagged. There was a slight swelling and bruising above his right eye.

Milly dropped to her knees. 'What's happened? Who would do this?' She crawled on her hands and knees, reaching for the door, shouting, panic rising through her body. The sudden fear and rancid smell made her nauseous and she threw up onto the steps.

Ben was standing halfway along the coach, passengers either side of where he stood. Five people in total, tied to their seats. Reading lights above their heads allowed him to see their sullen expressions.

'Laura, where's your phone?' Ben asked. 'Call the police. Dial 999 now. Go.'

His wife was in shock as she knelt on the floor, calling for Milly, searching for her daughter.

'Laura, your phone, hon. Where is it?' Ben shouted.

She was yelling, screaming for her daughter to keep hidden. Laura looked up. 'In the car. The phones are in the car.'

'Laura, I need you to concentrate. Please. Listen to me. You and Milly need to follow me down the stairs and outside. Stay right behind me. We'll get a phone and call for help. Let's go.'

As Laura mustered all the strength she had to lift her body off the floor, a phone rang from the dashboard. A deathly silence fell as Ben and Laura looked towards each other. The phone played an old-fashioned ringtone that made Ben picture a desolate house up in the hills, an echo sounding through the halls.

'Answer it, Ben. We need to deliver the news to whoever is calling and then we can get help,' Laura insisted.

Ben took a deep breath, straightening his body, filling his lungs with the foul, rusted odour inside the coach, then reached for the phone. 'Hello.'

Milly stood at the door. She composed herself, panting heavily, then turned around, watching her father. Laura was holding her hands over her mouth to control the screech which threatened to escape from her shocked body.

Ben pressed the speakerphone, thinking it was better if they all heard the caller. Again, Ben spoke, 'Hello.' Silence. Ben glanced towards his family. He shrugged his shoulders awkwardly, as if to say, 'What shall I do?'

They waited, their bodies numb with anticipation. Suddenly, they heard a voice. 'I'm so glad you came along when you did. I was beginning to think it was all for nothing.'

Ben was startled; he looked at Laura and Milly. He wanted to yell at the caller. Instead, he spoke, 'You sick bastard. Why would you do something like this?'

The caller's breathing was heavy, sharp from the phone. Then silence. Ben eyed his wife, who was instructing him to hang up.

Suddenly, Ben remembered the guy, standing at the foot of the road, waving his arms, forcing them along the quiet country lane. *It was a trap; we were meant to find the coach.* 'We're calling the police. I know who you are.' Ben waited, about to hang up.

'Here's how it plays out. I have your undivided attention now. I knew I would.' There was a slight pause. 'In total, there were eight passengers on the coach. I counted them. I saw for myself.

They're alive, but by the end of the night, some may not be so fortunate.'

'What the heck is your problem? You're ill. Why would you do this?'

The guy hesitated for a second, pausing. Then he took a deep breath. 'So, here's how it plays out. Tonight, you'll find out why they're here. You're going to assist me in the games I've set up. It's fate, you coming along when you did. I can't do it all on my own so you – and only you – are going to help me. Call the police, and I'll kill you all instantly. I have software which will monitor the phone. I'll know if you send a text message, make a call or if there's any activity other than answering my calls. The same goes if you untie anyone. I'll call again shortly with your instructions. By the way, I'd wipe up the vomit from your daughter's top. It's not a good look.'

As the phone went dead, a shuffle came from behind where they stood.

Someone was charging towards them from the back of the coach.

2

THE COACH

'Let me off. Let me off the fucking coach!'

Ben spun around. He sprung forward and dropped the guy like a concrete slab smashing onto the ground. He held his face against the floor of the coach. The guy was muttering, squirming and trying to wriggle loose.

'Who are you?' Ben shouted as he eased his right arm off the back of his neck.

'I'm the driver. I was hiding out at the back. I'm not a part of this.'

'So how did you get here?' Ben asked.

The driver said in a London accent, 'This guy approached me on the way home from work; he said he had a coach. Apparently, he drove for the company in the past and they let him go. He told me all I had to do was take the passengers to the airport. He paid me half and said I'd get the rest when the job was complete. If I didn't do it, he'd kill me. He knew where I lived; he knew my son's name. His instructions were to get in the driver's seat and not to look at anyone. If I didn't do it, he'd kill me. I have a fucking family, man. I agreed to do it; he gave instructions, where to find the coach.'

The driver, his face still pressed to the floor, continued, 'I hadn't heard from him and assumed he'd decided against it. Then, he turned up again as I came out of the depot, telling me what I had to do. I went to the address. I got on the coach, found the keys in the ignition. It should have been a simple job, there and back, return the coach where I'd found it. As I drove, this guy flagged us down. He told me the road was closed. Something about a tree coming down and there being no way around: he directed me along this road. He assured me it was a diversion. I shouted, knowing the road would bring us back around. A hood concealed his face but I knew it was him; I recognised the voice. As I turned up here, he walked in front. I kept driving, watching him in front until he turned towards me.'

The driver swallowed, and then said, 'He was holding a shotgun. I got off the seat and charged down to the back. He made his way up the steps, onto the coach. He fired. Two shots into the ceiling. The noise was deafening. I dropped to the floor.

'The coach was full of people screaming, begging for their lives. I could hear him, hitting people with the butt of his gun. Then it went quiet. I heard his footsteps, moving towards me. I kept still. I couldn't let him know where I was or alert him I was hiding. I guess he didn't look for me as his feud is with the passengers. A minute or so later, I heard people getting off the coach. He jumped onto the road and they walked away.'

Ben helped the guy up. He looked at him, seeing the anguish in his eyes. The pity. He wore a heavy jumper, jeans and his hair was long and scruffy. It looked like it hadn't been cut for months. He had a thick beard, but it was neat, shaped. 'He's watching us,' Ben informed the driver.

'How do you know?'

Ben pointed to the dashboard. He'd returned the phone where he'd found it. 'He called a few minutes ago, giving me instructions. Saying we'd find out why this is happening. If I let anyone go, he'll kill us all. The guy's messed up. What's your name?'

'I'm Andrew.' He held out his hand, gripping Ben's.

'Good to meet you, although I'd prefer if it were under better circumstances,' Ben joked.

'I heard a phone ringing. I couldn't make out the voice. I hoped it was someone who was going to help,' Andrew said. 'It's obvious that isn't the case.'

'We need to stay put. Keep calm.' Ben introduced his wife and daughter, then he moved to the door. He turned back to Andrew. 'What did the guy look like?'

Andrew hesitated, recalling. 'He was tall, well built. I only saw him from a distance. It was definitely the same guy who approached me, asking me to drive the coach. He wore a yellow mac which glowed, bright stripes or badges at the top of his sleeves. That's all I remember. He's going to kill us, isn't he?'

'Try not to panic. We need to stay focused.' Ben turned, addressing the passengers. 'Look, my name is Ben Stevens. We won't hurt you.' He placed his hand on his daughter's shoulder, edging her forward into view. 'This is Milly, my daughter. She's eighteen, and wants to study law. She still lives at home but is moving out soon. She has a boyfriend. I admit, he's a bit of an arsehole. But what father likes their daughter's boyfriend, right? Sorry, Milly.'

Milly was wiping the vomit from her mouth with the back of her hand. 'Talk, Milly,' he murmured to his daughter. 'Say something. Make them feel at ease.'

She stared at the faces of the passengers as they watched her, their eyes focused. 'Hi. We're on our way to the airport. We're going to Barcelona.' Milly went silent as the situation dawned on her.

Her mother stepped forward. 'Look, we're going to get help. I'm so sorry for what's happened. We'll do our best to get you all out of here safely.' Laura's voice cracked. She turned around, holding her hands to her face. Once she'd composed herself, she turned to Ben. 'We need to remove their gags.'

'We can't. You heard what the guy said on the phone. Release them, and he'll finish all of us.'

Laura thought for a second. Her body was shaking. She fought the sick feeling in the pit of her stomach, knowing she had to take charge of herself and gain control. The coach was like an ice bucket. She looked towards the windows, knowing the guy may be outside. Watching them. Trickles of water dripped down the glass as the condensation began to clear. 'He said we couldn't untie them. He never mentioned anything about removing the gags from their mouths.' Laura looked towards the elderly couple at the front. 'Quick, Ben. Help these people.'

They moved to each of the passengers. Laura went to the elderly couple first, gently undoing the knots in the cloths tied around their mouths.

Relief was clear on the old guy's face as he gulped air deep into his lungs. He pushed forward, struggling to get loose, turning his head to the left. 'Mary, are you okay?' There was fear in his wife's eyes but she nodded. Then, sharply, he directed a question to Laura. 'Our son and daughter-in-law were sat directly behind us. Have they been taken? It all happened so quickly.'

Laura was silent. She glanced at the woman behind, then looked at the empty seat next to her. After a few seconds, she crouched beside the older man. 'Your daughter-in-law is here. We'll find your son.'

'I heard the gunshots. I was asleep. He was like a wild animal, then he marched people off the coach. I'm Edward. This is my wife, Mary.'

Laura leant forward, pushing Edward's long grey hair out of

his face. He looked like a drinker; his cheeks were heavily veined. His skin was lined and wrinkled. His wife wore glasses, and her hair was brown and shoulder-length, resting on her black jacket. She looked slightly younger than her husband.

'I'm Laura Stevens. Sit tight for the moment until we work out how to get you off the coach,' she instructed. Laura joined her husband, moving slowly along the coach, making sure everyone was as comfortable as possible. She reached a woman on her left side who was sitting alone. 'I'm Laura. I'm here with my husband and daughter. We're going to get you help. As soon as it's safe, we'll get you out of here. Were you travelling alone?' she asked.

The woman looked up. 'I'm Lydia. We were brought onto this coach for a reason, my husband and I.'

Laura crouched, pushing Lydia's hair back, feeling the damp sweat. The woman had a certain vulnerability about her; she looked sad as if life had failed her. Laura didn't want to ask questions now. 'I'm so sorry,' was all she could think of to say.

Once Ben had checked on the remaining passenger, a lad who was sat on his own, he moved towards Laura. His voice was low as he murmured, 'What do we do?'

She spun in a circle. Her head was dizzy and confused as she took in the carnage around her. She glanced at the windows. 'I don't know if he can see us. When Milly moved towards the door, he saw her vomit. If we can keep the main lights off, it will make it more difficult for him to see inside. Let's keep the lights as low as possible.' Laura suddenly thought. 'Unless... A camera. Quick, Ben. We need to make sure. Check up and down the aisle. If there's a way he's watching us, we need to stop him.'

They moved along the coach, running their hands along the luggage hold, the empty seats and over the ceiling. They found nothing.

'What now?' Laura asked.

'I don't know. We wait, I guess. We need to keep everyone calm. Milly will be great. She has a way about her. People instantly warm to her,' Ben said.

Their daughter was now talking to the driver, Andrew. Her voice was raised slightly, and her hands were placed on his shoulders as she comforted him.

'We need a torch,' Ben stated. Andrew reached into the glove compartment and handed him a heavy duty torch.

'How are you bearing up, Andrew?' Ben asked. He moved the torch beam around the coach, keeping the light as low as possible. Worried faces and startled eyes looked back at him.

'I'm all right,' said Andrew. 'I feel a little claustrophobic. If I'm honest, I'm not great in these situations. I panic. I can't even get into a lift without freaking out, wondering if I'll reach the next floor. Usually I take the stairs. It's less hassle.'

Sweat was forming on the driver's brow, his cheeks were flushed, and he furiously wiped his forehead with the back of his hands.

'You can cope, Andrew. I know you can. Keep calm and inhale deeply, push out slowly,' Milly suggested.

The driver heaved air in through his nose, his broad chest expanding, contracting.

Ben looked out through the front window. It was so bleak. They'd been on the coach for an hour or so. In that time, they hadn't seen a light or any sign of civilisation. It dawned on him that they'd miss the flight and he felt guilty for a second as he thought about running and leaving the passengers to their fates.

'So let's go through our situation.' Ben's voice was low, hushed. 'We have an elderly couple at the front; their daughter-in-law is sat directly behind them. She was hit in the head, but she's conscious and with it, so to speak. Her husband, who was sat next to her, has been taken.

'Further down on the left, there's the woman sat on her own.

I spoke with her briefly. She was with her husband. Her name is Lydia and he's Jack. He's gone.

'And there's a guy sat a couple of seats behind her, Stephen. He's coping. He has a swollen eye, but it's not life-threatening. He was with a friend. Another male. Gareth, I think he said. That's about all I got from him. He seems to be calm – nothing for us to worry about at the moment.'

'Excuse me. I need water. Can I have some water, please?'

Ben turned, looking at Edward. His wife, Mary, was sat next to him; her eyes now closed, possibly her coping mechanism.

'Okay. Give me a second. We have a crate of water in the boot of our car.' Ben addressed Milly, Laura and Andrew, who were stood together at the front. 'I have to go to the car.'

'Ben, it's not safe. You can't go out there.' Laura crouched, looking towards the door which was still open. 'Do you think we can get the heaters going? These people must be freezing.'

Andrew climbed into the driver's seat, an array of buttons and switches in front of him. 'We can keep the reading lights on, it will enable the passengers to see and hopefully stop them freaking out. If we point them away towards the front, it will make it more difficult for him to see them from outside.'

Andrew started the engine, and flicked the row of green switches in front of the steering wheel. The heaters kicked in and began to warm the inside of the coach. The condensation began to clear which meant it was easier to see inside. But it seemed more important to warm the passengers.

Laura wallowed in the comfort of the heat, working its way through the coach. 'He said that no one could leave, but I'm guessing it's okay for us to keep warm.'

Andrew climbed out of the seat, then moved along the aisle, adjusting the reading lights above the passenger's heads.

When he returned to the front, Ben asked him, 'Why is he holding these people here?'

'Because he's a frigging nut job,' Milly piped up.

'There has to be a reason. Think about it. Five were left. Well, six if you include Andrew here. He's taken three passengers. Why not strap them all up? What's his reason? Why not take everyone?' Ben asked.

'A ransom?' Laura suggested.

'Please. Water.' Edward was licking his lips, trying to moisten them.

'I need to go to the car,' said Ben.

'Ben, no. I won't allow it. He'll kill you. Please.'

'He hasn't said anything about us leaving. His beef is with the passengers.' Ben moved towards the open door. He stepped down, holding the rail.

'Dad, please don't go,' Milly shouted.

'I have no choice, Milly. I'll be careful, I promise.' Ben crept along the outside of the coach. Every tyre had been deflated. He turned his head towards the windows. From out here it was difficult to see the passengers. They needed to keep the inside as dark as possible.

His car was around twenty feet from the back of the coach. The headlights were still on. The radio was off. The mobile phones were on the seats. He couldn't risk getting them. If the guy was watching Ben, he'd see it. As he slowly moved forward, he looked into the fields on his right. There was silence. He felt his stomach turn, a tight knot twisting in his belly.

Suddenly a twig broke. Someone was there. Ben estimated the sound to be ten, maybe fifteen feet from where he stood. He froze, struggling to focus, his ears alert, now frightened to take another step. The phone call played out in his mind – the guy's voice. *I'm so glad you came along when you did. I was beginning to think it was all for nothing.* What did he mean? Was he waiting for them? Were they chosen?

Ben waited. It seemed like hours since he stood on the

coach. He listened. Shadows danced between the trees. He could make out the blurred shapes, only just. His eyes darted left. Right. Then he ran towards the car. Panting deeply he reached the boot, and clicked the lock. The automatic opener whined. He moved the cases aside, picked up the water and hurried back, leaving the boot open. The noise of closing it would draw too much attention.

A minute later, he was back on the coach.

'Oh, thank God. Don't be a hero again. Do you hear me?' Laura grabbed her husband, kissing his cheek.

Milly passed through the coach, lifting water bottles to the mouths of the passengers. They gulped the liquid like they'd done a hike through the Sahara Desert.

The woman on her left thanked her.

Milly crouched. 'I'm sorry you're going through this. Lydia, isn't it?'

'That's right. And you're Milly?'

'You got it. How are you bearing up?'

'Apart from being held prisoner and Jack missing, fine.' She smiled.

Milly offered a smile in return. 'We'll find Jack. You have to believe me, Lydia.'

The woman stared ahead like something was on her mind, a sudden distraction.

'We were going on holiday in a couple of months. It was supposed to be a rekindle if you like. To make a lost connection. A patcher-upper. Things haven't been good between us for a while. I know he's not coming back.'

'He is coming back. Don't think like that,' Milly said.

Lydia turned her head towards the young girl. 'We did a bad thing.'

3

LYDIA AND JACK

'I'll be home late, hon, I have a meeting after work. You know how these things can drag?'

'Really?' Lydia pulled the blanket further up her body. She didn't want to sound like she was nagging her husband. God knows, it seemed all they did lately was argue. 'You've forgotten, haven't you?'

Jack turned, looking for his shirt. 'Forgotten? What? What have I forgotten, Lydia?'

She turned away, pushing her head deeper into the bedding. He'd promised to take her for a meal later this evening.

Jack picked up his shirt. He waved it, hoping to shake out the creases along the back. 'You don't need to wait up.'

Lydia didn't answer. She listened to the car pulling off the drive and closed her eyes.

She woke at just gone 10am, shuffled out of bed and jumped into the shower.

Lydia stood under the hot water. She and Jack had been married almost ten years. But lately, she'd had suspicions. He returned from work later and later. His phone pinged continuously. He brought flowers. Until now Jack had rarely brought her flowers.

Today, she had it all worked out. Enough was enough. Jack worked on Bond Street. He commuted daily from their four-bedroom semi-detached home in Surrey, and only brought the car when he had to visit clients. It was cheaper and much more affordable than living in London. They'd looked, but even a two-bedroom flat was out of the question.

But now, Jack had worked his way up, with an enviable wage packet and a desirable pension. His boss, Chloe, had often said she'd die without him. The company would never survive.

He had never introduced Lydia to Chloe. She'd checked her LinkedIn profile. Early fifties, the boss of a multimillion-pound company and as hot as fuck. She imagined Chloe waltzing through the office, short skirt, flaunting her bust. Jack was putty in her hands.

Lydia had no proof though, apart from the late nights, and the non-existent sex life. But today, she would find out for sure.

She turned off the shower and reached out, eyes closed, pawing for the towel. She stood on the mat, drying her body. As she moved along the landing to her bedroom and flicked on the lights, she noticed the power was off.

Click.

Click.

Nothing. 'Damn this.' She got her phone, unplugging it from the charger and dialled Jack's number.

'Hi. Is everything okay? I'm going into a meeting.'

'The electrics. There's been another power cut.'

'Okay. Downstairs above the front door, you'll find the consumer box. You'll need to get the small stepladder from under the stairs and the furthest switch on the right, just flick it up.'

'That's it?'

'That's it, Lydia. I have to go.'

'Jack?'

The phone went dead.

Lydia sat at her desk. She looked out of her office window at the front of the house, seeing the row of homes with empty drives. She felt so alone. She didn't have the confidence to speak with the neighbours. She envied Jack. He knew most of them and would often wave across the road when they'd go out together. That was seldom these days, and besides, Lydia preferred to be cooped up indoors. It meant she didn't have to face anyone. It was almost 3pm, and an empty wine bottle sat on her left side next to the heavy brass clock. Another, already half-finished, flashed in her peripheral vision.

She fired off the email she'd been writing – the satisfaction when you'd completed another task and swoosh. The sound was welcoming – the end of her day.

They didn't need the money, but working was a way for Lydia to keep sane. Yes, it was great at first, the opportunity to work from home, be her own boss. But the temptation to drink was always present. It started with a quick glass here and there. Then there were accusations fired towards her when Jack got home. She'd dismissed his comments, laughing them off. One glass led to two, then a bottle. Now, she'd easily polish off two bottles with a minimal hangover, still able to function, able to hide it from Jack.

An hour later, Lydia had started bottle number three.

Lydia stared at the fuzzy screen. She'd briefly nodded off. Now, the room was blurry. She blinked, focusing on a picture of her and Jack. A night out, a local restaurant, her arm held out with the bracelet Jack had brought her dangling from her wrist, capturing a selfie. Her husband wore a white jumper, his face cleanly shaven, hair forward, a wide grin. She hadn't seen him smile for so long. His arm was placed around hers, holding her tight. God, they'd been so happy.

Lydia fought the thumping at the top of her head, the early signs that the three bottles of red wine had taken its toll. The power nap had diminished the buzz. Now she felt sloppy, fatigued.

Water. I need water. Lydia stood, making her way down the hall and into the kitchen, holding the wall either side for support. She took a glass from the cupboard above her head, filled it at the tap and gulped. Water spilt from her mouth, drenching her top. She refilled the glass, gulped again, then placed it on the draining board, upside down. That way, she could put it away later when it dried. It wasn't officially dirty – no lipstick smudge or wine mark, so it wasn't ready for the dishwasher.

She stood, contemplating. She knew she shouldn't go out. Not in this state. But she'd had enough. Jack told her he had a meeting. He'd left for work in his expensive suit, fancy aftershave. She imagined boss lady clicking her fingers, her skirt pulled up high. *I need to go over a few things. Sod your wife and her two bottles of wine. No, three. Don't worry about her. I'm more important. You're going places, Jack Hargreaves. Right to the top.*

Lydia turned the lights off in the hall and slammed the front door.

She ordered a taxi which brought her to Woking station. When she'd reached London, she'd battled through the crowd of people, stepping onto the escalators, holding the black handrail tightly as it moved with her hand, waltzing through the aggressive barriers, opening and closing like the mouth of an alligator until she reached Oxford Street.

Lydia stood for a moment, composing herself. Floods of people steered around her, a torrent of unfamiliar faces with deep knotted brows, sighing and unwelcoming. She contemplated tackling the traffic by crossing the road.

A taxi driver pulled slowly beside where she stood. He stuck his head out of the window, wiping his brow, then pressed the horn, making Lydia jump. She moved quickly along the street, finding a pedestrian crossing, pushing the button and waiting for the little green man to appear. It reminded her of a Monopoly board. *Go. Collect two hundred pounds. Catch your husband with his slutty boss.*

Go to jail.

Lydia moved along the street, unnoticed, ignored by the masses, the stream of people rushing towards her. The dull pain which had started at the top of her head had now spread, an invasion, sprawling across her forehead. Her cheeks ached, her lips pulsed.

The traffic to her left was stationary, behind her, the taxi driver had crawled five or so yards. He'd stopped playing with his toy horn, accepting defeat: soon he'd be able to take it out on the accelerator.

Lydia crossed the street, edging around vehicles, pushing her hips gracefully left, right, like waltzing in a large ballroom.

She reached Bond Street. Jack's office was a hundred yards on her left, a large, corporate building, fit for purpose, bright, welcoming, secure. He worked on the fourth floor.

Lydia stopped. She glanced across the street at a man and woman sat by the front window of a public house with green glazed tiles and brass fittings. She moved towards the kerb, struggling to focus. The traffic had started to roll forward, pushing, tightly packed together. She backed up, crossed the street and moved closer to the front door of the pub.

The guy wore a suit, a smart tie, hair forward – a beaming

smile. The woman was in her early fifties, elegant and oozed sophistication. A candle flickered on the oak table, a large glass of white wine rested to one side, a tumbler next to it, probably filled with whisky and coke.

Lydia watched the conversation, fiddling with her bracelet. The man cared for this woman, taking an interest, smiling with her, listening. Only this was Jack. Her Jack. Why didn't he listen to her, take an interest in what she had to say, hold her, make love to her?

Lydia's husband reached forward, clasping the woman's hands with his. He passed her a napkin and dabbed her face as the mascara ran down her cheeks. *Not a good look*, Lydia thought.

She imagined the conversation. *I can't leave my husband. I simply couldn't do it to him. What about my kids? My house? My car? But you're good, Jack. You're going to the top.*

It was all so... cosy. So very easy for the two of them. Meeting up, a drink here, a bite to eat there. A quick fondle in the office lift as it approached the fourth floor.

Suddenly the woman stood, gulped the rest of her wine, seized her expensive handbag, and made her way out of the pub.

Lydia had two choices. Confront her husband, or follow boss woman. She decided on the latter. It could get heated if she walked into the pub – another glass of wine, leading to two... a bottle.

Lydia stood motionless as boss woman – Chloe – waving her arms frantically, hailed a taxi, opened the back door and swept inside.

Shit. What now? Lydia had to think, fast. She glanced to the right; another taxi was approaching, the traffic was moving now. Lydia hailed it and the taxi pulled in. Lydia sat on the back seat. She knew it was unwise to instruct the driver to 'follow that car'. It would draw unwanted attention.

'Where to, lovely?' the driver asked.

Shit. Where to? Oh, you see that taxi in front, well the lady sat in the back is fucking my husband. I'm going to confront her. Give her a little scare; you know how it works. Put your foot down, driver.

Lydia saw the taxi turning left at Marble Arch. 'Erm, keep going please.'

'Right you are.' The driver attempted to make conversation. She listened to the continuous babble of noise without answering.

Ahead, the taxi moved along Bayswater Road, turning left.

'Erm, take a left.'

The driver swung his arms, grappling the wheel, steering where Lydia had instructed.

Panic rose through Lydia's veins. She imagined sitting here for another hour. Left, right, straight ahead. How long before the driver was suspicious? He'd catch on any second now.

As Lydia leant forward, she sighed. The taxi in front was pulling into the kerb. She left it a few seconds, then shouted for the driver to stop. Lydia got out a hundred yards ahead, paying the driver and pacing along the street to where Chloe had exited.

Lydia watched her standing on the doorstep, fumbling for her keys, rooting about, shaking her handbag, dropping to one knee, sighing, standing, flicking her head back to move the hair from her face, straightening her skirt, then she opened the front door.

'Excuse me.' Lydia grabbed the door as it began to close.

The woman looked shocked. 'Can I help you?'

'Oh, I think you can.' Lydia forced her body against the door and moved into the hall.

'What do you want? I'm calling the police.'

The house was dark. Lydia peered up the stairs; the lights were off. She shouted. 'Hello. Hello.' No one answered. It was safe.

As Chloe reached into her handbag, removing her mobile, Lydia shoved her. She stumbled backwards, hitting her head on the tiled floor.

'You stay the fuck away from my husband. Let this be a warning to you.'

Lydia now looked properly at the woman lying on the floor, blood trickling from the back of her head, her eyes motionless, chest still. 'Okay, well, I'm going. That's all I wanted to say, Stay away.'

Lydia crouched, holding two fingers to the woman's throat. 'No, no, no. Please. I'm so sorry. Wake up. Wake the hell up.' She reached for her phone. *Jack would know what to do. He can tell me what to do.*

Her phone was dead. *Shit. The power cut earlier. My phone didn't charge.*

She ran into the kitchen, rooting through drawers, pulling out a selection of leads, finding an identical charger. She plugged it into a socket in the hallway, stepping over the dead body, waiting for the screen to come alive.

A voicemail. Jack was talking.

'*Lydia, I hope you're okay. I'm going into the meeting soon. I hope your day is going well. Love you.*'

Fifty minutes later. '*Hey, babe. I'm worried. You're not answering your phone. Call me.*'

A third message.

'*Hi, Lydia. I'm not sure what's going on. You always answer your phone. Listen, I have to talk to you. I know I promised we'd go for a meal. I remembered. Please accept my apologies. Let's do it later. My boss has had shocking news. Her partner, Dana, has been diagnosed with cancer. It's terminal. She's in bits. I'm going to take her for a drink, a bit of support. I'll be home for around seven-thirty. See you then. Love you.*'

Lydia spun around, looking into the living room. A picture of boss woman in a wedding dress, another woman stood beside her. They were embracing – another photograph of the two women exchanging rings.

Lydia glanced at the dead body of Jack's boss lying in the hall.

4

THE COACH

'Is everyone okay?' Ben directed the question to the passengers. His voice was loud, authoritative. People nodded, their expressions nervous. He was stood at the front of the coach, with Laura, Milly and the driver.

The engine was loud, and it caused the seats to vibrate. The windows had cleared, and warm air worked its way along the aisle.

The elderly couple at the front had relaxed, their voices low, soft. Behind, their daughter-in-law was silent. She stared at the seat in front, only moving her head occasionally to stretch her neck.

'Mum,' said Milly, 'I think we should deal with the injuries. Maybe there will be a first aid kit somewhere.'

'Good idea.' Lydia turned to Andrew. 'Where do you keep the first aid kit?'

Andrew reached under the driver's seat, brought out a small box and handed it to Laura.

Milly sat next to the woman directly behind the elderly couple and dabbed a cloth on her forehead. She found a bottle of antiseptic and pressed the cotton wool gently against her skin, wiping. The woman winced.

'Sorry, it's just to stop the cut getting infected. How are you feeling?'

She smiled. 'I've had better days. I'm Abigail. Thanks for your help. You are all heroes in my eyes.'

Milly held her expression as if she could feel Abigail's pain and thought that maybe staying as still as possible would stop the discomfort.

Laura was now standing across the aisle. She approached the guy who was on his own, two seats behind Lydia. 'Hey, can I look at that eye?'

'Is it that bad?' he asked.

'Well, it's swollen. Here, let me try and work some magic,' Laura insisted. 'Stephen, isn't it?'

'That's right. Sorry, I can't shake your hand. I'm a little tied up.'

'A comedian, huh? Well, I'm glad you've still got your sense of humour.'

Stephen sat still, grimacing as the antiseptic cream stung his eyebrow. His fingers curled, veins appearing on the backs of his hands like railway tracks. He was shaking, pulling his head away for relief.

'There you go. All patched up.'

'Thank you. I appreciate what you're doing. Why don't you just run? Leave us here? You don't need this shit. It's not your fight.'

Laura smiled. 'I'm waiting to be mentioned in the New Year's honours list.'

'Well, I'll put in a good word.'

Laura peered around the coach. She was unsure how this would end. There was a madman on the loose, that much she knew. Why these people had been taken was anyone's guess. She needed to find out more, question the passengers. Stephen seemed like he'd talk. He had a kind face, gentle, a wide smile and tender, deep brown eyes beneath a mass of black hair that had no particular style.

'Do you mind me asking how it happened?' Laura asked.

Suddenly, Andrew shouted from the driver's seat. Laura stood and made her way to the front.

He was pointing ahead, looking through the front window. Ben was crouching, asking Milly to get down.

'What's going on?' Laura whispered.

Ben turned towards the front window as Laura knelt behind him, placing a hand on his shoulder. 'I don't know. I think Andrew saw something.'

'Saw what?'

'There it is again.' Andrew turned the full lights on. The path in front of them lit up – shadows pirouetted, sweeping from the trees either side, casting an evil presence.

'Turn the lights off. It's better if he doesn't see us,' Laura suggested.

'He knows where we are. We're sitting ducks.' Ben turned, shining the torch at the passengers. 'Has he taken all of your phones?'

Everyone nodded.

'There.' Andrew pointed to his left, into the fields. There was a figure fifty yards from where they were parked.

'Andrew, the lights! Turn them off.' Laura's voice was loud, sharp.

'Mum, I'm scared.'

Laura reached for Milly's arm.

Andrew turned the key and flicked a switch on the dash-board. The lights went out. The whirring of the heaters cut instantly, the engine died and everyone was silent.

'I'm going to the door. I need to know if this lunatic is

outside.' Ben turned, facing the back of the coach. 'No one make a sound, not a peep, cough or spit. You hear?'

Edward and Mary, the elderly couple sat at the front, were starting to panic. 'I suggest you stay in here, young man, where it's safe. Don't do anything stupid. It's no use being a dead hero. Do you hear me?'

Ben held the torch, pointing it at the floor, and moved to the elderly couple. He glanced at Abigail, sat quietly behind them. 'Look, I'm going to get us out of here. Whatever it takes. I need to know if he's still outside. It may be a case that he's gone and had enough. But I need to know.'

Mary turned her head. 'I say we lock the doors, get that fellow at the front to drive like the clappers and if the bastard stands in our way, we take him out. God knows I won't be sorry. Putting us through this. I'm seventy, you know. I don't need this.'

Ben smiled. 'You look well for your age.'

Mary squinted her eyes, her cheeks flushed. Her way of thanking Ben for the compliment.

'Go on. Tell that fellow up the front to start the coach. Let's go.'

'It's a great idea but he's slashed the tyres. Okay. Please, everyone, no noise.' Ben moved along the coach, reaching the steps at the front. The door was open, and Andrew followed him out.

The path ahead was pitch-black, a stretch of total bleakness. Remote. Behind them, the lights from Ben's car pressed against the back of the coach.

Ben walked along the path, away from the coach. Only Andrew's footsteps told Ben the driver was with him.

After a minute, Ben turned. 'We need to, somehow, get these people out of here. We need to do something. It's getting late. He's going to move in on us.' Ben raised his voice. 'We have to get out of here.'

Andrew said, 'I don't know how. He has us where he wants us. I don't know how we're going to escape from this.'

The guys kept moving. Ben wrapped his arms around himself, trying to stay warm. Andrew was already breathing hard. He was unfit, overweight and fighting to keep up.

Ben stopped suddenly, looking into the fields on the left. He listened but all he could hear was Andrew blowing through his mouth, sharp exhalations of air from his lungs.

'So, tell me about you? What's your story?' Ben asked as he monitored his surroundings. Although it was still, there was no way of telling if the lunatic was near them.

'Well, I'm five foot four, thirty-nine.'

'No. I mean the coach? These people?'

'I've driven for the company for twelve years. Never had a problem. The odd stag-do, rowdy tourists, boisterous sing-songs, the occasional argument, raised voices, vomit on the seats.'

'Okay, I get your drift. I thought you never had any problems?' Ben asked sarcastically.

'Nothing like this. I sensed something was wrong, Ben. Call it an intuition. The guy who told me to do this... He– he knew things.'

'What things?' Ben asked. He was shining the torch towards Andrew.

'Where my kid went to school; where my wife worked; he knew what I drank at home, for Christ's sake. I know he was watching us. Anyway, he gave me an address, where I'd find the coach. He told me to get into the driver's seat and not look behind. I knew something wasn't right.'

'How? You mean with the passengers?'

'I was told they were going on holiday. As I said, the guy told me very little. My instructions were clear. Pick them up and drive to the airport. As I walked up the steps and climbed into the driver's seat, I got the smell. It nearly knocked me out. I'll never get it out of my clothes. That was the first thing I noticed. Also, they weren't happy. Not the jolly sort you get on coaches. People going to the airport, they talk to you, they talk between themselves. Conversation is rife. You can learn lots about folk. I quickly realised something was wrong. He's done this for a reason. They were meant to be here tonight.'

Ben listened intently. 'Then we have to find a way to get them out of here.'

Andrew turned, looking towards the coach. 'I've got an idea. Wait here.' And he started to walk back to the coach. Ben waited, wondering what the driver was thinking.

Suddenly, Ben heard his car start up. He lifted his hands to his face to deflect the glare and saw the headlights fading into the distance as his car was reversed skilfully back down the lane.

Andrew was gone.

5

STEPHEN AND GARETH

The barmaid tugged the rope for last orders. The bell was like a signal for boxers to get ready.

Stephen turned, looking across the table, wondering if he could steal in another swift one before they left. Gareth had sunk three large Jack Daniels. He had another on the table in front of him. Stephen hoped he'd maybe have a fifth. That way, he wouldn't feel so bad. He shouted above the noise. 'Gareth, another for the road?'

He looked at his half-filled glass. 'No. Come on. It's home time, Cinderella. I've got a lecture in the morning with the dreaded Dr Norris. If I don't turn up, he'll fail me. That's for certain. It's okay for you.'

Stephen peered down at his empty glass. 'One more? I'll slug it. I promise.'

Gareth lifted his phone. 'I'm calling a taxi now. They'll be here in ten.'

Stephen reached into his jeans pocket, pulling out his car keys. 'I'll drive.'

Gareth leant forward, whipping the air and missing by a

significant margin. Stephen snatched them back and held them under the table.

'Mate, Stephen, you're not driving. You've had two, maybe three. Not a hope. Come on. Hand the keys over.'

Stephen stood. 'I'm a student. A taxi will cost a fortune. I can't afford it. I'll drive. I'm fine.'

Gareth placed his phone back in his pocket, secretly pleased that he'd get a free lift home. 'Mate, are you sure? It's a half-hour drive.'

'I'll take the back roads.'

Stephen was fiddling with the radio, jabbing the automatic tuning device with his finger. White noise crackled through the speakers. As he leant forward, pushing his body to the edge of his seat, trees rushed past in his side vision, like a blurred mess scrambling his brain. He jabbed the brakes, realising he'd been speeding and lifted his head, watching the road in front.

He flicked on the full beams, wrestling with the steering wheel, holding it with his right elbow, his left hand searching for a station he recognised.

Gareth watched the road ahead, his fingers wrapped around the overhead rail. 'Mate, leave the music. We'll be home soon. How are you feeling?'

'I'm good. I just wish my brother wouldn't mess with the stations. I have everything tuned. It pisses me off. Hey, how fit is Nadia?' Stephen asked.

'Oh yes. What's the deal with you two anyway? She's in one of your classes, isn't she?'

'Yeah. Science. She sits behind me. She's a nerd. Clever as fuck. She's caught me looking at her on more than one occasion.'

'Bloody hell. Who wouldn't? She's so hot, mate. I saw the two of you talking at the bar.' Gareth pushed for more information. Secretly wanting her for himself.

Stephen lifted his finger from the radio. 'This will have to do. The DJ is a bit of a prick, but the music's all right. She said she'd join us, but she must have gone home.'

'Really. That's a shame,' Gareth said a little too enthusiastically.

'I do like her though. She's–'

'Watch out!' Gareth hammered his fist on the dashboard.

Stephen pulled the steering wheel to the right, slamming his foot on the brakes. The car skidded and turned abruptly to the side, coming to a halt. He'd hit someone. 'Where the fuck did she come from?'

'I don't know. Oh my God, you hit her. Did you see her, Stephen? I think she's dead. Oh my fucking days.'

'I was looking at you. I wasn't speeding. Shit. Shit. Shit.'

Gareth opened the passenger door. The car had smoke coming from the back, pumping through the exhaust. He stood alone, temporarily taking in the silence – the calm before the storm. The driver's door squealed and Stephen stepped out.

'We need to go back; I think she's lying on the road behind us. I can't believe this, Stephen.'

'She came from nowhere. She stepped out; I didn't see her in time. I swear. All I remember is her white nightdress. She had long, scraggy, black hair. She was old. She was on me before I had a chance to brake. What the hell is she doing out here at this time? I couldn't avoid her. She stepped out.' Stephen was tackling his conscience.

'What does it matter why she was out here? The fact is, she's probably lying on the road. We need to walk back, attend to her. Call the police.'

Stephen hesitated. 'No. No, mate. We can't. They'll throw the book at me. I'm in university. I have prospects. A career. A life ahead. I can't. I can't call the police. We can't do that. Do you hear me, Gareth?'

'So what? We just drive? Leave her here? Let her fucking die?'

Stephen waited, weighing up his options. The road was empty, and no one saw the incident. He felt he had too much to lose. He wanted to go back and help, to wait by her side, holding her hand until he heard sirens ringing through the trees. Stephen knew it was the right thing to do. He looked around him as he stood on the road, searching for the lights of an oncoming vehicle. They were alone. 'Gareth, I'm out of here. It's up to you. We've been mates since time. You do this, call the police, that's it. It's over. The plans, Thailand. Everything. Think about it.'

'We can't just go. We can't,' Gareth persisted.

'Well, I'm getting into the driver's seat. You stay, or come with me – your choice. But I'm out of here.'

The boys never spoke a word to each other for the rest of the journey home.

Stephen's mind was filled with outcomes, consequences if he drove back. He'd been drinking, although he said to Gareth he hadn't been speeding, they both knew it was lies. His head was now churning, hurling images on a loop. The old woman, wearing a white nightdress. That long, greasy hair. Her shocked expression as the car hit her. He thought hard. Had she been standing still? It happened so fast.

Maybe she ran out from the woods. She may have fallen into the side of the car. He thought about going back and checking the road once he'd dropped Gareth off. There'd be blood, skin, hair. But not his. As far as anyone knew, they weren't there tonight. This was bad. It was the worst thing he had ever done – but running was even more of a crime. Running was more serious.

Stephen pulled into the small block of flats and sat still in the driver's seat. Gareth got out, slamming the door, and went through the communal doors to his one bed flat.

Stephen watched as his friend disappeared into the building. He looked behind, then edged out onto the road. Guilt was now crippling him. His head was confused, cloudy. He struggled to concentrate on the road in front of him. He drove slowly, watching the traffic lights, red, green, his leg automatically pumping the accelerator or stabbing the brakes. He reached the end of a quiet road, eyeing the houses either side. It was almost midnight.

He imagined life inside these houses: couples kissing goodnight, cuddling, reading, a dim light on a bedside table, sleeping masks, pyjamas, nightdresses. He thought about the woman in the woods in her blood-drenched nightdress. She wasn't going home tonight. She wouldn't be lying in her comfy bed, listening to music.

Stephen swung the steering wheel to the left and pulled over, his front tyre bumping against the kerb. He dropped his head on the dashboard, gripping his hair. Then he screamed. 'Fuuuuuucccccccckkk.' He stayed still with the engine off, the locked doors between him and the outside world.

He sobbed uncontrollably, unable to deal with what he'd done. Questions catapulted to his brain. *What if she's dead? What if the police turn up at my door? What if they realise I'd been drinking? Learn that I left the scene? Hit-and-run. Cowardly Stephen. Stephen the coward. Killing the woman in the woods. Leaving her to die... Die in the fucking woods. People will talk.*

He imagined the headlines all across the papers.

Can you believe Steve? Steve leaves. He was driving, you know. Hit that old woman. It's hard to conceive Steve weaves and leaves.

Stephen lifted his head, rubbing the knot developing towards the front of his brow. It ached now, spreading across his face like an egg splattered against the wall, its yolk smearing the brickwork. Stephen jolted, his trance interrupted. He kept his head still, his heart raced, pumping through his jumper, pressing like a commuter during rush hour, pushing to get on a packed train.

Suddenly, he gasped. Stephen was sat alone, locked inside his vehicle, in a desolate street. But he had the feeling he wasn't on his own. He reached for the car door, making sure it was locked. In the corner of his eye, he saw a hand pressed against the glass of the passenger door.

He spun his head.

The woman from the woods, the long black hair, her white nightdress, her face contorted, twisted. She was closer now, pushing her face to the glass, her tongue lapping the window.

'No, no, no,' he moaned. 'You're dead. How did you get here? How did you find me?' Stephen shook his head, then unlocked the car door and gently opened it. He wanted to run; cowardly Stephen wanted to leave her again.

He stood on the side road. The lights of the houses were off either side; he was alone.

He moved around the car to where he'd seen the woman. She was there, real, right where he sat. He stood by the passenger door, waiting, observing. Behind him, the road was empty.

You're seeing things. This is the guilt, catching up, manifesting. Get a grip.

Ten minutes later, he turned the key in the front door of the building where he lived, walked along the communal hall and entered his apartment.

Inside, he looked along the hallway. The lights were out, the place still. Stephen stood for a moment, making certain the flat was empty. He was shaken, his legs were weak and struggling to hold him. He moved towards the kitchen, reaching for the light on the wall to his left.

The brightness caused an instant discomfort. He looked across at the fridge, contemplating another drink to calm his nerves, help him sleep better. Then he decided against it. He flicked the light off and went to his bedroom.

He looked over the room, reaching forward to open the curtains. Stephen pressed his face against the glass, looking out over the communal garden, which was lit by the glow of a small security bulb. There was the bowl with cigarette butts floating in water on a round wooden table. There were the cracked pavement slabs, and the barbecue which hadn't been operated for months.

He moved from the window, quickly swiping the curtains closed.

Stephen undressed, removing his boots, digging the tip of his left boot into the back of his right, kicking them both away. He threw his jeans and jumper over the back of the chair.

The blanket on the bed was curled over in one corner and he tugged it away, appreciating the look of the cool sheet underneath, the welcoming pillow which he couldn't wait to sink his head into. He opened the bedroom door slightly, enough to see into the hallway, then jabbed the light switch, feeling in front of him to climb into bed.

He lay there, staring at the ceiling, adjusting to the room. Gareth's face came into his mind: his best friend, soulmate. They'd known each other all their lives. Stephen hoped he could keep this secret. Was it too much to ask? Gareth knew he'd knocked an old woman over, probably killed her. Could he keep it under wraps, knowing what his best mate had done? How far would their friendship stretch?

A creak came from the hall. A low whine, then it stopped. Stephen sat up, pushing to hear, listening intently. Again, a creak, longer this time. The bathroom was more or less opposite, a little to the right.

Gently, he lay down, pulling the blanket up to his chin. The creaking had stopped. The flat was silent. He closed his eyes, fighting not to think about what had happened earlier. *Think of a blank screen. A clean white mattress. A wiped chalkboard. Don't think of a pink elephant.*

Suddenly there was a bang, like a broom toppling over, the handle bouncing on the wooden floor. Stephen debated whether to pull the blankets over his head, a shield from the monster. It couldn't work, could it? He had to get a grip. He'd shut and locked the front door, the flimsy security chain hanging in its holder across the thin wood. The window and curtains were closed in his bedroom. The back door at the far side of the kitchen was closed and locked, the key hanging on the rack beside the cupboard.

The bedroom door moved, he was certain, only slightly but it opened. No creak, no groan, it just opened.

He sat up. 'Hello.' He gripped the corner of the blanket, heaving it away, then swung his legs together, standing on the cold floor. 'Hello. I have a bat. I'll use it.' He couldn't move, his body was stuck to the floor, jammed to the spot under his feet. He felt paralysed with fear. After a couple of tries, he summoned the strength, forcing his legs to respond. To align with his brain and obey the instructions it sent. In his mind, he'd already raced out to the hall and was opening the door, screaming for help. He reached his arm forward, now able to command his body.

Stephen pulled the door slowly, edging it towards him. Then he stepped out into the hallway, debating whether to go back to bed, push something against the door, sit up all night and keep watch. Too late now. The noise was inside the flat. He tiptoed to the kitchen, switching the light on. Nothing was different and it was exactly how he'd left it a few minutes ago.

As he turned, pushing out a sigh to quash the stress, a shadow crossed the glass on the front door. It wasn't someone passing, making their way to their flat or going out and heading towards the communal doors. It was almost against the glass, like someone standing by the front door, moving to the side, trying to look in to where he stood.

He stared, flicking off the light in the kitchen, waiting. The glass was frosted, translucent, but he could make out the brightness from the communal hall. Stephen moved to the door, opened the lock, flicked back the chain and stood outside his flat. To his right, the communal doors were closed, to his left, the door to the flat opposite was shut. The occupiers were a mother and small child; he assumed they'd have been asleep hours ago. The stairs, further along, were empty.

Christ, Stephen, get control of yourself. This is ridiculous.

He stepped back into the flat, closing the door. He attached the security chain. As he backed away, the shadow appeared, moving swiftly across the glass from outside. It resembled a haze of smoke, a cloud pushing its way through the cracks. It became larger, forming the shape of a person: he could see the outline of a head. It was moving, darting left and right, like the person was continually passing his door. Carefully, Stephen removed the chain, his hands trembling, and swung the door open. The hall was empty. The stairs were vacant.

Again he backed into the flat, pushing the front door hard, flicking the chain, stepping backwards, watching the glass.

All of a sudden, the hallway light went off, a click and then bang. Lights out. *The communal light never goes out.*

Stephen panicked. A wash of stress rose through his body. He turned, moved quickly down the hall to his bedroom. He slammed the door shut and then slid the small bedside cabinet across the room. The lamp fell, smashing the bulb and spreading shards of glass across the wooden flooring. He darted to the window, pulled the curtains back and looked into the garden.

Stephen's heart felt like it had exploded. There she was. The white nightdress. The long, greasy black hair. The woman in the woods was reaching her left arm towards the bedroom window, fingers spread, moving forward on her knees, crawling towards where Stephen was standing.

'Arhhhh. You can't be here. You can't.' He ripped the curtains together, ferociously wiping his eyes with his clenched fists, tearing the curtains open again. Her face was now at the window, her hands slamming against the glass. Stephen stumbled backwards, falling to the floor. He turned around, lifting onto his knees, crawling towards the bedroom door, not heeding the shards from the broken light bulb. He forced the cabinet to his left, then he stood and ran to the kitchen door. He had to find out what she wanted. Stephen had to reason with her. Tell her he was sorry.

Outside, the garden was deserted. He walked across to his bedroom window, fear now crippling his body. He was struggling to take a breath; his bones ached with terror and his head pounded. The woman was gone.

Stephen grabbed his jeans, jumper, got dressed and then moved out to his car. He had to return to the woods. The alcohol had worn off, and was now replaced by adrenalin. He looked in the rear-view mirror, then pulled out onto the road.

I have to do this. I have to help. Gareth was right; I shouldn't have driven away, left her there. It's obvious I can't deal with it, live my life knowing I've knocked her down, left her in the woods.

Stephen drove, oblivious to his surroundings, in a trance state, numb and vacant. Side roads, trees, fields, sprawled left and right. He stared ahead, his gaze glued to the window, watching the road in front.

This is it – the place. Stephen gently tapped the brakes,

pulling the car over to his left. He opened the driver's door, stepping out into the cold night air. His mind returned to earlier, him and Gareth, driving along the other side of the road, Stephen was searching for music on the radio, remembering the buzz from the evening they'd had, how life can topple and plunge into darkness so easily.

He searched the ground, walking along the deserted road, looking for blood, clothes, anything. He didn't know what to expect, but he knew there'd be a body.

For forty minutes, Stephen searched the area, walking, searching then running a mile or so either side.

He found nothing.

The woman in the woods had vanished.

6

THE COACH

'Can you believe that arsehole? He's gone. He did a bloody runner.' Ben had joined Laura and Milly on the coach.

'Who? Andrew?' Laura was struggling to believe how someone could leave these people. 'You mean he's stolen the car? I saw someone getting inside, reversing, I thought you were moving it.'

'Yes, the coach driver has fled and left us stranded here. It would seem he's a dab hand at driving cars too,' Ben stated. 'Shit. This evening just gets worse. How are they coping?' Ben eyed the passengers, directing his question to Laura and Milly.

'They've been sat in the same position for hours. Their bodies are numb; the blood circulation is minimal. Imagine how uncomfortable they must be feeling.' She moved towards the elderly couple at the front, asking if they'd like more water. She thought of the food which she'd packed in the footwell of their car, but Andrew the driver would no doubt pull over somewhere and tuck into that.

Ben turned to Milly. 'I'm so sorry, love. This isn't how I envisioned the start of our holiday.'

Milly's eyes watered and her top lip quivered. Ben pulled her close, holding her tight.

'I'm so scared. But we're doing the right thing, Dad,' she whispered.

Ben kissed her head. 'I'm not going to let anything happen–'

A gunshot sounded, causing total panic. Ben and Milly ducked and Laura dropped to her knees. People were gripping the seats, stamping their feet, shouting.

Ben crawled to the door, then gripped the rail, looking out into the wilderness. He couldn't see anyone. After a few seconds, he turned, crouching on one knee. 'Please, everyone keep quiet. Calm down.' His voice was wasted on the passengers. They were shouting, asking to be cut loose. The elderly lady at the front muttered under her breath; her husband was trying to soothe her, telling her it would all be okay.

Lydia was pulling her arms upwards, yanking the rope that held her to the seat. She screamed out, then burst into tears.

The phone rang from the dashboard, the old ringtone echoing through the coach, a haunting offensive cry demanding attention.

Milly shouted, 'Quiet. Everyone shush!' She kept hidden and looked towards her father, watching his next move.

Ben stood, reached forward and grabbed the phone.

The atmosphere dropped instantly; trepidation rose thick in the air like a poisonous cloud. Ben hesitated, debating whether to summon the loudspeaker or hold the phone to his ear. He chose the first option. People needed to know what this guy had planned. They needed to understand the severity of the situation and why they had to obey the caller's instructions.

'Hello.' Ben waited eagerly, hoping it was someone else.

'That's what happens when you disobey a simple command.'

Ben looked behind, he felt like a teacher taking a class, eyes fixed on him, waiting to hear the next instruction. 'You're never going to get away with this. Do you hear me? You're sick. You need help. There are people on this coach, elderly people, women.'

'You need to follow the rules.'

Ben moved to the door, feeling the cold air press against his face. The rain had started again, drenching his hair, soaking his clothes.

He stepped down onto the road. Behind him voices were pleading for him to come back. 'What is it you want?'

'The gunshot you heard a minute ago, there will be another eight before the night's out.'

Ben did a quick calculation in his head, realising what the guy was insinuating. 'What's happened to Andrew? What have you done? At least let the old couple go. They're weak, vulnerable. They may not last the night.'

A moment passed, then the voice came back on the line. 'Oh, you're so right.'

Click. The phone went dead.

Ben had goose pimples developing on his arms as he replayed the last sentence in his mind.

7

EDWARD AND MARY

'Don't fret, Mary. Everything's organised. God, I wish you wouldn't worry so much. It's not the Queen coming for dinner, you know.'

'I wish it were. I wouldn't feel as wound up.'

Classical music played from a small stereo in the corner of the living room. The table was set, elegant, oozing sophistication: tall crystal wine glasses, red paper napkins, fine bone china plates, coffee cups, saucers, knives and forks laid, wiped and laid again.

Edward wore a black suit; his thick grey hair was slicked back and held with wax. This particular product smelled like strawberries and gave a slightly wet appearance, but his wife preferred the natural look. He had a thin moustache, which he shaped weekly, running the length of his top lip.

Mary gleamed in a simple but elegant green dress and matching shoes. Her brown hair was down, hanging loosely on her shoulders. Her thin-framed glasses rested on the end of her nose, and her face was flushed with the heat coming from the kitchen.

The doorbell rang.

'Oh God, here we go,' Mary said.

Edward stood beside her. 'Look, they've had their problems. God knows I wish he had not taken her back, but it's done now. Nigel knows his own mind. Let him be happy. He obviously loves her.'

'After what she did! How can he go on like nothing happened? That ghastly woman.'

The bell rang again. Edward glanced in the hallway mirror, wiping a speck of dust from his shoulders and straightening his tie. 'Right, are you coming? It's courtesy to greet visitors at the door with a smile. Try, darling, if only for your son.'

'I'm in two minds to greet her with a bat,' Mary answered.

'Must you, Mary?' Edward placed his right eye to the peephole before he pulled the door open. 'Nigel. Abigail. Welcome.'

Edward looked towards the flowers in Abigail's hands. His son clutched a bottle of wine. They smiled as if pleased to be there, although their expressions gave a hint of edginess.

Nigel was dressed casually, a brown suit jacket, blue shirt and jeans. His hair was too long at the sides, possibly making up for the receding hairline on top. He was clean-shaven and had a tired, troubled face with heavy bags under his eyes.

His wife wore a plain white blouse and a knee-length black skirt. Her long blonde hair was curled, and it bounced as she made her way into the house.

Mary reached a hand towards her guests; a casual, limp shake offered to both.

Once settled at the table in the living room, Edward moved to the kitchen, leaving Mary with her son and his wife.

'So, how have things been with you two?' Mary ran the question over in her head, not intending to be so direct.

Nigel looked at Abigail. 'We've been good. Work's busy. Oh, I must tell you, you remember our neighbours, Tom and Michelle?'

Mary pondered the question. She recalled a short introduction at the front door of her son's house while they made their way to the car. 'Yes. A nice couple.'

'He hanged himself a few days ago,' Nigel said.

'Oh, good heavens. That's awful.'

'Something to do with debt. Isn't it often the case? His poor wife, I saw her yesterday. I mean, what do you say?' Nigel looked at his mum as if he hoped she knew the answer. 'He was such a good bloke. I was gutted when I heard the terrible news.'

'Right. Who's for wine? Nigel? Abigail?' Edward placed the chilled bottle of white onto the middle of the table. Abigail grabbed her glass and pushed it forward. She received a critical look from her husband.

'Abigail,' Nigel said, hoping to divert her from the alcohol.

She ignored him as Edward fought with the cork. He placed the bottle between his legs, his face contorted and his cheeks going a weird purple colour. Abigail jumped as the cork shot from the top, and the wine overflowed slightly and spilled onto the table.

Edward poured, waiting for Abigail to lift her hand and declare when the glass was filled enough. The signal didn't come.

'Nigel, wine?' his father asked.

'I'm obviously the designated driver. Again.'

Edward returned to the kitchen where he opened the oven. The smell of garlic wafted into the living room.

Nigel turned to his mother, who was sat across from him. 'How are you, Mum?'

Mary longed to blurt out criticisms about Abigail. To ask how she could be so cruel to her son. To sleep with another man and think everything could be rosy. To ask how she could pretend the baby was her son's. He'd taken her back, working things out. She wanted to know how Abigail could watch him decorate the box room and buy a cot, clothes and nappies.

Nigel and Abigail had tried for years; they'd had tests. He was unable to have children. *A problem with his sperm. It doesn't make him a lesser man*, she thought. *If anything, he was brave, finding out and admitting it.* Mary had seen hope in her son's eyes when he'd told them, 'Abigail is pregnant. We're having a baby.'

Mary recalled the delight, a small celebration, just the three of them. Abigail had stayed home: she had to rest.

Then one day Nigel had called his mother, explaining that Abigail had walked out on him. She was staying with a friend and had fallen for another man. Nigel told his mother everything, confided in her.

Then, Abigail called him, begging to come back. She told Nigel she was pregnant and that the baby was his. Mary knew it was impossible, but she'd keep the secret for her son's well-being. He took her back, and now, they were having a baby. Mary knew it wasn't her son's, but she had to keep it quiet from her husband. He knew nothing of the beast Abigail had become.

Mary smiled, answering her son's question with a grin. 'I'm simply fine.'

Edward walked into the living room, balancing a roast chicken in his left hand and a baking tray full of roast potatoes in the other.

'Wow, Dad, this looks great.' Nigel found himself envying his parents' relationship, how they behaved together. He was determined to make things work with Abigail.

'Just something I rustled up.' Edward placed the plates on the table. 'Tuck in, don't wait for me.' Edward moved back to the kitchen for more food.

As Mary sat watching Abigail shovel her food away, gulping

wine, she wondered if she was pregnant at all. Her stomach was flat; she wore a tight blouse, and according to conversations with her son, there was no morning sickness.

She had to say something. 'Don't you think you should go easy?'

Edward heard the question as he sat. He reached forward, placing his hand on his wife's arm. 'Let's not start anything, Mary. This is a simply joyous occasion.' He turned to his son. 'So, how's work going?'

'Oh, you know, working all the hours, never seeing the benefits. The usual.' He placed a roast potato in his mouth but found himself uncomfortable with the sudden heat, wishing he could remove it and set it back on his fork but knowing it wasn't good manners.

'Oh yes, they've just come out of the oven,' Edward commented. 'Well, you'll have to work all the hours now the baby's on its way.'

Mary saw Abigail blush. She wanted to question her, see what the heck was going on with this woman.

Abigail reached for the wine and topped her glass to the brim.

Mary hammered her fist on the table. The three of them jumped. 'How dare you?'

'Mum, leave it.'

Abigail calmly composed herself, wiping her mouth with a napkin. She didn't answer; instead, she stood and made her way out into the hall.

'For heaven's sake, Mary. What is wrong? Can't you just let it be?'

She glanced to her son, who went to stand. 'Sit back down. I can't hold my feelings in, seeing her sat there, as if butter wouldn't melt, after what she's done to you.'

Nigel sat, then held his head in his hands. 'We're working

things out. Christ knows I'm trying, can't you just be happy for us?'

'Happy, how can I be happy?'

'Mum. Please. Let it go.'

Mary took a sip of her water. 'She's not pregnant, is she?'

Nigel paused. It looked like the entire blood content of his body had moved to his cheeks. 'There were, complications. I'm not sure what happened. She had pains during the week. Abigail went to the doctors. She's lost the baby. I know they say it's early, just cells, but it doesn't take away the pain.'

'Good God, Nigel, I'm so sorry.' Edward stood, moving to his son, placing his arms around him. He peered across the table at Mary. For one slight second, he thought he saw a smirk on her face. 'I'll check on Abigail. She's been gone a while.'

As Edward left, Mary turned to her son. 'You must be devastated. You have my condolences. It's simply awful news.'

'It's not like we can try again. It was going to be mine. Although, well, you know the truth, but it's a tough blow to take. I would have treated that child as if it were my own.'

'And you were okay with that, were you? Knowing she's slept with someone else. It wasn't your child. How could you hide that fact? She shags someone else, and it's all okay. Is that fair on you?' Mary took a swig from her glass. 'She waltzes back into your life, expecting you to pick up the pieces and father her baby. Not yours. Hers and her bloody fancy man's.'

Out in the hall, Edward was looking for his daughter-in-law. 'Abigail, come on. Come back into the living room.' He opened the door leading into the utility room. Abigail was standing in the far left corner.

He walked over, pulling her close and unbuttoning her blouse, then he kissed her breasts.

'Not here. We'll be caught.' Abigail threw her head back, wrapping her leg around Edward's thigh.

Edward pushed his body against Abigail's. She could feel his arousal. 'It makes it all the more exciting. Oh, by the way, it was the best decision. The baby, I mean.'

8

THE COACH

'I think he's dead. The shot we heard, I think he's killed Andrew.' Ben pressed the lever on the dashboard, closing the door. He'd kept it open earlier so they could hear if the caller approached. Now, they knew what this guy was capable of, and they needed to barricade inside. He glanced at the passengers, then back to Laura and Milly stood with him at the front.

'Oh no, Ben, this is a horrible nightmare. We're going to wake up in Barcelona any second now by the pool, me with a cocktail, you and Milly playing blind man's bluff in the water.' For a second in Laura's eyes there was hope, but it disappeared just as quick. Creases appeared on her brow.

'I think he's planning on doing the same to the rest of them. He mentioned something on the phone, something about eight more shots before the night's out. He's close by. How else would he know that Andrew ran?' Ben climbed into the driver's seat, contemplating the caller's next move. He leant forward, his head in his hands, then jabbed his knuckles into his forehead as if knocking his brain into motion. He wanted to drive the coach, race along the road with his family and the passengers as far from here as possible. The flat tyres instantly quashed that idea. He couldn't move this thing more than a couple of yards.

'What's happening, young man?' Edward called out from the front seats.

Ben stood and pointed the torch towards the voice. He moved along the aisle. 'I don't know why he's doing this. I don't know his name, what he looks like or what he has planned. All I know is that none of us are allowed off the coach.' Ben thought about the gunshot. He continued. 'He's armed and very dangerous. That much is obvious.' Ben had to make conversation, ease the tension. 'Where do you both live?'

'Surrey,' Edward replied. 'We live in Surrey.'

Ben remembered the coach driver saying he lived there too. He was beginning to see a connection.

Edward flashed a glance towards his wife, then back to Ben. 'Untie me; I'll take my chances.'

'Edward, what are you thinking?' Mary asked.

'I'm sorry, sir. I can't do that,' Ben insisted. Edward was going to be trouble.

'Untie me, I said. This instant. I'm not waiting in this seat to die. Do you hear me? Now,' the elderly man shouted, commanding attention from the other passengers.

'Please, you'll get us all killed. Don't be so stupid,' Lydia shouted from her seat further back.

'You're not going anywhere. None of us are. We're staying put until further instructions,' Ben ordered. He stood, then moved to the front.

The coach became silent.

'Can we put the heaters back on? I'm freezing,' Mary said.

Ben sat in the driver's seat. He feared for a moment that Andrew had run with the keys. He shone the torch and reached forward, relieved to find them in the ignition. Then he turned on the engine and the grills kicked into life, slowly warming the coach again. The passengers needed light and warmth. So far, they hadn't been instructed to leave the engine off. Ben knew they could be seen from outside, but he also knew whoever was doing this could get on the coach whenever he wanted.

He looked outside, taking in their surroundings, wondering if there'd be another gunshot, a phone call. Ben speculated whether the guy could hear them. He doubted it. They hadn't found any hidden devices when they'd searched earlier. Maybe he was listening now, out there, stood alone in the fields. He could see them. That much was obvious. Ben remembered the area being a mass of green when he and his family had arrived. The land was flat, barren and wild. They had pulled off the M25 and then they drove for miles through a landscape that became more secluded, empty and deserted.

The passengers were looking out of the windows on either side of the aisle. Lydia muttered a prayer under her breath from the middle of the coach, then called out, 'Am I going to see him again? Jack, I mean?' She turned to the side, speaking to Stephen who sat a couple of rows behind. 'What about your friend? Is that it? We'll never see them again.'

Milly moved along the coach and sat beside Lydia. 'You can't give up. I won't let it happen, do you hear?' She raised her voice, looking along the aisle. 'No one is giving up. We're getting off this coach together, all of us,' Milly proclaimed.

Laura's face gleamed at her daughter's bravery. Ben reached behind, holding his wife's hand. 'I'm certain he's out there now, waiting for us, watching us from the darkness. He's able to see us, to view our every move. We're sitting ducks. We have no chance of knowing where he is.'

'Hon, don't talk like that. I know you'll think of something.'

'What? What can I think of, Laura? It's pitch-black outside. We haven't seen a light for ages. He's steering vehicles away, diverting them, he's probably a few yards from here. He can listen for a car, move along the fields and keep anyone from coming up this road. He has a hi-vis jacket. No one is going to question him. No one is going to come along this road.'

Laura placed her hand on his shoulder. 'I love you.'

Ben smiled. 'Why couldn't this have happened on the way home from Barcelona?' Ben turned, then stood, slowly moving down the coach, observing the passengers. He peered to his right, Edward and Mary were sat in silence. Behind them, Abigail was focused on the seat in front of her. He moved further along. His daughter Milly was sat beside Lydia, trying to comfort her. A couple of rows back, Stephen was resting and had closed his eyes. The swelling above his eye had diminished slightly.

Laura called from where she was sitting at the front. 'Ben, come quickly.'

He came along the aisle. 'What's up?'

Laura was pointing ahead. 'Look. There.'

Ben moved his head closer to the glass. 'I don't see anything.'

'Look harder. A light.'

'Oh yes.' Ben saw it in the distance, around 300 yards or so from where they sat. A small speck which appeared to be enlarging.

'Do you think it's another vehicle?' she asked, hope in her tone.

'I don't know. It's possible. The light is moving towards us. There are two of them. I'm certain it's a car,' Ben said.

'What if it's the guy, walking towards us with a torch?'

'No, Laura, there's definitely two lights. It's a vehicle. I'd bet my life on it.'

'Two torches?' she stated firmly, mildly deflating his anticipation.

As the lights gained, so did the apprehension. Ben and Laura kept it quiet from the others. The last thing they wanted was to build up the hopes of the passengers. They'd been through so much already.

Suddenly, the lights halted. Ben and Laura peered through the window, looking for a shadow, a figure exiting the vehicle, moving towards them, but they couldn't see anything. Then the lights went off.

'That's strange? Surely whoever was driving would move along the road, approach us, realise they couldn't get past, then back up.' Ben hit the dashboard.

'Maybe they've broken down?' Laura suggested.

They kept watching; seconds turned to minutes. The sudden hope started dissolving, the possibility of help was fading fast.

'Should I go down and take a look?' Ben asked.

'Yeah. If you're mad. No, Ben. Stay here with us. Maybe someone's broken down. What could we do anyway? The caller is never going to let us leave the coach.'

'But–'

Laura stuck to her guns. 'So what, you go down there, get the driver to call for help? Or we get as many passengers as possible in the vehicle. It won't work. Or we call 999, but as soon as the emergency services turn up, he'll hear the sirens, shoot the lot of us and run.' Laura was puffing quick breaths from her mouth.

'So we just sit and wait, hope he has a heart attack or gets bored?' Ben was agitated.

Laura didn't have the answer. She waited, letting her husband gain control of his emotions and gather his thoughts.

Ben rubbed his face; the bristles of his stubble were sharp against his hand. His back was aching; stress was taking its toll on his body. He wondered how the passengers were coping. The elderly couple, Abigail, whose husband had been taken, Stephen and his friend on the coach together, one of them gone. Lydia, worried sick about her husband Jack. Why had he chosen these people? What were his plans? Would he kill Ben and his family?

'We should be at the airport now, departure lounge. Sipping a beer, you with a gin and tonic, Milly with her headphones on, listening to grime.'

Laura eyed her daughter, conversing with Lydia. She was so caring, a beautiful young lady. They were so proud of her. Milly was confident, generous and understanding. They'd struggled with her at school: the usual, not putting effort into her lessons, revision troubles, late nights and even later mornings. She loved her bed, like most people her age. But in the last year she'd shown incredible maturity. They'd worried less about her, understood her more. In the end, Milly had passed her exams with top marks. She'd gained a place at the University of Leeds, and things were on the up. Ben and Laura were approaching their twentieth anniversary, hence the trip to Barcelona.

They'd opted to take Milly; it was too risky giving her the run of the house. It wasn't the mistrust of their daughter as much as the people she'd have over while they were away. Teenagers and alcohol were a dangerous combination, especially with parents out of the country. Luckily, when they'd asked Milly, she'd jumped at the opportunity.

This wasn't how they'd expected to start the holiday.

The atmosphere became placid; the low, hushed conversation was a testament that the passengers were a little more relaxed, despite the circumstances, they seemed to be coping with the situation.

Ben and Laura watched from the front seats, searching the distance for the lights. They'd seen little evidence to confirm whoever had been on the country road was still here. The passengers behind were beginning to communicate, chatting, mixing with each other. It was a good sign.

Suddenly, the phone rang. Ben jumped. Laura squeezed his

leg a little too hard. He turned, facing everyone. 'Quiet. Please, keep quiet.'

The voices dropped as if someone had tapped a fork against a wine glass in a packed room.

Ben reached forward, lifting the phone off the dashboard, his heart quickened, pumping through his chest, his hand numb with fear. The phone felt like a lead weight. 'Hello?' He put the speakerphone on.

'You're going to do something for me.'

Ben threw a quick look at Laura. 'What is it you want?'

'There's a passenger on the coach. Stephen Holmes. It's amazing what you can find out. Social media these days is an entry to everyone's world. He's on his own, sat towards the back. Recently he was involved in a hit-and-run. He thought it was okay to drive off, leave the old lady on the country lane. What he didn't comprehend was that he was being watched. I saw everything. I saw him pull over, get out, then flee the scene. Now it's his turn to correct his actions. To put it right, so to speak. He's going to be the one on the receiving end.'

Ben replied, 'I don't know what you want from us.' He raised his voice. 'You need to let these people go. You can't do this.'

'Move away from the driver's seat and untie him,' the voice demanded.

Ben shivered. A wave of shock darted through his body as he realised the caller could see him, sat at the front, him and Laura. Any second he could kill them all.

The guy's voice came over the phone again. Deep, husky, calm. 'Once he's untied, bring the phone, get off the coach and walk along the path round the front. You'll find a vehicle a couple of hundred yards from you; the keys are in the ignition. You have ten minutes, otherwise, bang.'

The phone went dead.

Ben stared at the screen, a multitude of outcomes raced

through his mind. The guy on the phone said that Stephen had been involved in a hit-and-run. Now he was going to put it right. *What did he mean – 'Put it right'.* He said, 'I need to untie Stephen.'

'Ben, you can't go out there,' Laura insisted.

'I have no choice.' He stood and went to where the young lad sat. His eyes were still closed, and the side of his face was pressed against the cold glass. Ben reached his arm forward, tapping Stephen's shoulder, shaking him gently. 'Hey. We need to go. Wake up.'

Stephen's eyes opened. The lad momentarily forgot where he was. 'What's wrong?'

Ben crouched, keeping his voice low so's not to agitate the other passengers. 'Look, this is extremely difficult, but I have no choice. We have no choice. You need to understand. If there were another way, I'd find one.'

Stephen went to stand, forgetting he'd been tied to the chair. 'I'm listening.'

Ben looked over his shoulder, then back to Stephen. His daughter was trying to calm Lydia. 'This guy, whoever he is, whatever he has planned, is watching us. He said I had to untie you, then we walk together, away from the coach. If you don't come with me, we're dead.'

9

BEN AND STEPHEN

They were alone, walking towards the vehicle. Ben and Stephen were roughly halfway between the coach and the car further along the road.

'What did you do exactly?' Ben asked. He stopped, turning towards the young lad, realising how direct his question had been. He wanted to prepare himself for whatever the caller had set up.

Stephen hesitated, he took a deep breath, filling his lungs with the cold air. The blood had started to return to his body, the temporary paralysis evaporating. 'It was a mistake. I'd had a couple of drinks. Christ, I didn't mean to do it. Gareth told me we'd get a taxi; but I couldn't afford it, I'm not working, I had college fees. I didn't mean to hit her.' Stephen broke down. He turned to the side and covered his face.

Ben placed his hand on Stephen's shoulder. 'I'm not here to judge. My family's safety is my priority but we can't walk away from this. Whatever this bastard wants us to do, let's get it over with so we can get on with our lives.'

The two men continued walking. They were roughly fifty yards from the car.

Ben stopped suddenly. 'I think it's mine. The car, I mean. Andrew drove it away earlier. Can you see anyone in the driver's seat?'

'I don't think so. It's too dark.'

They approached the car and Ben opened the driver's door. It was empty.

'Shit. What's happened to him?' Ben asked. He looked on the seats, searching for bloodstains. He presumed the caller had pulled him out of the car before shooting him. He quickly reached under the driver's seat, pawing on the floor for his phone. He found nothing.

They were alarmed when the phone rang from the back of Ben's pocket. 'It's him. Keep calm; we need to let him think we're in control of our emotions.'

'And how are we supposed to do that?' Stephen asked.

Ben lifted the phone to his ear, struggling to keep his hands still.

'Get into the car,' said the caller. 'You'll find the keys in the ignition. Start the car and drive along the road.'

Ben moved into the front, and Stephen sat in the passenger seat.

'Not the young lad. He stays outside.'

Ben turned to Stephen, knowing the caller was close. 'You need to get out.'

'What?'

'Outside. Stand outside,' Ben demanded.

Stephen slowly reached the handle, opened the door and stepped out of the car.

'Now, you're going to drive as fast as possible,' the voice instructed.

'This is ridiculous. I'm not playing these fucking games. People's lives are at risk.'

'You're right, including the passengers on the coach. Don't do anything to jeopardise their situation.'

Ben placed it and the torch on the passenger seat, started the engine, turned on the lights and slowly tapped the accelerator.

'I want you to speed up.'

'The road's narrow. How do you expect me to speed?' Ben's arms were shaking. He pushed his body forward, trying to see outside.

The voice was calm. 'Press the accelerator to the floor.'

Ben switched on the full lights. The road ahead edged to the left. He watched the speedometer; the car was moving faster, the wing mirror clipping bushes, branches swaying with the force.

He worried about Laura, Milly, the people stranded, held prisoner on the coach. Questions powered through his mind. *Why would he do this? How the heck would it all finish?* Ben needed to be strong, positive. Now wasn't the time to panic. He had to hold his shit together. It was going to be a long night, and this lunatic only seemed to be starting his games.

Ben followed the road around in a circle; his hands were wet and sticky with sweat, his eyes glazed, his head aching.

The voice on the line was urging him to speed. He had little choice. In his side vision was a haze of darkness, shadows darting, racing, swirling like a spinning top. Ben glanced at his speed: forty-three miles an hour. On a motorway, it would seem like a stroll, the first lane, tightly jammed between cars, lorries clinging to your bumper, traffic slowing, drivers passing and giving you the finger, horns blaring, an ebb of agitation as people passed.

Now it seemed dangerous, beyond lunacy. Ben needed to draw a conversation with this person. It was worth a shot at least. He took a deep breath, shifted in the seat, then began. 'Can I ask you a question? I have a family, a beautiful daughter called

Milly. She's eighteen, getting ready to go to university. She's a bright child. She looks after people. She cares. My wife, Laura, is the love of my life. We're going to Barcelona, a celebration of our twenty years together. Yes, we have cross words, we niggle, who doesn't? But she's the most incredible lady I've ever met. I'm asking you to stop now. They've suffered enough. Let's end this and move on with our lives. Let the people on the coach go. Whatever they've done. For whatever reason they're here. Let them go. Please.'

There was a long pause. Ben thought the guy had hung up.

But then the voice came out of the phone. 'Let me explain something to you. The world has become an excruciatingly, cruel place. Laughter has been replaced with tears – joy with contempt – gratitude with jealousy. People's souls have been replaced with hard, putrid rock.'

Ben was taken aback. This guy was messed up, hurt, bitter. He was unsure of how to answer. 'So what, you make it worse by doing what you're doing? Is that it?'

For the first time, he heard laughter, then it stopped. 'It's a sick, twisted life we live. No one gives a rat's arse. They couldn't care less.'

Ben needed to play the psychiatrist suddenly. 'There are good people as well as bad. Surely you realise that? This isn't the way to right the wrongs in our world. It's not the time. My family and I, we've been caught up in this mess, we didn't ask to be here, we don't know you.'

'You're right. But it's destiny. Our paths were meant to cross. I can't do this alone. It's a shame for you that you came along when you did but that's the way it goes sometimes, and now, you and your family are going to help. You're a part of it you see? I've planned this for so long. People need to pay for their sins, to replenish, wallow in the fountain, cleanse, to be reborn.'

Ben hesitated. 'You're not making any sense.' He jabbed the brake, turning the steering wheel, then sped along the country lane.

'You need to go faster. Before the night's out, you'll get me. You'll understand. I promise you that. The passengers on the coach, the sinners, they'll all be sorry for what they've done. Believe me.' Suddenly, the guy shouted, 'Stop.'

Ben hit the brakes.

'Your young friend, he left a woman to die in the woods. Now, you have the chance to save him.'

Ben wiped the bead of sweat which had trickled down the side of his face, causing his nose to itch. 'How so?' The full lights illuminated the stretch of road. Ben could hear heavy breaths, like the caller was moving fast, running along the road.

'Put the car in reverse and hit the accelerator. It's a long road; you can build speed.'

'No, I'm not doing it.'

'Then you leave me little choice.'

Ben waited. He knew this guy was serious. He wasn't willing to wait or bargain. 'Okay. I'll do it. What happens then?'

'Just drive.'

Ben braced himself, eyeing the bleak darkness either side of where he sat. He grappled with the gearstick and pressed his foot on the accelerator. The car picked up speed.

'Faster.'

'I can't go any faster. The speed has to accumulate.'

'Faster, I said.'

'For Christ's sake, I'm doing my best.' Ben watched his speedometer, eighteen, twenty, twenty-three. It was building fast. He fought with the steering wheel, ripping it left and right, jabbing the brake, his head turned as he struggled to look out of the back window, the car swerving. Twenty-five, twenty-seven. 'That's it; I can't do this. I'll crash. It's too dangerous.' Suddenly he heard a crack, something snapped. Ben hit the brakes. He shouted. 'Stephen.' Ben grabbed the torch and the phone which he'd placed on the passenger seat and opened the driver's door.

The phone disconnected.

Ben stood for a moment, then turned behind him. He was back where he'd started, the coach was a little further up the path. He shone the torch on the ground; his mind flashed images of the young lad lying on the road, his legs mangled, his body crushed. Blood flowing along the tarmac like a stream. 'Hello. Stephen. I'm sorry. I'm so sorry.' Ben jogged away from the car and along the road towards the coach. He swung the torch side to side; then he saw something on the ground – a sandbag the size of a large pillow which the caller had thrown. Ben crouched, lifting it, then hurled it into the field to his right.

'I'm okay. I'm alive.' Ben heard Stephen's voice in the distance. 'When you drove I carried on running along the path. I saw you reversing so I stopped,' Stephen said.

He looked to where the young lad was standing. The full lights of his car bringing the tall, gangly figure into view as Stephen stepped onto the road.

'Thank God. I thought I'd hit you. Are you okay?'

'Yes. Fine. I'm sorry you had to go through that, Ben. He's playing with us. A torment he's not going to stop. I watched the fear as you thought you'd hit me. He's making us play out the mistakes we've made. I'm going to run for it. I'm young. I can make it.'

Ben was instantly agitated. 'Don't do it. Don't be so selfish. You'll get us all killed. Do you hear me?'

'Sorry, mate. You're on your own. I'm getting out of here. Good luck, to you and your family, I mean.'

'Stephen, don't do this to us. I'm begging you not to do this.'

'He has our phones. If I make it, I'll get help. I'll make a call as soon as I can. As soon as I'm out of here. I promise. Be safe, mate. The best of luck to you all.'

'No, Stephen. Look out!'

The caller was now in the driver's seat of Ben's car and it started moving, gaining speed, racing towards where Stephen was standing.

10

LYDIA AND JACK

Lydia stood in the hall of Chloe's house, the body of her husband's boss at her feet. The courage the three bottles of wine had given her had evaporated, as if shock had driven the alcohol from her body.

She was startled by a thumping on the front door. She crept forward, placing her ear to the wood. 'Is that you, Jack?' She'd managed to get through to her husband and explain what had happened.

'Yes. Open the door.'

She slowly twisted the lock down to let him in.

Jack wore a coat and had the sleeves pulled over his fists, making sure he didn't leave any fingerprints. 'Christ, Lydia. What the fuck have you done to Chloe?'

Lydia was babbling; she stood on her tiptoes, her eyes unfocused, her mind confused. 'I thought – I saw you and assumed – I didn't mean to kill her. I shoved her, thinking you and her were, you know, an item.'

Jack looked past his wife, seeing his boss lying on the floor. The blood had covered one of the small square tiles and was working its way to the next one.

'You're not going to tell anyone, are you? I'll go away for life. Please tell me, Jack, that you won't say anything?'

Jack covered his hand with his sleeve and reached forward, awkwardly pressing his fingers through his jacket to feel the side of Chloe's neck. He stood, then grabbed his wife. 'You've murdered her. She's not going to recover, Lydia. She's not going to regain consciousness, sit up, brush herself down and tell you she's okay. You understand that, right?'

Lydia backed away, then steered her eyes towards Chloe. It suddenly dawned on her. She fell to her knees, pulling clumps of her hair.

Jack moved beside her. 'Find a mop, something, anything to get rid of this blood. We'll have to carry the body out – you and me. Where else have you been? Think, Lydia. Where else did you go in the house?' Jack asked.

She froze, unable to think.

'Lydia, concentrate. Who saw you?' Jack raised his voice to get his wife's attention.

'Erm, the taxi driver.'

'Did you say anything to him?'

Lydia thought for a second. 'I don't think so. I just told him where to go. That's it.'

'How did you know where she lives?' Jack asked.

'Well, I saw you drinking together. I waited outside the pub. She came out, jumped in a taxi. I jumped in another a few seconds later and followed.'

'You mean you travelled all the way from Surrey? On your own?'

Lydia kept an embarrassed silence.

'Did the taxi driver say anything to you?'

'Like what, Jack?'

'Did he ask what you were doing? Where you lived? What you were up to?'

Lydia thought. 'No, I'm pretty sure he didn't ask anything like that. He kept talking, but I wasn't listening if I'm honest.'

'We need to clean this up. Her partner, Dana, could be back any minute. Then we're screwed,' Jack warned. He found a mop stood next to the fridge in the kitchen and filled a bucket he'd found under the sink with water. Then he spent ten minutes mopping the hallway floor. The thick blood oozed and stuck to the mop head. Jack winced at the squelch as it dropped into the water.

'Lydia, did you go anywhere else in the house?'

'No. I came into the hall, shoved her – Oh, the kitchen. That was the only other place. I was looking for a charger.'

'You're sure? Did you go upstairs?'

'No. Nowhere else.' Lydia wondered suddenly if she had gone upstairs or into the garden. She fought to determine the facts, to get it straight in her mind.

Jack went back to the kitchen and took a cloth from under the sink. He wiped along the table, the chairs and finally, he ran the mop over the kitchen floor, hoping Chloe's wife didn't become suspicious when she returned home. He couldn't use detergent; the smell would arouse suspicion.

'Right, we need to place the body in the boot of my car. We have no choice. It's dark and if we move quickly, it should be okay. We lift her and bring the body straight outside. Are you ready?' Jack was concerned they'd be seen. He was an accomplice to murder.

Lydia had gained a little composure. She was more confident now that Jack was here. 'I'll check if anyone's outside.'

'Okay. I'll wait. Be quick, Lydia.'

She returned a minute later. 'It's clear.'

Jack placed his arms under Chloe's shoulders. She was heavier than he'd imagined – the realisation of what Lydia had done suddenly dawned on him. 'Oh Christ, this is awful. Quick, grab her legs. We have to be fast, Lydia. Hurry.'

Once they had the body in the air, they manoeuvred Chloe out to the car. Jack drove a dark blue BMW and kept it in immaculate condition. The body was going to cause a stench. Lydia was panting heavily and had to drop Chloe's legs a couple of times. When they reached the end of the drive, they placed her down on the pavement to open the boot and then dropped her body inside.

Jack moved back into the house and picked up Chloe's handbag and phone. He'd have to hide her belongings under the car seat. He wiped the splurges of blood that were left by the body in the hallway, then cleaned the door and lock on the way out.

He shut the front door, and wondered where the hell they were going to hide his now ex-boss.

Jack drove along the Bayswater Road, heading to Surrey.

Lydia sat in the passenger seat. Her body was aching from stress. She continually watched in the rear-view mirror, checking every car that pulled up behind them, every person that stepped out onto the road. Her body was tense, and her mind agitated. She sat forward, straightening her back, hearing her spine click. Her head ached from the three bottles of wine she'd had earlier; the adrenalin had sobered her, now she felt like she'd been dragged through a thorn bush. 'Jack, I'm so scared. What if we're stopped? How will we explain what happened?'

Jack noticed how his wife used the word *we*. 'Keep calm, Lydia. We need to make it home, sleep on it. We'll think of something. How do people get rid of bodies? I don't have a clue.' He turned to his wife. 'Do you?'

Her body slumped in the passenger seat. 'I remember watching something on the telly. A documentary about a serial killer: he used to get rid of bodies by dropping them in a bath of acid. Apparently, it dissolved the flesh and just left the bones.'

Jack struggled to believe they were having this conversation. 'How conspicuous will it look going to a hardware store at this time of night, asking for tins of acid? Come on, Lydia, you're not thinking straight.'

'I'm only trying to help.'

'Shit, Lydia, we're in over our necks. What the hell are we going to do?'

She turned to her husband. 'We get rid of the body. The taxi driver was the only person that knew I was there. He's probably picked up loads of people since then. I don't think they keep a log of the passengers and addresses. It's all in their heads, unlike a private firm where everything is pre-booked. Maybe they do log everything. I don't bloody know.'

Jack thought for a second. His wife had a point. The only other concern was Dana, Chloe's wife. How long would it be before the alarm bells rang and she made a call to the police? There'd be DNA, hair, fibres, fingerprints. No matter how much they cleaned the house downstairs, there was always the possibility of something being left behind as evidence that could incriminate them.

An hour later, Jack pulled into their drive, opened the car door and stood for a moment, eyeing the US style mailbox planted at the front of the house with the word 'Hargreaves' written in gold letters.

He imagined seeing the name splashed over the internet. *Murderers. Hargreaves husband and wife team hide dead body.*

Lydia joined him a few seconds later in front of their white-painted house. 'What are you thinking?' she asked, watching her husband's face as he mulled over what had happened tonight. She knew Jack would deal with it. He was so much better at handling situations and resolving problems.

'The garden. It's the only way.'

'Oh, Jack. Are you serious? We can't.'

He turned to his wife and felt the stones from the front drive dragging under his shoes. 'Have you got a better idea?'

Lydia paused for a second, thinking of ways they could dispose of Chloe. 'No. Of course not. It's just... the garden. It's not right.'

'An hour ago you wanted to drop her in acid.'

Lydia stepped forward, holding her husband. He gripped her tightly. 'Jack, I need a drink. Let's think about it tonight. I suggest we leave her in the boot. If we decide to bury her in the garden, we'll do it early tomorrow morning.'

She went into the house, and Jack followed.

'I'm home.' Dana hung her jacket on the stand by the front door and removed her boots. 'Chloe, are you in bed?'

She listened for a reply. The lights were off upstairs. Chloe always turned on the lights when she got home. Not just a habit, she was terrified of the dark, and if she came in before Dana, she automatically switched them on.

In the kitchen Dana looked at her watch. It was almost 10pm. She had a bad feeling; something was wrong. Chloe would have called her, left a message to tell her where she was going and when she'd be home. The last time she'd spoken with her partner was mid-afternoon. She was going for a drink with Jack after work.

Dana walked out of the kitchen and into the hall, getting the phone from her jacket. She dialled Chloe's number, listening to the brief message and leaving a quick, sharp reply. 'Chloe, it's me. Not sure where you are, and I haven't heard from you, which is a little concerning. Call me. Love you.'

Dana dialled Jack's number. He answered on the sixth ring. 'Jack, it's Dana. Have you heard from Chloe?'

'Err. No. Nothing. Why?'

She detected an irritable tone in his voice. 'Oh. It's nothing. I'm worrying unnecessarily I'm sure. Did you go out this evening?'

'Out?' Jack asked.

'Yeah. You and Chloe?'

'No. What makes you think that?'

'Well, it's just Chloe said she was meeting you later, that's all.'

'No. I came straight home.' Jack realised the trouble lying could cause. He was tongue-tied, and at this moment, he knew he shouldn't have fibbed.

'So you never saw Chloe this evening?'

'No. Look, I have to go. I'm sure she'll turn up.'

'Okay. Thanks, Jack. Sorry to have bothered you.'

Dana ran the conversation over in her head. Jack knew something. She was certain of it. She debated calling him again, pressing him, firing questions. She didn't want to appear rude, but it was late, Chloe wasn't home, and she'd never do this without a phone call or a text to let Dana know she was okay.

Dana sat at the table in the kitchen. The seconds loudly clicked as the hand swept around the clock. She picked up her phone, again dialling Chloe's number, deciding not to leave another message.

Jack is hiding something. He knows where Chloe is. She specifically told me earlier she was meeting him for a drink. The two of them had to have been together. Surely Chloe couldn't be with him now? Could she? The two of them, wrapped in each other's arms, sharing food, a bottle of wine, under the duvet.

She fought the paranoia. Wrestled it, punched it, kicked it and threw it to the back of her head.

I'll call him again. Sod it. This is my life. The phone rang. Eventually, a recorded voice answered. 'You're through to Jack. Leave a message.'

Dana hung up, then redialled. The same thing, the ring, then his voice.

He was refusing to answer.

That was all the proof she needed.

'We have a problem.' Jack walked into the living room.

Lydia was sat at the table, already working her way through a bottle of wine.

'What is it?'

Jack relayed the phone call he'd just received. 'Dana knows something isn't right.'

Lydia's voice began to slur. 'Well, we deny everything. What can she prove?'

'You're not getting it, Lydia. It's not something you can brush under the carpet. You murdered someone. We removed the body, wiped the scene and we're going to fucking hide her.' Jack's voice was loud, harsh.

She gripped the glass, throwing her neck back, the contents emptying into her throat. She seized the bottle, holding it like it was a baby.

Jack poured a large whisky into a glass, tasting it and then grimacing at the strength. 'Look, Dana is suspicious. But at the moment, she knows nothing. She has no proof in regards to us. We keep a low profile, play it cool. Early tomorrow, I'll dig a grave in the garden and keep Chloe hidden.'

'I'm not comfortable with this. A dead body in the garden. Jack, it's not right.'

He lifted the bottle of whisky, pouring another measure. 'So what do you suggest?'

'I don't know. Why don't we dump her somewhere? If it's out there in the garden it's just a constant reminder, you know.'

'Christ, Lydia. What were you thinking?'

She placed her head in her hands. Her shoulders began wobbling and she cried uncontrollably. 'I'm so sorry. I thought you were having an affair. I saw red. I didn't intend to follow her, but this rage... it came over me, and I couldn't control myself. When I turned up at her door, I intended to scare her, frighten her off, warn her to keep away. I didn't realise she had a wife. Jack, I'm so sorry. I'm scared.'

He placed his hands on hers. 'Look, we'll get away with it if we're clever. We need to keep quiet and be sensible.' He stood. 'Come on, let's call it a night.'

Lydia finished the glass of wine, and they went upstairs.

At 5.10am, Jack was in the garden, towards the back with a shovel from the shed. He'd turned on the sprinkler before he went to bed to soften the earth and make the digging more manageable. Now, he left it on to drown out the sound of shovelling. The garden was vast and there was little chance the neighbours would hear. Still, Jack had to be careful. The high fences either side would hide what he was doing. He peered at the neighbour's houses: the bedroom curtains were drawn.

The air was chilly as he rammed the end of the shovel into the soil. The earth was thick and clumpy and stuck to the end of the shovel. The sky was clear, sprinkled with stars and the frost was patchy on the grass. Jack would dig the area where the sprinkler had soaked overnight. He wore a jacket and an old pair of jeans. Despite the cold, sweat beads on his face made the work uncomfortable.

Eventually, the hole was big enough for him to stand in. He tested it: it was deep enough to cover up to his knees.

Visions of his boss circulated in his mind. He recalled a recent awards ceremony. Her face gleaming with pride, she had held Jack's arm aloft, telling him she couldn't have done it without his hard work. She had worn a plain red dress, had her black hair back, tied tight. She had been so pleased with the direction the company was headed. Chloe grafted, starting early, leaving last, wining and dining clients, calling Jack at the weekends and at ungodly hours. She lived and breathed the company.

Now, she lay dead because of a terrible mistake. Lydia had killed her. Jack knew his wife wasn't a bad person, but she was ill. She suffered delusions, paranoia.

As he dug, he recalled numerous occasions when they'd had friends over. She'd clasp his arm in the kitchen. 'Claire and Ted, they've been talking about me. The room went silent when I walked in. Claire blushed. She giggled and then the conversation changed.'

Whenever they'd eaten out, she had to sit facing the kitchen, watching the chef, making sure they didn't poison her food.

Jack knew his wife would never survive prison. Lydia wasn't a well person but she refused to get help. She found it a weakness to speak to anyone about her problems, about her thoughts.

Jack loved her; he'd do anything for his wife. Even hide a dead body. He stood, straightening his back. His fingers were numb; his forearms ached, his right shoulder throbbed with pain.

He looked at the thick soil, stood back, taking it all in, then moved to the house.

He closed the kitchen door, peering outside as the heating warmed his body. He thought about the future, Lydia and him, how they would come to terms with what they'd done. How they would deal with it. *One step, one day at a time.* That's what his father had told him years ago. *Embrace and face.* That's what he'd said.

Jack stood at the kitchen door as the minutes passed, his mind a whirl of emotions, a knot deep in his stomach, widening, spreading, rotting his soul.

He drew a deep breath, held it, five seconds, ten, then let it out, forming a patch of condensation on the glass. He stepped back, his eyes never leaving the garden. The security light went off.

He left the kitchen, moving along the downstairs hallway towards the front door. He listened for Lydia stirring though he was certain she was still asleep.

Jack opened the front door.

The car had gone from the drive.

Chloe was still in the boot.

11

THE COACH

'Stephen, run!' Ben's car, driven by the caller, was heading down the track straight to where the young lad was jogging. Moments ago he'd said he was going to leave, to try and escape. Ben had pleaded with him, begged him not to do it. Now, Ben stood on the path, watching as the car hurtled towards him.

Stephen turned, racing backwards, facing the full lights, holding his hands in front of him to reduce the glare, stepping left, right, stumbling, his body clumsy as the car approached. He threw himself towards the ditch, grasping clumps of grass as he pulled his body upwards.

Stephen screamed as he climbed the verge, his trainers sliding and scraping into the mud as he struggled to get a grip. He separated the barbed wire and dived head first into the field, landing heavy on his stomach. At the same time, the car rammed into the side of the bank.

Ben was unsure if Stephen had made it. He raced towards the car. The reverse lights flared, the engine revving, and the driver pulled back. There was a crunching sound, like an axe against a wooden door as the car jolted forward and the bumper cracked. Again, the driver manoeuvred the car backwards, then pulled away.

Ben reached the spot where Stephen had been standing seconds ago, praying he'd made it into the field. His head was swamped with visions of the young lad lying on the grass, his legs mangled and crushed. As Ben called Stephen's name, he saw the car suddenly stop. He knew the caller could get out, enter the field and shoot Stephen where he lay. The gunshot earlier was testament he was armed and threatening. He could kill them both, then move to the coach, pissed off that his instructions weren't being followed. He pictured his daughter, Milly, Laura and the elderly couple sat at the front of the coach.

Everyone relied on him to do the right thing and get them to safety.

Ben worked in a warehouse; he drove a forklift truck. When he left school, he flitted between jobs, always the drifter and never staying in employment for more than a few months. He'd fall out with a boss or dislike how he was spoken to, then leave, onto the next one. But meeting Laura changed his perception of life. He settled for working at a local factory. Ben's grandfather had worked there, and his dad had said, 'If it was good enough for my old man, it's good enough for you.' Ben saved every penny he made and with Laura managing a local florist they quickly got enough money together and moved into a small flat in North London.

As Ben progressed, he'd been offered managerial roles, which meant working behind a desk and barking orders. It wasn't him. He wanted a relatively stress-free life, collecting his wage packet every Friday afternoon.

Once they were able to afford a house and a mortgage, Ben cut back on the overtime. He spent every spare minute with his family. Ben lived for his wife and daughter.

Now, standing on the side of the road, searching for Stephen, he realised he wasn't cut out for this; he didn't see himself as a hero, he wasn't an individual with superpowers. He was plain and simple Ben, on his way to Barcelona for a week of relaxation with his family. That was all.

He felt sick with fear. Ben debated whether to go back to the coach. He stood still; his legs were weak, unable to follow the commands his brain gave out. His head was sore; an aching throb now pushing from the back of his neck and making its way along the side of his face. He worried it may be a stroke. He could drop here, and lie hidden for hours.

The door of his car opened. The guy – the caller – stepped out.

Ben wanted to run, screaming through the fields, shouting for help at the top of his voice, flagging a car down, begging the driver to assist. *'Yes, I'm so glad you're here. Only there's a problem. You see that coach? Well, there are people tied up, about to meet their maker but you're going to help us. How does that sound? Oh, come on. It'll be fun. Call it your good deed for the day if you like.'*

The caller stood on the road. He was motionless, staring at Ben. The glow from his jacket reflected in the lights of the car. His eyes were focused, his face expressionless, watching, waiting.

'What are you going to do?' Ben's voice was as calm as he could muster, but he still felt weak. The low tremble that came from his mouth exposed how he felt. His breath made a small cloud of condensation. He stamped on the ground to gain the courage he needed and wake his body from the trance that had taken over.

He couldn't run: there was nowhere to go. So many times he'd told Milly to stand up to bullies. Conversation was key. He had to try and talk, somehow reason with this man. 'I want to know why. Why are you doing this?'

The caller had a hood pulled tightly over his head. He was

tall, maybe six-four, possibly bigger, and well built, strong-looking. Ben could outrun him, he was certain of that, but it was the last option. The final choice to flee, chicken-legged along the road, lock the coach door and admit he was shitting himself to the passengers.

Suddenly, the guy started speaking. 'What does sin mean to you?' He paused, making sure Ben was taking everything in and understanding what he was saying. 'To me, it's wickedness, desire, lust, greed; all the other words you can muster. People's actions speak volumes – the way they're programmed, how they act. The betrayal is rife among us. Take the people on the coach, for instance – the old couple at the front – the man. You'd imagine butter wouldn't melt in his mouth. He's a powerful person, a husband, provider and a scheming wretch who lives a double life. A fraud to anyone who knows his mucky secret.'

'I don't know where this is going,' Ben said.

The guy continued, 'The girl sitting towards the middle, do you know what she did? Her and her husband? An act of pure, unadulterated immorality. This young lad, out in the woods, did a selfish deed of the lowest, depraved form. He chose to drive away for his own self-regard. See, sin is profuse. It festers in the lives of the people we meet. It's the biggest weakness. If it goes unpunished, it will continue to grow. It will start to escalate, ooze from the souls like a potent virus and spread; it will scar the world we enjoy, the places we visit, the food we eat, it will hang in the air and cause doubt, negativity, despondence.'

'Is that what it's about? Wrong choices, bad decisions? People do it all the time; it's how we're built. We make mistakes. That's part of the learning curve. We're human; we make mistakes,' Ben answered.

'Are they mistakes? Or options?' The guy pointed along the path and behind Ben. 'The people on that coach, they could have done the right thing, made the correct decision. We all have the power to change our path, to walk along the correct road. We get a feeling deep within; some people call it a premonition, a sixth sense. Imagine, if you like, that you are walking along a path. The sun is beaming, the sky clear, birdsong in the air. You're surrounded by trees and you're alone. You come to a fork in the road. There are two signs pinned to the bark of a tree, near the base. One points left, one to the right. The sign on the left says, "Stay as you are". The sign on the right says, "All the wealth you'll ever need". Me, I'd go to the left. But how many people would choose the path on the right? See, we're never satisfied with what we have.'

The caller continued. 'Greed is a horrible trait. The next-door neighbour gets an extension, builds on top of what they have. Maybe they live alone, a semi-detached house with a hundred-foot garden, but it's not enough. They need more rooms, more space. You become envious, enraged with jealousy, needing to know how it will look, the price it's costing. You start to wonder if you can afford the same extension yourself. You ask your boss for more hours, cut back on going out, save a little. But now the neighbour has a better car, a more exquisite holiday, further afield.

'Think about work colleagues, the "yes sirs" of this world, striving for a better position in their job, swapping a uniform for a suit, a higher pay cheque, company car, longer hours, their own office, a large desk, a swivel chair, pictures of their family hanging on the wall behind them. Their former colleagues now have to make an appointment, knock on the door. They need to ask him to make time for them. The same people he trampled on while making his way to the top of the tree.'

'Isn't that just people, trying to make a better life for themselves?' Ben asked.

'The world has become a haven for rogues, parasites. Look at what I'm doing as a punishment if you will. A child, he steals from the local grocery store. He's chased home by the owner. The young boy races down the street, an apple under each arm. He makes it, flicks a look behind, the street is deserted. His mother greets him at the door; he pretends he picked them from the local field, maybe he tells her he found them on the ground. She rubs his head, goes back to the kitchen, flicking through a recipe book, making a large pie. Her nan's ingredients which were passed down are not good enough anymore; she wants to make a better-tasting one, more flavour, more succulent. The boy goes back to the grocery store again, this time he grabs more apples, over and over he steals from the owner. One day, he reaches for a melon, as big as his head and he rips it from the shelf, his eyes wild, filled with excitement, but the shopkeeper is waiting for him outside. As the boy runs, the owner sticks out his foot, and the boy drops to the floor. The owner is holding a rolling pin, and he beats the boy's legs until they're bloody and bruised. The shopkeeper lets him go and, needless to say, the boy never returns to the store.'

The guy got back into the car. He turned to Ben as he closed the door.

'That boy was me. You see, sinners require harsh lessons to learn from their mistakes.'

He hit the accelerator and Ben saw the car disappear into the distance.

12

THE COACH

Ben climbed into the field. The ground was wet, and his shoes sunk into the grass.

He called out. 'Stephen, are you there?' The guy had driven Ben's car away a few minutes ago. Ben wondered whether he'd drive full circle and park near the coach or if he'd gone somewhere else. He kicked the long grass with his feet, battling through, and shone the torch at the ground.

Ben wanted so badly to call for help, let someone know what was happening out here. But the caller was monitoring the only phone they had. Their own phones were in the car. Ben could have snuck one of them in his pocket but he couldn't risk the caller seeing him do it. He hadn't seen another vehicle for so long. There was nothing he could do. The guy was out here, hidden, watching them all. He had taken three people from the coach: Stephen's friend Gareth, Edward and Mary's son, and Lydia's husband. How long before he took the others?

Ben looked out over the terrain, wondering if they were close by, tied up somewhere. Maybe they were being tortured. The caller could easily return and come back for the others, do the same to them. A sharp chill made its way along his back and his body spasmed. Ben briefly considered running, grabbing Laura and Milly and racing towards civilisation. He couldn't and wouldn't. These people relied on him. Ben was their only hope. Their only way out.

He thought how it would look to the passengers and his family, what they'd think if Ben ran and left everyone to die.

Suddenly he heard a groan, close to where he was walking. Ben lowered the torch, shining the small light and sweeping it across the grass. He saw the young lad, Stephen, lying on his stomach around five metres from where he stood.

'Hey. Thank God you're still alive,' Ben said, keeping his voice as low as possible.

Stephen lay still.

Ben moved closer. 'Stephen, are you okay?'

The young lad lifted his head and rolled over onto his back. 'Shit. He almost killed me.' Stephen had crawled along the grass, keeping low, too frightened to stand up.

'I saw him drive the car at you. Then you were out of sight.'

'He charged towards me. I think the bonnet smacked against the verge. I just escaped. I dread to think what could have happened.'

Ben offered his arm. 'Can you walk?'

'Yeah. I'm okay.' Stephen reached up and let Ben pull him to his feet.

'I say we make our way back to the coach; I'm sure we'll hear from him shortly. Come on, let's go and make sure the others are still alive,' Ben said. He wiped the mud from Stephen's clothes.

'Thanks. I'm so glad you're here.'

Ben smiled; he didn't want thanking. They walked together, side by side.

'I'm sorry you're in this mess. I can't thank you and your family enough.'

'I'm sure anyone else would have done the same thing,' Ben answered.

Stephen paused a second. 'Not me. I wouldn't have helped.'

Ben was unsure of how to answer. He appreciated the lad's honesty, if nothing else. 'You're scared now. Confused. But you would have helped. I know you would.'

'I left that woman to die in the woods. I drove away. What does that make me? What does it say about my character?'

There was silence as the guys walked towards the coach. Ben kept an eye on the road, hoping to see another vehicle.

Stephen was contemplating their situation. 'I'm sorry I ran. I'm sorry I'm not braver. Christ, I could apologise all day,' Stephen acknowledged. 'I see her, you know?'

'See who?'

'The woman I knocked over? Sometimes she's in my flat, standing in the garden or when I'm driving, she's on the road ahead. I hear her in my room; I often see her shadow pass my front door.'

Ben kept his eyes on the ground, watching where they were stepping. 'Tell me what happened. That's if you feel the need to talk,' Ben said. 'I understand you hit someone from what the caller said earlier. Did you kill her?'

Stephen rubbed his face with the back of his hand, panting, struggling to keep up with Ben. 'We were out drinking – Gareth and me. It was late, I'd had a little too much. He said not to drive, to get a taxi, it wasn't safe, but I didn't listen. I thought I knew it all. That we'd be okay. That I could drive safely. When I hit her, Gareth told me to get out, to help her. I had my life ahead of me. I didn't want to face up to what I'd done. So I drove away. If it happened again, I'd do the same thing. I'm ashamed of myself, but honestly, I'd drive away again.'

'At least you're being truthful,' Ben said.

'I envy people like you. I don't need to ask what you'd have done, how you'd have dealt with the situation. I'm not built like you. My parents, they never taught me anything, right from wrong, correct decisions, etiquette. They weren't around half the time. My father was abusive, my mother a part-time junkie. We fended for ourselves. My brother and me. He's much older, so I never had someone to guide me properly. To educate me. Most of the time, I was left to my own devices.'

'Where are your parents now?' Ben asked.

'Mum's in care, a type of rehabilitation programme, and my father ran away with his secretary. I haven't heard from him in years. I don't ever think about him or what he's up to these days. He left us, so why should I contact him?'

Ben felt for the lad. He'd made a mistake and was brave enough to admit he'd do it again. He respected his honesty at least.

'That's your only daughter? The girl on the coach?' Stephen asked.

'Yeah. Milly. We've had our problems, don't get me wrong. Show me a family who hasn't. But she's going in the right direction. Don't get any ideas, by the way,' Ben advised. He laughed to show Stephen the last sentence was more in jest than a threat.

Stephen smiled. 'She is kind of hot.'

'Hey. I'll pretend I didn't hear that last remark.'

'I see her everywhere.'

'Who. Milly?' Ben asked.

'No. The woman in the woods.'

'The mind can do that sometimes. The subconscious can play tricks.'

Stephen stopped abruptly. He was looking towards the coach as they approached it. He turned. 'It's not my subconscious. It's her ghost. I'm sure of it.'

Ben was uncertain of how to answer.

'I see her spirit everywhere,' said Stephen, his voice brittle.

'The thing is, when I went back to help, to rectify my mistake, I couldn't find her.'

'You mean she'd vanished?' Ben asked.

'Yes.'

'Are you sure you returned to the right place? It was late. That's what you told me.'

'It was the right place.'

Stephen went on to tell Ben where it happened and how the woman came down and appeared from nowhere. He went to say more but was suddenly stopped, distracted. He pointed down the road. 'See. There she is now.'

Ben looked to where Stephen was pointing.

'There's a shadow. The silhouette of a person, standing by the coach. She appears in many forms. She's haunting me, Ben.'

'That's not a spirit. Someone is standing beside the coach. Shit! Laura. Milly.'

13

STEPHEN AND GARETH

Stephen stood alone in the woods. He'd searched for the woman he'd hit with his car for over an hour. Now, he had choices.

He could keep looking. Maybe the old woman was further along the road. It's possible he was mistaken about where it happened; the woods were dark and he may be confused.

Or he could call the police. This went against his earlier actions. He imagined the conversation when the officers turned up. Yes, he'd sobered up a little, but they'd know, they'd work out what had happened. Stephen had been drinking with his best friend, had driven home, knocked over a woman in the woods and fled the scene. He'd wrestled with his conscience, and then gone back to do the right thing.

You say you hit someone? An old lady? She wore a white night-dress, you say? Had long, scraggy hair? Well, she sure as hell isn't out here now. What's that? She was in your flat earlier, and then out in the garden? Have you taken anything tonight, sir? Had a little too much to drink perhaps? Is that it?

Stephen pulled his phone from his jeans pocket and contemplated calling Gareth. He'd said he had a lecture tomorrow morning. It was late, too late to call anyone. He stood in the middle of the road. For a moment he wallowed in the tranquil surroundings. The woods were serene. He was on his own with no other sound but his breathing, his body warm with anticipation. He shivered through fear, now struggling to stop his teeth clunking together in his mouth. He composed himself. The trees either side of the path were at rest; the wind had halted and the air was still.

Suddenly he heard a clicking.

Tap.

Tap.

Tap.

Stephen moved towards his car. It was unlikely that another vehicle would drive along here so late, but he needed to leave.

Tap.

Tap.

He eyed the mobile in the palm of his hand. He blinked, struggled to focus.

Tap.

Tap.

'No. This is not happening. It can't be happening.' He brought the phone to his face. A string of letters appeared.

I'M BEHIND YOU.

He spun around, dropping the phone.

'Leave me alone! Why are you doing this?' He reached down to the ground, pawing in the dark. He grabbed the phone, jumped into the driver's seat and shut the door.

Stephen glanced in the rear-view mirror, slightly adjusting it. *Breathe, Stephen. Breathe.*

He placed the phone on the passenger seat, then started the engine. Steadying himself, he contemplated what to do.

She had to be out here, lying on the road somewhere. There was no way she had got up, smoothed out her nightdress, pushed her long hair out of her face and left. Stephen couldn't understand what had happened to her.

He sat, eyes closed, the scene playing in his mind over and over. Him in the driver's seat, speeding, playing with the radio, hearing the loud bang.

Minutes went by as Stephen sat, thinking, pondering his choices, composing his thoughts, his mind now spewing out images, frightful visions. He opened his eyes and tried to move his foot to the accelerator, but it felt trapped in a vice, held down and confined. *Move, you bastard. Obey my command. Lift and slide. Lift and bloody slide, damn you.* His foot just would not obey.

The agitation was building. *Get a grip on this situation*, he told himself. He looked down and said aloud, 'Okay, after three, leg, you're going to move. You'll hit the accelerator, and we're out of here. Do you understand the simple instruction? One. Two.'

Bang.

The car jolted forward and conked out. Stephen viciously turned the key in the ignition until his fingers were sore, cut with the pattern of the key fob. He reached for his phone, lifted it to his face and unlocked it. The words that appeared a couple of minutes ago had gone. The screen was clear.

Stephen opened his messages; the last one he'd received was from Gareth, instructing him when to swing by and pick him up for their evening out.

Stephen laughed as he sat alone in the car. His heart rate was slowing, his mind emptying of the thoughts he'd had. His leg moved freely. He circled his right ankle, one way and the other, up and down, moving his foot and letting the blood circulate. He pushed back in the driver's seat and inhaled, then slowly pushed a long, smooth breath from deep within his aching body.

Once he'd composed himself, he slowly turned the key in

the ignition, listening to the engine crank, the smooth purr, then the click of the seat belt as it engaged. All the comforting sounds and motions of a car working as it should.

Again, he adjusted the rear-view mirror. Something was lying on the road behind the car; making its way towards where he sat. The white nightdress. The long black hair. She'd come from nowhere.

'No,' he moaned. 'It can't be. Leave me alone. I'm begging you. Leave me the fuck alone. How did you get here? I checked. The road was empty.'

He threw his face violently into his hands, then pushed his head back on the seat, gripping the cloth with his fists in frustration. He glanced again; the road was empty. A second ago, the old lady was crawling along the road, lying on her stomach, pulling herself along the ground like a wounded animal, slowly making its way towards him.

He turned the key and switched the car lights off, then stepped out onto the road. His hands were shaking as he lifted the phone, turning on the torch and checking the area around where he stood.

He paused, aware of his breathing, controlling it as best he could. He remained motionless for a couple of minutes.

Once he was sure he was alone, he glided the torch from his phone to the front of the car, then back and into the woods. The tall trees stood like soldiers, side by side, compacted, ready to march forward. Mist crept through the trees towards where he stood, writhing like a snake as it worked around the trunks. Stephen backed away, watching as the fluid coalesced. Enlarging. He swiped the phone torch along the path once more.

'Right. I'm out of here. You're on your own. I don't need this shit. I saw you, crawling behind the car a minute ago and now you're gone. If you don't want my help, then stay here. I don't care anymore. I'm not playing your games. You're dead. I can live with this. I can live with it, you hear me?'

Stephen got into the car, started the engine and turned on the lights.

The old woman was standing at the bonnet, her face bloody and sinister, staring at him.

'No!' he moaned. 'I killed you. I ran you over. You're dead. You can't be here.'

Tap.

Tap.

Tap.

Stephen reached for the phone as the car lights went off and the engine died. He hadn't turned the key. He sat in darkness, whimpering, stamping his feet on the floor of the car, shuffling on the seat, waiting as the minutes slowly ticked. He had to drive away from here, away from the woods.

Once he gained the courage, he focused on the front window, manoeuvring himself with his hands against the seat, like a gymnast on a pommel horse.

He turned the key, the lights came back on, ahead of him was an empty road. The old woman had gone.

Tap.

Tap.

He looked at the message.

I'M SAT BESIDE YOU.

Stephen was numb; his body felt temporarily paralysed. He fought the terror as he sat in the darkness, but sheer dread had exhausted his body. At this moment, he had never experienced such horror.

He saw his body as if he was viewing it from above, like he was hanging in the air, floating, looking down on himself. The car was spinning, a broken parachute that had got tangled around the person jumping. The car continued turning, revolving.

He slowly reached his hand towards the ignition; the air in the car had turned from fresh to stale in an instant. A stagnant, putrid, rusty odour as if blood had leaked onto the seats. The stench seeped into his lungs, poisoning them.

Stephen heard someone arranging themselves on the passenger seat, shuffling, getting comfortable. His hand touched the key, feeling it swing. Again, the engine went dead. He edged forward, holding his breath, and turned the key to summon the engine. The lights sprang to life, lighting the road ahead.

Stephen turned his body sharply.

The passenger seat was empty.

He pressed the accelerator and drove.

Stephen woke in his flat and lifted the alarm clock from the floor. It was just gone 10am. He'd slept lightly, waking every hour or so.

He'd left the woods after the woman had disappeared from the passenger seat. He reached for his phone, opening the messages. The last one he'd received was still Gareth's. He hadn't contacted Stephen this morning. He wondered if his friend had made it to his lecture; if he'd told anyone what Stephen had done.

He sat up in the bed, stretching his arms above his head. He looked at the bedside cabinet, pressed against the door. He remembered last night, going back to the woods; the messages on his phone; the old lady crawling behind the car, making her way towards him.

His head was a mass of confusion. Had she been real, or was it his imagination running wild?

He threw the blanket back, stepped onto the cold floor and went to the window. The curtains were closed, and as he pulled them back, he expected to see her face.

The sun shone, causing him to shade his eyes. The sky was clear blue with only a light haze. Despite what happened last night, he felt good, alive. Then the guilt set in. He had driven from the scene of an accident. Stephen was the lowest of the low.

In the shower he turned on the water and stood. It felt like his body was melting; his sins discharging into the plughole.

He spent the rest of the day indoors, lounging on the sofa. He didn't have the confidence to face anyone. He flicked through his social media, liking posts, comments, pictures.

He ate at lunchtime, two pieces of toast, lightly buttered and a cheese single slammed on top of each one. He continually listened for the buzzer, a noise in the communal hallway. Anytime someone passed his flat, he sat up on the sofa, pushing to the edge of the seat, holding his breath.

He kept the radio on in the background, listening for news bulletins.

There was nothing reported about the woman he had run over in the woods.

Gareth sat in the lecture theatre, watching Dr Norris drawing numbers on the board, stabbing the piece of chalk for effect and discussing a recent law case which had made the news. His droning voice was monotonous and uninspiring. His lecture was a long, tedious waffle that Gareth had no interest in processing.

In any case, his mind was preoccupied. The events of last night were taking their toll; his concentration was non-existent.

Gareth closed his eyes; the tiredness was now taking over, his mind closing down. The information the lecturer provided was slamming into a brick wall. There was no way into Gareth's head. There was no room.

'Gareth! Are you still with us?'

He opened his eyes, found his head resting against the desk. 'Sorry, I'm not feeling well. I think it's something I ate.' Gareth waited, knowing the lecturer didn't like him.

He sat through the torrent of abuse, taking it all in like a large sponge. Dr Norris didn't need an excuse; he tore into Gareth for the simplest of things.

'You'll flunk the test papers. You wait, young man. You haven't a cat's arse in hell of passing. You sit there with your glazed expression, unwilling to take my course seriously but you'll be the loser in the end. I still get paid.'

Gareth was seething inside. He turned his head to the right, seeing the piercing eyes, the disgust on the faces of his classmates. Marette Donoghue, Simon Johnson, Paul Gates. They stared with revulsion at him: another interruption causing a sidetrack in their education.

Gareth stood. He was fuming. 'I'm sorry. I have to go.' Amid tuts and quiet sneers he left the lecture theatre.

He stood in the car park. He was unable to drive and too distracted, so he opened the door of his battered dark blue Volkswagen Golf and lay on the back seat.

Gareth woke. It was late. He sat up, forgetting where he was.

The car park was more empty than it had been. The main

doors of the university building were closed. The lights in the windows of the classrooms were out.

He thought about Stephen. Last night. Was he now a factor in what had happened? Did his actions make him a part of the crime his best friend had committed? He wanted to go to the police, tell everything. He couldn't. They'd been best friends for years.

Gareth opened his car door and moved to the front seat. His body was numb as he stretched to rid the paralysis. He felt heavy, sluggish, like he was suffering a carb overload, although he hadn't eaten for hours.

Suddenly, Dr Norris came out from the main doors and moved towards the back of the car park, pushing his hand into his pocket and retrieving his keys. His suit was immaculate, his hair perfect. His shoes were glistening.

Hatred rose from the pit of Gareth's stomach.

The lights of Norris's expensive jeep pinged to life with a small beep as he stepped gracefully into his vehicle. The lecturer waited in the driver's seat, the lights on, unaware that Gareth was watching him.

Why aren't you going, you arsehole? What are you waiting for?

Gareth was about to leave when he saw the jeep pulling out from the car park.

Gareth couldn't explain why he followed Dr Norris, why he needed to get into his private life and interfere in the business of someone he knew little about.

But he followed him.

Gareth struggled to keep up with the jeep in front. The lecturer drove erratically, taking turnings at the last second without indicating, racing through a village and ignoring the signs stating the speed limit.

Gareth despised him. He wanted to crush Norris for the way

he humiliated him in lessons. If there was anyone to blame for the deterioration in his education, it was this man.

He thought about ramming the jeep into a ditch or pushing it into the oncoming traffic at the lights. Of course, it wasn't in Gareth's nature to do something like that, but it didn't stop him taking pleasure in fantasising about it.

He pulled back from the jeep as it wound up a steep hill, while keeping close enough to see it.

Suddenly the jeep slowed down, the brake lights blinking, and the lecturer pulled into a small car park in the middle of the countryside.

Gareth knew this place. It was a picnic area with amazing views over Surrey. On a clear day, you could see for miles. He slowed the car, stopping in the middle of the road. He needed to wait for the lecturer to settle. If he drove straight in, he'd risk being spotted.

Gareth waited, watching in the rear-view mirror, prepared to leave if another vehicle approached.

He gave it five minutes, then slowly pulled forward.

As he approached the entrance for the car park, he rolled the car into a space and turned off the lights. He looked further down. Norris was parked roughly fifty yards from where Gareth sat. He saw another car about ten yards from where the lecturer had parked. Someone was in the driver's seat with the internal lights on.

Dr Norris sat still, so did the driver of the car next to him.

'What the hell is going on? It must be a drug deal. Dr Norris has a dealer?'

Gareth stepped out of the car, making sure to keep obscure. He left the driver's door open and moved slowly towards where both people were parked. He crouched, edging closer.

Suddenly, the other person opened the driver's door and stepped out. She stretched, pushing her arms above her head.

She shook the cramp from her legs, adjusted her skirt and made her way towards the lecturer. Dr Norris opened the door, walked around his jeep and stood beside her.

Gareth gasped. He recognised the person the lecturer was meeting.

Marette Donoghue. His classmate. *So she's a dealer. Wow. I have you now, you bastard. You wait until I get this out on social media.*

They stood beside each other; a smile passed between both participants, nothing more, then Dr Norris undid his belt, dropped his trousers and Marette knelt beside him.

'No. No. No. You sick bastard! She's your student!' Gareth realised he'd said it too loud. He waited, holding his breath. He felt sick. She was nineteen; Norris was mid-sixties at least. This was how he dealt with grades and achievements.

Gareth grabbed the phone from his pocket and started clicking, photographing their every move. Gareth didn't realise the flash was on.

Dr Norris turned, spotting Gareth in the darkness. 'Who's there?' He quickly pulled his trousers up and tightened his belt.

Gareth ran, he slid and tripped on the stones, falling forward and landing on his hands.

The lecturer was charging towards him, his footsteps loud on the gravel. Gareth managed to get to his feet and wiped his hands on his jeans. He had to get out of there. The lecturer would kill him for what he'd seen. Gareth would never get through his course. The lecturer would make it impossible for him. He couldn't contemplate future classes and how this man could destroy his education at the drop of a hat.

Gareth reached the Volkswagen, and Dr Norris stopped in his tracks, turned and ran back to his own vehicle.

He was going to give chase, and was determined not to let this get out.

14

THE COACH

Ben and Stephen ran along the road, never taking their eyes off the figure stood beside the coach.

They expected at any moment to hear gunshots.

As they approached, Ben shouted, 'Move away. Don't do it. Leave them alone.'

Laura was making her way down the steps. She joined the person standing by the coach.

Now Ben was close enough to make out the figure. It was Edward, the elderly guy who'd been sat at the front.

'What the hell is going on here?' Ben asked as he reached the door of the coach. His voice was raised, authoritative. Edward was putting the other passengers in immediate danger.

Laura turned. 'Ben. Thank God. He won't listen to me.' She moved forward, holding her husband.

'What in heaven's name are you trying to do?' Ben directed the question at Edward. He saw Milly standing on the steps of the coach with a confused expression.

'Milly and I were looking after the passengers. She was talking to Lydia, and I was speaking with Abigail. Suddenly I saw Edward stand and move towards the door. Somehow he managed to free himself.'

Ben turned towards Edward, his voice critical. 'Do you realise you're putting yourself and the others in severe jeopardy? The caller instructed that no one leaves the coach. That includes you.'

'I'm not staying in that wretched thing for a second longer,' Edward shouted.

'What about your wife? Your daughter-in-law? Your son? So you're just going to leave and think only of yourself?' Ben asked.

'I'm going to get help. I can make it. I'm stubborn enough to succeed.'

'I don't doubt that, Edward, but think about your family for a second,' Ben suggested. He was desperate to get through to the older man. This was a deplorable task that could go either way.

'I'm not deserting them. I'll get help goddamn it, I can make it.'

Ben grabbed Edward and pulled him closer. 'I'm telling you, we stay here. No one leaves until it's safe to do so. Do I make myself clear?'

'You're not giving me instructions, young man. I'm too long in the tooth to listen to anyone. I make my own decisions. Now move out of my way,' Edward insisted.

'I'm not letting you go,' Ben said through gritted teeth. His body tensed.

Edward was acting like the last man standing in a bar, too stubborn to drink up and leave with the others as staff turned stools upside down on tables and began switching the lights off. As the two men grappled with each other, they heard a car racing towards them. They all looked, wondering if it was help.

The car stopped around a hundred yards from them. The passenger door opened, the full lights causing them discomfort.

Something landed on the floor with a thump. The car door closed and the lights moved backwards out of view.

Ben, Laura, Milly, Stephen and Edward all stood motionless. They were unable to speak as they stared into the darkness.

Ben broke the silence. 'I guess it isn't Amazon.'

'What do you think he dropped?' Edward asked.

'I doubt it's food,' Ben said. 'I'll go and check it out. Stephen, can you come with me? Edward, wait here with Laura and the rest.'

For once, Edward listened.

Ben led the way, pointing the light from the torch towards the ground. Stephen followed close behind. As they walked closer to the object lying on the road, Ben turned, shining the torch towards the passengers. On Laura's face he could see the anticipation. He turned, looking at Stephen. 'This isn't good.'

Stephen didn't need to say anything. The fear had struck him mute.

'Stay calm, compose yourself,' Ben instructed.

As they got nearer to the large shape, the two men braced themselves; the apprehension was rife. Ben could hear muttering from behind him as the gravel crunched under his shoes. The road was uneven, like it hadn't been finished and he could feel the large holes as he stepped.

Laura called out, 'Be careful.'

Ben obeyed without responding. His mind was focused. He needed to deal with this.

They were now standing over the object. The first thing Ben saw were the shoes. The person was lying on their side. He scanned the light over the jeans, a jumper. Ben crouched. He gasped at seeing the remains of the person's head. The image would haunt him and Stephen for the rest of their lives. They could tell from the clothes it was Andrew. But half his head was missing. A large, gaping hole left the insides on display like a presentation in a freak show.

Ben looked towards Stephen. 'The bastard must have shot him as he drove away. He was waiting out here, watching as he attempted to escape. To do this type of damage, I'd say he was standing pretty close. We can't let the others see this. It's something they'll never forget.' Ben turned, looking into the fields and wondering whether the caller could see them now. The hairs stood on his arms, prickly pimples covering his skin as he watched for a shadow in the darkness. 'This is what's going to happen if we try to escape.'

Stephen turned. 'We're never going to leave, are we?' He burst into sheer panic, sliding his hand down his face, pulling his mouth downward. He grabbed a fistful of hair and ripped his head back.

Ben moved forward, held Stephen tightly, clasping him around the shoulders. 'We'll get through this. We need to follow the guy's instructions.'

Stephen pointed to the body on the ground. 'Look, for Christ's sake. I've never seen anything like this. Look at his head.' Stephen turned, crouching, holding his mouth, and then vomited on the side of the road. Once, he'd finished, he stood, wiping his lips with the back of his hand. 'How the fuck are we going to get out of here? A person capable of this won't think twice about finishing the rest of us. I have to take my chances. I have to cut loose.'

Ben shook Stephen to try and make him see sense. 'You leave now, and this is how it ends for you. Is that what you want? To finish up like this? You're young. You have your life ahead of you. You can be anything you want to be. Are you listening?'

Stephen broke down, crying hysterically. Ben held him until the panic had passed, then he knelt beside the body, turning Andrew onto his front, face down. He shone the torch towards his head. The hole was so deep that the head looked as if it could come away from the body at any second.

'We can't leave him here. If we move the body and place him on the coach, there'll be hysteria that we can't control. The less people know about this, the better, for everyone's sake. Here, hold his legs,' Ben ordered.

Stephen froze. 'I can't.'

'Yes, you can. We need to lie him in the field. If we survive, we'll get him a proper burial. Until then, we need to keep the others safe.'

Stephen summoned all the strength he had, fighting with the terror that attacked his body. He knelt beside Andrew, pushing out a sharp breath, an intense groan released from deep within his frame. 'I can't do this.'

'Stephen, watch me. Look into my eyes. Lift on three. Keep looking at my face, okay?'

'Okay.'

Ben and Stephen carried Andrew off the road and placed his body on the grass. Ben knelt, saying a prayer while Stephen clasped his hands together with his head down. They were silent; the two men had witnessed an atrocity they'd take to their graves. Once they'd paid their respects, they joined the others.

'We're keeping it quiet. No one finds out, okay.' Ben was talking more to Edward than Laura and Milly. Edward nodded. The older man was shaken, and he finally seemed to be taking the situation seriously.

'What kind of animal are we dealing with here?' Edward asked.

The question was too obvious to warrant an answer from the other four.

'We stay on the coach, together. There's safety in numbers.' Ben looked towards Edward. 'You need to sit back with your wife. I don't need to explain the consequences.'

Edward climbed the stairs to the coach and joined Mary.

Laura, Milly, Stephen and Ben followed close behind.

'How's everyone doing?' Ben called from the front. He placed the phone on the dashboard and shone the torch along the coach, watching the passengers. Milly was now standing in the aisle. He regretted that his daughter had seen the body being dumped on the road. The only saving grace was that she hadn't seen the damage. She was young, delicate. He wanted to shield her from all of this. He moved along the coach.

'Hon, are you okay?' Ben asked.

Milly slowly moved towards him. 'I've had better days.'

He reached out and held his daughter tightly. 'I'm so very proud of you. You know that?'

'Likewise, Dad.'

'I'll keep watch from the front. You and Mum keep an eye towards the back of the coach. If you see anything, let me know. This guy is a psychopath, Milly; I think it's only the beginning.'

Suddenly the phone rang. Concern seeped from every pore of every person on the coach.

Ben swung around, looking away from Milly. He briefly turned back, clocking his wife and daughter who had moved close together. He swept his right hand in a downwards action, bouncing it as if gently calling for calm.

The phone was on the dashboard. They knew who it was.

Ben stepped forward. Again, he felt the hairs rising on his arms, a multitude of strands standing, preparing. He pressed the loudspeaker button and listened.

'How did you like your present?'

Ben didn't answer. He stayed looking out the front window of the coach.

The voice continued. 'I enjoyed talking with you earlier. We spoke at great lengths in regards to people and their wrongdoings and how they should be dealt with – the consequences of their actions. I do hope I enlightened you a little. I'd hate if my ramble was for nothing.'

Ben held the phone out, wanting to smash it on the dashboard with frustration. 'Why did you do it?'

'Disobedience. It's one of my biggest bugbears.'

'So you shot him dead?' Ben realised he'd said his words a little too loud.

The caller's voice raised in volume. 'See, this is what pisses me off. Listen, Mr Do-Gooder, and I'll explain. The coach driver is paid to look after his passengers, to make sure they get from A to B safely. We agree on that, I'm sure? If not, stop me at any point. He loads the luggage, he has enough fuel, the tyres are pumped, and he makes sure everyone is seated before *bon voyage*. He'll keep to the speed limit, drive carefully, be considerate, obey the road rules. There'll be a pit stop, a bite to eat and toilet duties. He'll wait, he's carried out a headcount and won't go until every passenger is packed into his road ferry. He'll wear his uniform, proud to be carting passengers forward, new beginnings, a better life, a hotter climate. Wherever their onward journey takes them, he'll be a bit-part in their travel arrangements.

'Now, Mr Do-Gooder, you work in a café. I'm speculating here. You turn up in the morning, and you tap the alarm code as you walk through the door. The place is spotless. Your task starts. Maybe the chairs are upside down on the table; maybe the sign needs changing to, "We are open. Come in and fill your face". You've planned for a delivery. It needs to arrive way before anyone comes through the door with their tablet tucked tightly under their arm and their meetings scheduled over a coffee and a bun. The food is placed on display, neatly arranged, the menu spread across the board in thick felt pen. You feel good; it makes you feel good, making people feel good.

'Now suppose you turn up late, later than the people who

have formed a queue outside your eatery. The delivery hasn't arrived, the alarm goes off as you open the door, the screech ringing through the street. The chairs are still placed upside down from the night before; the sign still says "Closed" as people sweep inside. The smell is off-putting, the floors grubby, the menu smudged, the food decaying on display behind the grimy counter.

'You are now the sinner. Putting people's lives at risk. That, Mr Do-Gooder, is why the driver of the coach had to face the consequences of his actions. I gave him one job, and this is how he repays me.

'He ran. Mindless of anyone in his care. He is a sinner, Mr Do-Gooder. A scoundrel, a loafer. Taking my money for haphazard work. A thief, wouldn't you say?'

Ben wanted to challenge the caller. He could push, but he wasn't sure how far. 'So how does that make you any different? You're putting the passengers at risk. You're a sinner.'

'To avenge the violation and transgression of others? How so?'

'You're no different from any of these people,' Ben stated.

'If you wish to think that, be my guest. Only some people are going to pay for their wrongdoings before others. We'll all pay in the end, only some much sooner. I believe if someone sins against you, or you witness this evil, then you have the power to put it right. It simply must be dealt with. That's what I'm doing. An eye for an eye. My revenge. Their penance.'

Ben wanted to question more, to ask what he knew about the people on the coach. Why he'd taken it into his hands to dish out punishment, thinking it was okay for him to play the higher power. There was more to this story. The passengers had told him very little. It seemed to Ben that there was history between these people. His thought process was interrupted.

'I want you to get Edward,' the voice demanded.

Ben turned, looking at the older couple sat at the front. 'Why do you want him?'

'I saw he got up a few minutes ago, so there's no need to undo his rope.'

Ben sighed; the frustration was taking its toll. 'You're playing with people's lives here. You understand that?'

The guy ignored Ben's plea. 'Take him to the front, and the two of you get off the coach. This is something I've very much looked forward to. At the end of the road, I want you to turn left. Then walk along the dirt track. You'll find an old derelict barn towards the back of a field. I've rigged up a light on the roof so you won't miss it. I want you and Edward to walk along the path until you find it.

'Inside the barn is Edward's very disorientated son, Nigel. Let's say I've roughed him up a little. He's armed with a sawn-off shotgun I gave him earlier. He has one bullet. Edward is going to explain everything to his son. The affair he's having with Nigel's wife – who incidentally is sat behind him as we speak – and the little situation of aborting the baby.

'I'm certain Nigel will be cross. Oh, so cross. Now, if he shoots Edward in a blind rage, of course, it goes without saying, Edward loses. You know the other outcome. You all walk out like one big happy family and back up the yellow brick road. It's a game called shoot or scoot. Oh, best of luck to the both of you. I feel you'll need it.'

15

STEPHEN AND GARETH

Gareth sped along the road, watching in the rear-view mirror. He saw the jeep pounding out of the car park. Dr Norris had seen him taking photographs with his mobile phone.

Shit. What have I done? Why the hell didn't I just go home? I had to follow this idiot. Now, he's going to make my life hell. He's going to tear me limb from limb every time I enter his lecture. He knows my car, the registration plate, he'll see me. He'll know it's me.

But there was no way the lecturer could have seen his face. That was the only thing Gareth had on his side.

He could see the jeep gaining in the right-wing mirror, becoming larger, enveloping the glass. He ripped the wheel to the left and pressed the accelerator, darting down a side road.

The jeep went past the turning. *Yes, you bastard.* Suddenly, he saw Norris reverse and pull into the road, now moving behind him.

No, Gareth! Think. I can't go home. I'll park up, race inside, and a minute later, he'll barge against the front door. He'll grab my phone and ram it down my throat. I need to keep driving and maintain a reasonable distance between us. I'll lose him. I have to lose this idiot.

Gareth reached the end of the road. He waited briefly,

looking left and right, then he pulled out. There was no sign of the jeep. He tapped the brake, rigorously checking the mirrors. He slowed, wondering why the lecturer hadn't reached the end of the street. Gareth realised he needed to get out of here – no point in waiting. *Maybe he's crashed. He could be lying in a ditch now, cut, his head on the dashboard; the airbag engaged – the car alarm ringing out across the remote road.*

Gareth waited. He gave it another minute, taking in his surroundings, weighing the options. His mind went back to last night. The woman in the woods. He wasn't going to do what his friend Stephen had done. He needed to do the right thing. Go back and make sure Dr Norris was all right.

Slowly he pressed the accelerator with his right foot, pushing it gently. He'd turn around at the next roundabout. *Go and make sure–*

He looked to his right. A vehicle was stationary, waiting on an adjacent road – the lecturer in the front seat.

Gareth hammered the brakes as the jeep pulled out. He grabbed the gearstick and forced the car into reverse. The top half of his body was twisted to the left as he peered out of the back window. The lecturer was following, moving quickly towards him.

Gareth swerved along the road, slowing as the car manoeuvred left and right. As the jeep caught up, Gareth hit the brakes and quickly moved the car into first gear. He pulled away as the jeep stopped and attempted a U-turn.

In seconds the lecturer would be tailing him again. He thought about what he had on his phone. A college lecturer in his sixties, a respected man. Norris was married – Gareth knew he had a family. He often referred to them during study periods. But Gareth had pictures of him in a desolate car park with a student nearly fifty years younger, performing a lewd act on him. Norris would lose his job, his credibility. Probably his family too.

The seriousness of the situation dawned on Gareth as he wrestled with his conscience. He wondered why he'd taken the photos; he questioned if he was ready to ruin another man's life. The lecturer had spent years building his reputation, gaining trust, working hard to establish honour, respect. One click and pow! The end of the legend.

He saw the lights in the distance, two pinpricks enlarging, rapidly growing and making their way towards him. The lecturer wasn't going to give up. His life was on the line, and he'd do anything to get the photos back.

Gareth drove with the jeep on his tail. He feared the outcome if the lecturer caught up with him. He was now struggling to hold off a panic attack which threatened to paralyse his body. It seemed as though hours had passed. Gareth couldn't chance going home. He couldn't have the lecturer knowing where he lived. He'd be a sitting duck, weak and vulnerable, a target waiting to be splattered – an open invitation.

Gareth pulled into a side street and drove to the end of the road. He pulled the car into a space and waited. He locked the doors, released the catch of his seat belt and waited. He sat for an hour.

A couple strolled past, walking a dog; a group of lads possibly swigging a bottle of alcohol, wrapped in a brown paper bag as they passed it between them. A young woman brought out a white bag filled with rubbish and struggled to lift it to the lip of the bin.

He wanted to ring Stephen, tell him what had happened and ask him to help. He was the only person who would understand and who really cared. They had been best friends since childhood. Gareth told him everything. Likewise, Stephen confided in him. The trust was mutual.

He suddenly felt embarrassed about what he'd done. For a second, Gareth wanted to take the phone, delete the pictures and move on with his life. Forget about what he'd seen. It was a sordid little secret, a tale that spirals. The sort of story that once you hear it, you keep it to yourself and think about what you've been told. You hold on to it. After a day or so, you share it, tell others. As you watch the shock on their faces you wish it was you hearing it again for the first time. You miss the buzz as your brain processes the shocking information. Gareth knew he'd opened Aladdin's cave and he wanted the world to see it. But was he ready for the consequences?

He waited another half hour. He grew tired of watching a cat rolling on its back, the figure to his left through the window pacing along the living room floor with his earpiece and dramatically talking on the phone with his hands – the flashes of light across the road from the telly and the woman who smoked on her doorstep and flicked the cigarette butts onto the pavement.

He started the car and pulled slowly out onto the street. He imagined Dr Norris at home now, speaking with his wife, looking into her eyes, telling her he loved her, sipping a glass of wine and spooning pasta that she'd prepared for him into his mouth. He sits opposite, telling her about his day, the clown that will flunk every exam paper put in front of him, how tasty his lunch was, the uneventful journey home.

Gareth felt enraged. Angry that this bastard could do this, go home to his wife and pretend everything was perfect in his fraud of a marriage. He needed to steer his mind away from the lecturer. He had him now. He had one over on this disgusting excuse for a man. Whatever happened, Gareth had the photos, the proof. His life was going to change. For too long the lecturer had made his progression in life difficult. It would change.

Gareth pulled out onto the main road. He was going home to eat a light snack, shower and hit the sack. The long day and the stress had caused an ache which was working along the front of his forehead. His eyes were starting to blur and his ears were ringing with pressure. He wiped his brow with the front of his hand, straightened his back, listening to the satisfying crunch of his bones and then adjusted the seat, exhaling a long breath.

As Gareth drove, his eyes darted to the right-wing mirror. He'd checked a second ago. The road was empty. Now suddenly, lights were gaining, getting closer.

It can't be? Surely he's gone home, given up the fight?

The lights were on top of him, blinding his vision. Gareth grabbed the mirror, adjusting it so he could see better, to dim the glare. He jabbed the accelerator, eyeing the petrol indicator. He had enough to get him home. The lecturer had waited, bided his time. This was serious. The guy could kill Gareth for what he had on him.

Gareth had pulled into the side street, waited. He didn't know for how long, but it felt like hours. Here he is though, on his tail, prepared to go the full hog to destroy what Gareth had.

He was fearful for his life, afraid of what Norris would do to him. He envisioned the lecturer bursting into his room in the middle of the night and stabbing him in the bed, or running him over in the car park outside the flats. Gareth sped up; the lights stayed close behind.

He turned up side streets and indicated left and right. He swerved, trying to lose the jeep behind. Wherever he went, the lights followed.

Shit. This is it. The guy has been pursuing me for hours. I can't get out of this situation. I can't win.

The accelerator was pressed as far as it would go, the engine was loud and struggling – a long whine which added to his already aching brain. His mind was addled, and Gareth had never felt pressure like this.

As the two vehicles came to the end of a small town, the road became a double lane. The jeep caught up and rammed the back end of Gareth's car. He felt the steering wheel spin out of control, and his body shook. He forced the accelerator, willing his car to push, to keep going. He knew it wasn't built for a pounding like this. He envisioned smoke from the bonnet, the tyres dropping off or the car collapsing and him sitting in the middle of the road in just a seat.

All of a sudden, a truck pulled out from a side road. Gareth saw it in the distance. He doubted the lecturer would have time to process what was happening. He was watching Gareth's car. The truck driver signalled for Gareth to slow down, but the jeep kept going.

The tail end of the truck swung out onto the road and Gareth managed to steer around it while the lecturer slammed on the brakes. It gave him a couple of minutes to pull into a side road.

Gareth parked his Volkswagen, jumped out and raced along the road, checking the vehicles on the drives. He got lucky a quarter of the way up the street. One of those chance-in-a-lifetime opportunities. A car parked on a drive with the key in the ignition. A US style mailbox planted at the front of the house with the word 'Hargreaves' written in gold letters. This was the break he needed.

He reversed out and drove slowly along the street, watching the lecturer pass him on his right-hand side.

Gareth drove home, mechanically following signs until he reached the main road, barely noting the details of his surroundings, unaware of his location. He was also unaware there was a dead body in the boot.

Dr Norris drove along the street, knowing he was conspicuous. His head was hazy, addled with the stress the mystery photographer had caused. A stream of perspiration worked its way down his forehead, and he swiped it away with the back of his hand. He was clammy, his clothes were damp, a temperature was building. What he'd do for a drink now. A large glass of water, room temperature, no ice. He drove, watching the houses both sides, knowing he had to find the driver of the car. His life was over if he didn't get the phone.

He drove for another half hour, up and down the quiet road, slowing up when he saw someone on the street.

'Shit. How could I lose him? How could I be so bloody stupid?' He slammed his fists on the dashboard, screeching as he swung the steering wheel, manoeuvring the car along the road.

He wondered if Marette could have set him up, then shrugged the possibility away. She was a good student, not great, but intelligent. He did her favours, helped her, adjusted her marks where possible. She'd be an idiot to throw it back in his face. He'd gotten away with it before: there were other girls, flunkers who didn't stand a hope in the big world, dossers who turned up late, left early and as soon as they entered his classroom, their minds drifted. He knew the ones to pick out. The women who needed a break, who thought that life owed them a favour; they turn up to one of his lectures and expect their world to change.

He had that power.

But it came at a price.

The lecturer checked his watch. It was late. Too late to tell his wife he'd broken down or lost his way. Too late to say he'd had a meeting, but still time for a quick stop-off.

As he drove, the roads became a mass of lines, curling and twisting like a snakes-and-ladders board in his peripheral vision, an illumination holding him in a trance. He struggled to focus, he felt beaten, knocked senseless and dropped into a bottomless pit with no way out.

Finally, he reached home. The lecturer parked on his drive. He got out of the car and stood for a moment, fearful for the future. It was going to get out. The nineteen-year-old student and him, the car park, the lewd act caught on camera. He was bang to rights.

As the lecturer opened the front door, he heard a familiar voice. 'Edward, is that you?'

'Yes, Mary. I didn't feel well. I had severe chest pains and had to pull over. I'm better now.'

'Oh, you poor dear. I've made dinner. I'll warm it up. You've just missed Nigel.'

The lecturer closed the front door and went into the kitchen.

Mary turned towards her husband. 'So, how was your day?'

'Oh, nothing exciting.'

16

BEN AND EDWARD

Ben and Edward reached the end of the path and turned left, following the caller's instructions.

Edward walked in silence; the shock of the evening was hard to swallow; he had a mass of nervous energy pulsing through his veins. He wanted to run and sod what the rest of them thought. He didn't care. He thought, *I am the most important person in this situation.* He recalled his wife Mary and the things he'd done. They'd been married for over thirty years, and to an outsider, they were the perfect couple.

Edward knew he had a problem, that it was a struggle to 'keep it in his pants'. He felt that if something was there and looked good, it was his to take.

Deep down, Edward knew he was a rotten husband. Yes, he showered his wife with expensive gifts, extravagant holidays, he opened doors, complimented her, held her, made conversation and listened to everything she said; but he abused his power. Edward always used his authority to get what he wanted. He also had a remarkably close relationship with his son. They spoke most evenings, met at weekends and now that Nigel and

Abigail were back together, they'd started to come for dinner every couple of weeks.

Now, Edward had to meet with him. Explain his actions as Edward the adulterer. But this time he'd crossed the line. Even by Edward's standards, having an affair with his daughter-in-law was very wrong.

As Ben and Edward walked along the quiet path, Edward broke the silence. 'I'm sorry you're mixed up in this. I haven't had time to thank you.' He found it astounding that he'd admitted his feelings to this stranger.

Ben was holding the torchlight to the ground. 'There's no need to thank us. I'm sure anyone would do the same.'

'I doubt that. You and your family are remarkably brave.'

The two men remained mute for a few moments.

'How is Mary coping?' Ben asked.

'She's an incredible lady. She's strong, not just in spirit, but mentally. I love that woman. She's my rock. I've done bad things, Ben. Things I will have to live with until my dying day.'

Ben was unsure whether to push the conversation. It was Edward's business; he was the one who had to live with the way he'd acted.

As they walked, Ben saw the light on the barn in the distance, a small glow towards the left side. 'Are you ready to speak with your son?' Ben asked.

Edward stopped. He turned, facing Ben. 'How can anyone admit the ultimate betrayal? Nigel is a beautiful lad. He cares for us, he's great to me, to Mary. I don't think he's ever caused us a problem. I don't know if I'll be able to deal with him cutting me out of his life.'

Ben said, 'Aren't you more worried about the gun he's supposed to be holding?'

Edward was silent for a moment and then said, 'Nigel

wouldn't know how to fire a gun. He's... he's not a violent person.'

The two men continued walking along the road, getting nearer to the barn.

Ben stopped, looking at the small brick building. The heavy clouds from earlier had parted slightly and a section of the moon reflected off the roof, lighting its felt.

They climbed the grass verge. Ben helped Edward through the barbed wire fence and they pulled themselves between the poles and rough bushes into the soggy field. The barn was roughly a hundred yards from where they stood.

Edward took a deep breath. 'Let's get this over with.'

The light from the torch played across Edward's face and Ben noticed tears streaming down the older man's cheeks. 'I'll be right behind you. Nigel will take it badly, I'm sure. He has a firearm. He's disorientated, but we'll deal with it. We'll get you both out and back to the coach. I can't say for sure how your life will pan out, but the main objective is to get out of this situation alive. You ready?'

Edward had his hands resting on his hips. 'As I'll ever be.'

Ben went first. His eyes darted towards the patchy grey sky, and he prayed to whoever was up there to look after Edward. He knew he'd done bad things; he had the morals of a rat and the way he lived his life was the complete opposite to the way Ben lived his, but tonight, he said a small prayer asking for Nigel to forgive his father.

Ben pushed the door; the loud creak grated his ears. It was stiff, jammed on the mud below. Ben shoved hard, pressing his body to get inside. He held the door for Edward who followed. A dim bulb hanging on an old, flimsy electrical cord in the middle of the barn provided adequate light.

'Nigel, are you here? I'm with your father. My name's Ben and we are helping your family and the others. Your mum and dad are okay. So is Abigail.' Ben shone the light towards the back of the barn. Hay was scattered across the floor, and there was a smell of manure. A small wooden trailer sat in the middle.

'Nigel, it's your father. Are you in here?'

A figure appeared from the balcony which ran across the right side of the barn, reached via a wooden ladder with slim rungs. The person was standing at the front towards the railings and looked down towards the two men. Ben shone the light to where he stood. He noticed a man standing still, looking dishevelled. His shirt was ripped, his hands bloody and he had the sawn-off shotgun by his side.

'Dad. Thank God!' Nigel called out. 'Where's Mum?'

'Your mother is fine. She's coping. Abigail too. We're here to get you out.'

Nigel climbed down the small ladder which sounded as if it could crack in half at any second. When he reached the ground, he moved towards his father and dropped the gun to the floor. He lifted his arms, holding his dad tightly, wincing with the pain.

Edward stood back. 'My God, what did he do to you?'

Nigel shot a look at Ben. He placed his hand out, shaking it and introducing himself. 'Nigel, good to meet you, although I wish it were different circumstances.'

'You and me both,' Ben answered.

Nigel recalled his version of events. 'The guy came to our house. He kidnapped us at gunpoint. Placed us on the coach and tied us to the seats, gagging our mouths tightly so we couldn't speak or call for help. It all happened so quickly. One minute we were preparing dinner, Abigail and me, the next, we were marched onto the coach. There were others too. I thought he wanted a ransom. I thought you'd pay him, Dad, and that would be that. He drove, with everyone strapped tightly to the seats and parked at the back of a driveway, out of view. He left us overnight. People soiled themselves, Ben. The smell... We were vulnerable. It was early the next morning, a guy climbed onto the coach and got in the driver's seat. He didn't look at anyone. He just drove.

'The next thing we knew, a man stopped us out here, waving a shotgun in our faces. He marched us along the road and put me in here, tying me up. I don't know what he did with the others. He came back a while after, sticking the gun in my mouth. I thought he was going to kill me. I was scared, shitting myself. I tried to wrestle the gun from him, and he grabbed a large knife from his trousers.' Nigel lifted his bloodstained hands and showed the cuts. 'Needless to say, I came off worse. The stupid thing is, when I came around, he'd left the gun.'

The phone rang.

Edward braced himself.

Ben answered. 'Hello.'

'I'll be listening. Don't hang up.'

Nigel darted a confused look between Ben and his dad. 'That's him. That's his voice. What the hell is going on here?' Nigel reached for the shotgun, gripping it in his right hand. He lifted it and pointed the barrel over the room; his eyes were wide open, the fear evident on his face.

'Nigel, we need to talk,' Edward stated.

'What's happened? Is Mum okay?'

'Yes. As I've stated, your mother is fine.'

'Abigail? Has something happened to her?'

'No. She's fine too. Everyone is fine,' Edward answered.

The room fell silent; a sense of gloom rose in the air. Edward watched his son drop the gun to his side, resting the length against his hip.

Ben knew it was an illegal weapon, created by cutting off the barrel to make it shorter and easier to conceal. It seemed its main objective was to kill people.

Edward spoke to his son. 'Nigel, what I have to tell you can't wait. You need to listen. I beg you not to judge the man standing in front of you. I, your father. The person who, along with your mother, moulded you into the man you are today.'

Ben noted the clever tactics Edward was using. He glanced at Nigel's right hand, at his finger curled around the trigger.

'What's going on, Dad?'

'Nigel, I say this with embarrassment. With downright shame of what I've done to you, your mother and Abigail.'

Nigel glanced towards Ben, then back to his father. He was confused, trying to understand why they weren't leaving the barn and why the person who abducted him had been talking on the phone.

'I want you to know I love you. I love my family. I'd do anything for you and your mum.'

'I know that. You're scaring me. What's happened?' Nigel brought his left hand to the top of his head, preparing for what his father had to say. His deep brown eyes were becoming glazed. His body was tense, his face strained.

Edward took a deep breath, then glanced at Ben, who nodded as if to offer some encouragement. 'I've done some terrible things. I'm ashamed as I stand here before you. You recently split with Abigail. Your mother and me, we were devastated. Mary took it bad. She didn't trust Abigail; she said she led you on, that she was no good for you, that you deserved better. Well, she's been having an affair. With me.'

The atmosphere in the barn dropped like a brick from a ten-storey building.

The shotgun fell from Nigel's hand. His body was trembling as he dealt with the shock of what his father had told him. He went to speak, but nothing came from his mouth.

Edward's eyes never left his son's. He was trying to read his next move and anticipate the result of what he'd just delivered.

Ben stood, holding the phone, expecting the caller to burst into laughter.

Suddenly Nigel clasped the sides of his head with his hands, banging them against his temples. He murmured something, then gained the control to speak. 'I don't believe you. Abigail would never – you wouldn't do this. The two of you... You wouldn't.'

'I'm afraid it's true. It was my doing. Abigail called me one evening. Your mother was out at a church meeting; you were at the pub with a friend. She was in a state, crying down the phone. She said she'd never loved anyone like she loved you. She wanted it to work out, for you both to get back together. I tried to comfort her; I told her to give it time. The more she spoke, the more desperate she sounded.

'I got in the jeep and drove over to her place. When I arrived, she greeted me at the door. She spoke, I listened. I got up to go when she'd calmed down. I assured her you'd both be okay, that things would work out. As I went to leave, she offered me a drink. You have to believe that's all I intended – the one drink, offering a little company. Yes, if I'm honest, I find her attractive. What man wouldn't? But she was my daughter-in-law. My son's wife. There are boundaries. We sat on the sofa. Abigail told me how much she thought of your mother and me. How much she wanted her marriage to work. She was envious. Can you believe that?

'As I stood to go, she moved close to where I was standing. She placed her arms around my waist, thanking me for listening, for being there. I held her; I pulled her closer.

'Whatever came over me and I'm not making excuses, but I had a desire. Something I struggle to control. I removed my arms from around her and placed them either side of her head. I kissed her hard on the lips.

'She pulled away at first, saying it was wrong. I saw the shock on her face, the realisation of what could happen. She didn't want to. Blame it on loneliness, dejection; I don't know, but as I went to leave, she beckoned me to come back. I'm embarrassed to say that I slowly undid her clothes, and we made love on the floor.'

Edward stopped talking. He searched his son's face for a reaction – something to denote what would happen next.

Ben waited, watching Nigel, the gun. His fingers twitched and his smiling facade sunk into a grimace.

Edward stood in front of his son, waiting, expecting at any minute to get a bullet in the head. 'I'm so sorry,' he offered.

'Sorry? Sorry for what exactly?' Nigel struggled to conceive what his father was saying.

Edward moved his head forward, staring towards the ground. He didn't answer the question.

'You and Abigail? I don't believe it. It's not true. This is a nightmare. I'll wake in a minute, and I'll find myself at home with my wife, under the duvet, the telly on in the background, and I'll be sipping warm coffee. It's a bad reaction; it has to be something I ate. Any minute now, I'll wake up.' Nigel was babbling to himself.

Edward lifted his head. 'I didn't mean for it to happen.'

'Wait – the pregnancy. We were having problems. I found out I'm infertile. I've had the tests. We can't have children. I took her back, prepared to father another man's child. Christ, I'd do most things for a happy marriage. I was prepared to deal with it. To accept it.' Nigel turned away for a moment. He composed himself, then faced his father. 'Are you telling me the baby was yours?'

'Please, Nigel. Don't make this any more difficult. Yes, the baby was mine.' Edward's face turned red. He fought to stop himself from passing out.

'So what happened to the baby?'

Ben stood between the two men, his eyes, darting back and forth as if he were watching a tennis ball being smashed across a net. He could hear the caller's breathing rasping down the phone.

'Nigel, I'm begging you.'

'Did she lose it?'

'Son. Please.'

'It makes sense now. You terminated it, didn't you? Your sordid secret. The baby would remind you every time you saw it of what a cruel manipulating bastard you really are.'

Ben took a step back, now facing both men. 'Guys, this isn't the time. Let's go back to the coach. To Abigail, Mary.'

'But then again,' Nigel continued, 'you've always been a selfish bastard. Abusing your position. When I think back, you've always done what you wanted, regardless of anyone's feelings. You stamp on people, crush them and move on.' Nigel lifted the shotgun and looked at Ben. 'Get out of my way.'

'Don't do this. It's what the caller wants, can't you see? He's put us in this position, beaten you black and blue and made your father confess. Drop the gun, Nigel,' Ben shouted.

'I said, move out of my fucking way.'

Ben stood his ground.

Nigel moved to the side, holding the gun to his father's head.

Edward stared ahead; his eyes were closed as he mumbled a prayer to himself.

'Don't do it, Nigel. You'll work through this. You'll sort it out. It will take time. That man in front of you, regardless of his actions, is your father. Your flesh and blood.'

Nigel turned his head to where Ben was standing, keeping the shotgun aimed at his father. 'Why didn't he think of that while he screwed my wife? Terminated her child? He's my father, but he's a selfish, arrogant, pig-headed bastard. I'm doing all of us a favour.'

'You won't achieve anything.' Ben braced himself for the explosion as Nigel squeezed on the trigger.

Edward screwed his eyes tighter; sweat dripped down his face, and he had a damp patch on his groin. He screwed his fists tight, mumbling to himself.

Nigel pulled the trigger a little more; his hands were shaking, his expression contorted. Suddenly he dropped the gun and fell to his knees. He sobbed hysterically, ashamed that he'd almost murdered his father.

Ben sighed with relief while Edward opened his eyes and crouched by his son. 'I'm sorry. I'm so very sorry.' Edward held his son, who was crying like a child. He pushed his face into his father's shoulder, and they clasped each other.

After a few minutes, Edward stood. 'Let's go back to the coach. Your mother and your wife need you. I need you.'

Ben blew out another heavy breath.

The caller had failed with his trap.

Nigel stood, brushing himself down. He would struggle to walk the distance, and his hands were severely cut and would need attention.

Ben told him that Milly had a box with bandages and antiseptic back on the coach. Ben moved to the door of the barn.

There was an almighty bang. He swung around, his ears ringing, seeing the back of Edward's head and what the older man was staring at.

A body lay on the floor.

Nigel had placed the sawn-off shotgun under his chin and pulled the trigger.

17

LYDIA AND JACK

Jack stood on the drive, staring at the empty space where his car had been parked. He stared down at the glistening marble-style paving slabs. His hand, pressed against the white painted brick. He moved out onto the street, wondering if he'd left it along the road. He hoped the pressure was playing tricks on his mind. He moved quickly along the pavement, searching for the vehicle.

No, no, no. This isn't happening. It can't be happening. How can I lose the car? Think, Jack. We arrived late last night; I distinctly remember parking on the drive. I'd have no reason to leave the car on the road, especially in the circumstances. With a body – with Chloe in the boot I'd have all the more reason to park the car close to the house.

He stopped, turned and walked back the other way, checking. He heard the birds' morning song. The sky was clear, the sun rising and he'd normally go to the corner shop, buy a paper and come home to look at the Saturday football fixtures over a hot coffee. He'd bring Lydia her tea at around 9am, kissing her gently on the forehead. She'd stretch, thanking him, and then turn over for another hour of sleep. Later she'd gulp the tea and call down for a warm one.

He needed routine, normality. But it could never go back to how it was. Lydia had killed Jack's boss. He was knee-deep in the appalling crime; and now they'd lost the body.

Jack stood on the drive for a few seconds, focusing. He stepped into the house and sat on the bottom of the stairs. He rubbed his eyes, circled his head and swung it left and right to clear his mind, then stood.

It has to be a dream, a brain freeze. It's a temporary lapse in normality. That's it. That's what has happened. The car is on the drive. It has to be.

Jack held his breath as he reached for the front door, pulling it hard. *I'm going to see the car.*

The space was empty. This was real. The car had been stolen.

Jack slammed the front door, edging back, holding the bannister for support. He couldn't go upstairs to Lydia and tell her what had happened. She couldn't deal with this. There was no way she could get to grips with what had happened. The car had been stolen from the drive, and Chloe was in the boot.

Jack walked into the kitchen. He had to think logically. If someone had stolen the car, he had to find it. It may have been dumped somewhere close by. The thief could have found the body already, in which case, Jack couldn't report it missing. Jack didn't want to contemplate the other scenario. The thief had been pulled over, the car searched and it had led the police back to their drive.

The more Jack thought, the bigger the problem. He imagined putting an ad out on social media. A reward for the safe return of their car.

Hey everyone. This morning, I opened the front door and POW! Our car was gone from the drive. Stolen. Some shitbag got into the front seat and helped themselves.

I'm asking for your help because it's not a normal situation and Lydia and myself are desperate to get it back.

See, there's something different about this plea. My boss, who I think the world of, is dead in the boot. Lydia killed her – by accident, I'll add. Anyway, if anyone sees it about, give me a call.

Oh, just to add: don't open the boot.

Just call me if you know where the car is, and I'll look after you.

If by any means you do open it, don't mention the corpse in the boot. I'm really stressing this.

Thanks again,

Jack and Lydia.

Jack decided against the ad.

He sat in the kitchen, listening for Lydia. He was sure she was still asleep. He had an idea.

Jack went into the garden and started to fill the hole. There was no way Lydia would know if Chloe's body was buried there. She'd see the turned-over soil and assume Jack had buried the body. Lydia would never go out and start digging, wanting to see it. She'd have no reason to believe anything else. Jack would tell her he'd done it, that he'd buried Chloe.

His forearms ached as he began filling the hole. He had a vision of finishing, maybe sticking a small cross on the mound by way of respect. He imagined Lydia coming downstairs, thanking him for his effects, then seeing the car back on the drive, finding the body in the boot and asking what the hell he was up to. That would be a little tricky to explain.

Of course, Lydia would ask about the car. How the hell would he explain that? This situation was getting more complicated by the second.

Okay, think, Jack. Here's what you say. I got up early and dug the hole. I went to the car and moved the body. You were asleep, and I didn't want to wake you, Lydia.

I pulled the body through the house, I know, it was horrible, some-

thing which couldn't be helped. Then, I brought Chloe into the garden, dropped her into the hole and filled it all in again. Done. Job's a good one as they say.

But about the car... I'm sorry, I couldn't drive it again knowing what had been in the boot. I just can't face getting into it again. It's been tainted. I can't deal with the thought that my boss was lying in the boot so I drove it to the nearest reservoir and pushed it into the water.

Hey, we'll get another one. A new car. One that has never had a body in it. How does that sound?

Jack patted the earth with the shovel and stuck it into the ground. It was another way to hopefully convince Lydia that Chloe was buried in the garden.

He walked back into the kitchen. He needed to think of an excuse as to why the car was gone from the drive.

He heard Lydia upstairs, going to the bathroom. He went to the hall and called up, 'Do you want a tea, Lydia?'

She grunted back, 'Umm. That would be nice.'

Jack filled the kettle and switched it on. He listened to her moving around upstairs, wondering if she'd looked out the front window onto the street below. The front of the car would normally be visible from there. If she had seen the car was gone, she hadn't said anything yet. Jack braced himself; it wouldn't be long before she realised. He had to think of something. The steam rose from the kettle, billowing into the kitchen.

'I'll bring it up in a minute,' Jack called. He waited for a response.

He heard water running and then the creak of floorboards as she went back to the bedroom.

He finished making the tea and climbed the stairs. He needed to act as normal as possible, wait on the end of the bed until she turned over and nodded off.

He pushed the bedroom door with his left hand and entered the room.

Lydia sat up. 'Thank you. I need to rest, Jack. I didn't get much sleep.'

Jack placed the tea on the bedside table as relief washed over him: he had another hour or so to think of an excuse. 'Okay. See you a bit later. It's Saturday. You don't need to get up for anything.'

'Is it done?' she asked.

Jack turned and headed towards the bedroom door, making sure she couldn't see his face. 'Yes. It's done.'

Gareth.

The first thing Gareth did when he woke was call Stephen. He'd missed a few calls from him, and he needed his friend, now more than ever.

He had a lucky escape last night; Dr Norris, his least-favourite lecturer, had seen him in the car park and followed him for what seemed like hours. He recalled how he'd dumped his own car a few miles from home and stolen another one that had been left parked on a drive with the keys in the ignition. But now he had to get rid of this car. Maybe drop it back. This wasn't him. It wasn't the way Gareth acted. In the last twenty-four hours, he'd been involved in a hit-and-run, became a voyeur, obtained obscene photos for use in blackmail and robbed a car.

He dialled Stephen's number. His friend answered on the third ring. 'Gareth. How's it going? I called you a few times and texted. I thought you were ignoring me. What's happening?'

Gareth explained the events of yesterday evening.

'Shit, mate. That makes what I did seem a bit less severe,' Stephen said.

'I'm in trouble, Stephen. I don't know if Dr Norris saw me. I can't go in on Monday. Everything is a mess, mate.'

'I think he's the one in more trouble. Do you have the photos saved on your phone?'

Gareth pressed the loudspeaker button and flicked through the pictures. 'Yes. They're a little dark, but you can tell it's him.'

'Well stop worrying then. You have him by the balls.'

Gareth laughed nervously. 'What are you going to do about the woman?'

'I went back to the woods. She was gone,' Stephen said.

The phone went silent for a second. 'What do you mean, "she was gone"?' Gareth asked.

'I drove back to where we saw her – the same spot. I don't know how long after, but I drove back.'

'Stephen, she can't have gone. It's not possible. You hit her. You left her on the road. How could she have gone?'

'I saw her,' Stephen said.

'Hang on. You said a second ago that you didn't see her.'

'I saw her at my flat. At the window, in the garden. She kept appearing. I had to go back, put it right. When I arrived in the woods, she'd disappeared. She must have got up, brushed herself down and left. But then I saw her on the road, crawling towards me; and she messaged me, telling me she was sat in the passenger seat.'

'Are you listening to yourself? For Christ's sake, Stephen.'

'I know how it sounds, Gareth, but I've been seeing her. I think she's coming for me.'

'Okay. Look, I have a few things to do. Let's hook up later,' Gareth said.

'Yeah. I need to sleep. Come over later. See ya, mate.'

Gareth spent the rest of the day indoors. He tried to revise, but struggled to take in the notes and diagrams. After a while, he went to the window and glanced down at the car he'd stolen last night. He had to do something. So he showered and dressed then flicked through the telly channels, scanning one trash programme after another. He contemplated a box set, but his mind was too addled.

He was unable to stop thinking of Marette, the lecturer and what he'd seen. *Christ, why did I do it? Why couldn't I have driven home when I left the class? Minded my own bloody business?*

Gareth was too exhausted by stress and fear to take control of his terrified mind and in the end it shut down and he fell into a deep, merciful sleep.

Gareth woke at just gone 4pm. He jumped up and went to the window. The dark blue BMW was still there. For a second, he'd hoped someone had come for it. He took the keys from the kitchen worktop and went down the two flights of stairs to the car park.

Outside, he stopped at the corner of the building, making sure there was no one around. He glanced at the vehicle parked in the bay marked number four, the disabled badge on display on the dashboard. A small scooter in bay three; the elderly owner rarely came out anymore. Gareth remembered his wife had died a few months back and he seldom left his flat. He'd knocked the door a few times to check the elderly widower was coping, but he never answered.

Once he was sure he could get into the car without being seen, Gareth opened the driver's door and sat inside. Now it was daylight he could see that the car was immaculate, much cleaner and tidier than his. It looked like the owner was a careful person and proud of their car. But it smelt like something had gone off, the slight whiff of rotting meat hung in the air. *They've dropped a sandwich under the seat, I bet.* He didn't have time to look for it now.

He reversed out of his space and onto the road. *Right, let's get this car back onto its driveway, and I'll pick up my car and–*

As Gareth pulled onto the main road he realised that he had no idea where he had left his car, and no clue which suburban driveway he had taken this car from. The only thing he recalled was the US style mailbox.

The flashy BMW had started immediately and was a smooth, luxurious drive. But he felt a sharp longing for his own blue Volkswagen Golf. It was old and on its way out. Dr Norris had rammed it, so it was probably damaged. But it was his car, and he'd be able to drive it without guilt, without fear.

He turned left and drove towards Stephen's flat. Stephen, with his background of buying scrap, may know how to get rid of an unwanted car. And he owed Gareth a massive favour.

His mind was distracted. He felt guilty, but he couldn't remember where he'd snatched the vehicle from, the house, the road, what part of town.

Paranoia had set in, and Gareth worried what he'd say if he was pulled over. The police would have a field day.

He slowed as he drove along the main road, trying not to look conspicuous, edging the brake to let cars out from side turnings and being over-polite. He found himself scrutinising traffic lights, always acutely aware of pedestrians who might step onto the road.

He turned on the radio, hoping the music would soothe his nerves. But he still felt sick – knowing he was driving a stolen car... and that smell was getting worse. He opened the windows. Gareth had to get rid of this car. He turned various plans over in his mind.

Suddenly, he found himself turning into the block of flats where Stephen lived. He struggled to remember how he had got here, like he'd been transported through time.

Stephen lived on the ground floor of a small block of flats, mostly occupied by elderly folk. Gareth pressed the buzzer and waited to be let inside.

'Whoa. You look like death,' Stephen announced. He was standing at the front door, wearing tight jeans and a loose black T-shirt.

They hugged, and Stephen stood to the side of the door to make way for his best mate.

'How are you feeling, if it's not a dumb question?' Gareth asked. He sat on the sofa, taking in the small living room with the oversized telly in the corner, photographs neatly aligned on a low shelf and a stack of eighties comic books resting under a coffee table.

'I've had better days.'

'I need your help, Stephen.'

'Go on.'

'Last night was horrible. I don't know what came over me. So much happened. I'm struggling, mate, and need you to do me a favour.'

'What do you need?'

'I want you to get rid of the car I came here in.'

Stephen's eyes were confused, empty and lacking emotion. 'Can't you take it back?'

'No. I can't remember where I took it from. I can't do it, I can't drive or function at the moment. My head's so confused with everything that's happened and I'm struggling to think straight. I need your help. I'm desperate.'

Stephen stood up. He sighed, letting Gareth know he wasn't happy with the request. 'You're suffering with the shock. I get it. Look, rest up here and I'll drive the car somewhere. I'll call you to come and get me when it's done. Where are the keys?'

Gareth leant forward, removing the keys from his front pocket and dropped them on the table. 'Not a word about this to anyone. I need it gone.'

Stephen opened the car door and sat in the driver's seat. The smell almost knocked him out – a mixture of shit and rotten cabbage. 'What the hell?' He opened all the windows, then stood outside.

It felt like his lungs were infected, drowning inside his body. He waited by the car until fresh air washed through it, then sat back inside. He looked over the vehicle, thinking where to dump it. He wondered if this would come back on him. Was Gareth asking a little too much?

By the time the smell had dissipated enough that he could drive the car, he had decided to dump it in the woods.

Jack was pacing the floor. It was gone 11am, and Lydia was still asleep.

In a way, it was a good thing; he still hadn't thought of anything to tell her about the car. He'd have to play along when she noticed, make out he knew nothing about it being taken. This posed a threat. If she reported it, Jack would have to tell her about the body still being in the boot. He'd have to tell her he didn't have time to retrieve Chloe and that the grave he'd dug was empty.

His mobile rang, making him jump. Jack looked at the number, realising it was Dana.

Shit. This is all I need.

He answered with a bright, cheerful voice. 'Hey, Dana. Did she come home?' Jack already knew the answer.

'No. That's why I'm calling. Her phone goes straight to voicemail. I'm worried. She's never done this before. What am I going to do, Jack?'

Like a teacher writing a maths equation on the board at the front of the classroom, asking the pupils to work it out, put their hand up and give the answer when they knew, Jack had the information. He knew what had happened to Chloe, but he didn't know how to answer Dana. 'I'm so sorry. It's not like her. She was fine at work; she never mentioned anything was wrong. Chloe was her usual, ambitious self,' Jack answered.

'What time did she leave?'

'I'm not sure. I left work a little after six. She was still in her office. I promised Lydia a night out. It's been a while.'

Dana pushed for answers. 'Did she say anything about drinks? About our news?'

Jack remembered sitting in the pub, Chloe pouring her heart out to him about Dana getting the awful news of having cancer. She was in such a state, crying, telling Jack how much she loved Dana and that they'd fight it together. 'No. What news?'

'It doesn't matter. Look, please, Jack, if you hear anything, call me straight away. I'm calling the police again.'

The phone went dead.

The conversation with Dana had added to their mounting problems.

Jack opened his laptop, searching for news of a dead body being found in the boot of a car. His hands were trembling; his tongue felt stale through dehydration. He stood, walked to the sink and drank two cups of water. A headache was working its way along the right side of his face and spreading rapidly.

He sat back at the kitchen table and scanned recent posts on Facebook, then went onto a page with up-to-date local news. There was nothing about Chloe. Nothing about a body in the boot of a stolen car. Jack shut the laptop and stared at his phone, tempted to block Dana's number. It would look suspicious. He had to help, be supportive. He needed to hone his skills at lying, now more than ever.

Lydia stirred in the bedroom. Jack stood, his hands were clammy, and his heart raced, beating through his T-shirt, like fists pounding on his chest. He moved to go upstairs, then paused and sat back down. This would crush Lydia. She was vulnerable at the best of times. More recently, she'd turned to alcohol to suppress the demons that festered in her head. This could send her toppling over the edge.

He heard her at the top of the stairs, slowly making her way down. He listened to her light footsteps, her hand sliding along the rail.

Jack moved to the door, stepping into the hallway. 'Hey, babe. Did you sleep well?'

Lydia smiled, reaching forward and kissing Jack on the cheek. 'Not as bad as I'd expected.' Her face looked swollen, her cheeks puffy, and she had a bed mark along the right side of her face, like stitches, stretching across her skin. She looked out into the garden through the kitchen window, seeing the grass, the mud which had been turned over. 'Jack, I can't. This isn't right.'

'What else are we supposed to do, Lydia? There's no other way. It has to be the garden.'

Lydia moved to the window. 'I want you to dig her back up. Right now.'

Stephen.

Stephen drove with the windows open; the breeze made the stench more bearable.

He was driving through town and paranoid that he'd be pulled over any second, asked to produce his driver's licence while the police officer called in the number plates. He saw himself waiting, watching the officer's eyes, then pressing the accelerator and racing away with the car hot in pursuit. He needed to get to the woods, dump the car and get Gareth to pick him up.

A few minutes outside of town, a tractor was holding up a queue of traffic.

The breeze eased up, causing a lack of airflow. Stephen was

feeling sick. He would have to park somewhere, move out of the car and get rid of the smell. His stomach was turning around, spinning one way, then the other. He pulled over to the side and got out. The tractor ahead went into a field and the road cleared.

What is making that smell? He opened the back doors, searched under the seats, pulling the carpets forward, checking the floors. Then, he moved to the boot and opened the lid.

Stephen jumped back. *No. This isn't happening. You're dead. You're fucking dead.*

He fell to his knees and vomited over the road. When he'd finished, he stood. He stared at the dead woman and he screamed, holding the side of his head. He turned around, looking along the empty road. Then, he moved to the boot, reaching forward. Touching the corpse.

The body is real. Someone must have seen me. Someone has dumped the woman in the woods in the boot of the car.

He grabbed his phone and dialled Gareth.

'Yo. Have you got rid of the car?'

'Got rid of the car? You didn't get an odd smell? Like say, the fucking dead body of the woman in the woods.'

'Mate, you need to simmer down and calm yourself. That shit isn't real. She's not haunting you, Stephen.'

'Then why is she lying in the boot of the car you asked me to get rid of?' Stephen looked again, making sure his mind wasn't playing tricks. 'I need you to see something. She's dressed differently, but I'm certain it's her. Turn on FaceTime.'

'Mate, you need to stop this. She's not coming for you. The things you're seeing aren't real. Stop this shit. Now.'

Gareth hung up.

Stephen called back, hearing the phone go to the answer machine.

I don't believe this. I need to get petrol. I'll have to burn the car.

Stephen edged forward, seeing the woman in the boot, and

slammed the lid. He got back into the car and drove, unable to comprehend what was happening, questions forming in his mind that he couldn't answer. Ever since the night of the accident, he'd been plagued by visions, a ghostly apparition of the woman he'd hit. He saw her, appearing in different places, haunting him. This was real. He knew the difference – the smell for one. The stench was still filling the car, poisoning the air he breathed. He touched her while she lay dead in the boot.

He saw a petrol station and pulled up next to one of the pumps. Stephen needed to do this right, carry on in a normal manner. He bought a petrol can, and filled it at the pump. The woman behind the till looked out. She seemed to smile.

Back in the kiosk, he placed a box of matches on the counter, and the container he'd filled.

'Having a bonfire?'

Stephen looked up. 'What do you mean?'

'I'm just joking with you.'

She gave Stephen the price, and he rushed out to the car. As he sped away, she watched him.

He drove, incapable of concentrating on the road ahead. He had so many questions. Why would someone do this? Why place her body in the boot? Did Gareth have anything to do with it? Would he arrive at the woods and find she'd gone from the car? Was his mind, playing with him, tormenting him.

Stephen pulled over and got out. He checked his phone for any crazy messages, remembering when he'd got texts from the woman saying she was sitting in the passenger seat. There was nothing.

He listened for vehicles, then moved to the back of the car and opened the boot. The smell was repugnant. He turned, puking up water, then slammed the boot aggressively. He stood in the middle of the road, then dropped to his knees, crying out for someone to help him.

Once Stephen had composed himself, he got back in the car and continued driving.

He tried Gareth's number again, cursing him. *Why had he wanted me to do this? Why wasn't he answering? Did he know the woman in the woods was in his boot? He made out he'd stolen the car after the lecturer had given chase. Was he lying about that too?*

Stephen jolted suddenly, realising he'd reached the same area where he'd hit the woman.

He pulled the car onto a path which led to the woodland. Stephen sat for a moment. He had to do this. To exorcise the demon. To rid himself of the visions. She'd been put on a plate, and now, he had to deal with her and finish it.

He got out, took the petrol container from the back seat and poured the contents over the car.

Then he took an old rag from the boot, dipped it into the container, lit it and threw it onto the back seat. He stood back and watched as flames engulfed the car. As the smoke rose, spewing toxic fumes into the air, he dialled Gareth's number again. He was pissed off that his friend would do this and then ignore the phone calls.

A dazed voice spoke on the other end. 'Hi, Stephen.'

'I can't believe you didn't answer the phone. What the fuck is wrong with you?' Stephen's voice was raised; he watched the smoke building, realising the urgency.

'I'm sorry. I powered my phone off and fell asleep. The stress is playing with my emotions and wearing me out. Shit. Where are you?'

'I'm at the spot in the woods. You need to get your arse in gear and pick me up.'

Gareth sat forward on the sofa. 'I'll take your car. I'll see you in about twenty minutes.'

Stephen interrupted before the phone went dead. 'There's so much smoke. I'm worried someone will come. I'm going to cut through the woods. Meet me on the other side. As you drive, you'll see me. I'll hide in the forest. Hurry, mate.' Stephen pressed the button to end the call.

The smoke was getting into his lungs, making him cough. He was breathless, unable to inhale properly. The fire was roaring. Any minute now, someone would pull over and ask what had happened. The emergency services might even be on their way.

Stephen ran, charging into the woodland; his arms reached out in front, swerving through the trees, the leaf litter and sticks crunching under his feet. He hoped it was over. The woman in the woods was in the boot of the car, which was now a blazing wreck. His mind raced, wondering if she was real. He'd seen her lying still, the smell so strong, so evident. What if it *was* just a mirage, a figment of his out-of-control imagination?

She's dead. She has to be dead. I saw her in the boot. I set the car alight; I saw the flames, the smoke curling, into the atmosphere.

Stephen stopped suddenly. The smell of smoke had disappeared. He was struggling to see; his eyes were watering, his lungs full, seeming unable to take anything into them. He bent forward, placing his throbbing hands on his knees, listening to the silence. He was surrounded by wood, stumps, leaves piled knee-high. He remembered how as a child he had come here with friends in autumn, building with the leaves and charging head first through them like a diver on the edge of a swimming pool. Stephen straightened his body. He needed to get to Gareth, flag him down. His life had to return to normal and he needed to forget about what happened.

As far as he was aware, no one had reported the woman; no one had come forward for the missing car or mentioned the body in the boot. Gareth didn't believe him. Maybe it wasn't real, after all.

He heard a crunching, the noise of a stiff leaf being trodden on. He paused, taking in the area, watching. The world remained motionless. He edged ahead, one foot slowly in front of the other. There it was again, like someone was there with him.

Stephen turned in circles. 'Is anyone there?' He looked through the trees, straining to see in the distance. He waited, a minute, two, three, then moved on, slowly placing his feet on the ground. As Stephen walked, he continually checked behind. The shapes which surrounded him formed pictures, dark figures, patterns which played with his mind. He ran suddenly, unsure which way to go or how to make it to the road.

He pulled his phone from his back jeans pocket, seeing the screen bouncing as he charged through the forest. The signal was gone. Stephen moved it left and right, lifting the phone above his head. He crouched, swinging the phone in semi-circles. 'Sod this shit!' he shouted, panic in his voice. 'Gareth.'

As Stephen turned, he saw a figure in the distance. A man, watching him.

Shit. You're not real. I know you're a mirage, a shadow, a form of brain confusion. Leave me alone. This isn't fucking real. He glanced at his phone, still no reception. The light was minimal; the woodland had closed it off, acting like a blanket. He took a deep breath, his lungs aching. He looked down to the floor, then back to where he'd seen someone standing. The figure was moving fast, racing towards him. Stephen dropped the phone, glancing at the shape, gaining on him.

'Shit. What do you want? Leave me alone.' He bent forwards, searching the ground, swiping his hands over the leaves. *Where the hell is the phone? No, what am I doing? I'll have to leave it here. There's someone charging towards me. He's going to kill me.* And then his fingers found his phone. He placed it in his pocket; then he ran for his life.

18

BEN AND EDWARD

Ben rushed from the barn door, blocking Edward's view. He desperately tried to stop the older man seeing his son, lying on the floor.

Edward screamed out, fighting to get to Nigel.

'Don't look. Please, Edward.'

The older man forced his way through, kneeling beside the dead body of his son. He reached out and touched the remains of his son's head, cradling him and pulling him to his chest. Edward looked at Ben. 'What have I done? Oh God, please, no, no. Son, don't die like this. I'm begging you, don't die on me here.' Edward fell to the floor and he lay on his stomach, unable to deal with what had happened.

Tears streamed from Ben's eyes at the sight of a father grieving for his boy. The soul had been ripped from Edward, and as he lay on the floor, he screamed, filling the barn with hysteria, pressing his hands to his face and crying uncontrollably.

Ben stood beside Edward and the dead body and let the man grieve. He didn't say anything; it was their time together – their goodbye.

The Coach.

Laura and Milly were stood at the front of the coach. They heard the bang in the distance and knew it was a gunshot.

'Mum, I need to go and see if Dad's okay.' Milly was already moving towards the door of the coach.

Laura caught hold of her daughter and stroked her hair. 'Milly, you can't go out there. Baby, the guy has a gun.'

'I don't care. I need to see if Dad's all right.'

Laura looked back towards the passengers. 'Everyone, sit tight. We need to check on Ben and Edward. Don't move or try to escape. I'm begging you. This guy will think nothing of shooting us all. Do you understand?'

The passengers murmured their agreement. 'Milly, I'll go alone. You stay here.' Laura thought it was a safer option for her daughter to stay on the coach.

'Mum, I'm coming with you.'

Laura spun around as an arm reached up outside and hammered on the glass. The passengers screamed. Laura and Milly ducked.

'Stay down, Milly. I think he's outside. Oh my God. He's going to get on the coach.'

Again, the hand thumped against the glass. The person was outside, shouting desperately. 'Open up. It's me.'

Laura crawled towards the door and saw her husband standing outside the coach. She reached across the driver's seat, opened the door and quickly climbed down the steps. 'Oh, thank goodness. You can open the doors from the outside, you know. You scared us half to death. Where's Edward?' She searched Ben's face and saw his fearful expression. 'What is it, Ben? What's happened?'

He explained the phone call, told them about Nigel blowing his head off and how he had been unable to move Edward from the barn.

'Oh shit. What do we tell Mary and Abigail?'

'He's hysterical. He heard and saw his son taking his own life. He's blaming himself, his selfish actions. I don't know what we're going to do, Laura. I think if there were another bullet, Edward would have shot himself. The caller was clever, knowing what would happen – the trap he set. We thought Nigel would either shoot his father or drop the gun. I didn't see this happening. It's not over. This maniac is just starting.'

Laura looked across the fields. 'Where is he now?'

'His only communication is this phone.' Ben brought the mobile out from his back pocket. 'He called us when we reached the barn. He was listening to everything unfold. Nigel played right into his hands. He's out there somewhere now, planning the next game. He's having the time of his bloody life with these people.'

Laura waited, processing what her husband was saying. 'We're not going to make it, are we? It's only a matter of time?'

Ben held his wife tightly. 'I'll do anything to protect you and Milly. I won't let anything happen to you both. That's a promise. I love you so much, Laura.'

She rested her head on her husband's shoulder. 'I love you too.'

Despite pleas from his family, he couldn't leave Edward alone. He needed to give Edward time with his son to grieve, but it wasn't safe with the caller out there. He assured everyone that if he saw the caller moving towards the coach, he'd get back, untie everyone and they'd run together. Then he walked back along the path to the barn. He thought about what Laura had said and how they would break the horrific news to Mary and Abigail. It was Edward's responsibility. He was the one who had to tell them, his way.

Back at the barn, Ben found Edward dragging the body along the floor. He searched his mind for the right words. *What do you say in a situation like this? What words could you use to console the bereaved? He had a good innings. What an exit. Bang. Did you see that? Such an awesome way to go, it certainly won't be forgotten.*

Edward looked up. 'Can you help me? I want to bring him back to the coach. Let Mary say goodbye.'

'Edward, I'm sorry, but I don't think it's a good idea. Do you really want Mary to see him like this? Her state of mind isn't strong at the moment. Please consider your actions here.' Ben didn't want more confrontation. They needed to work together.

'Then what do you suggest?' Edward asked.

'I know it's difficult. I can't imagine the pain you're feeling. But you need to think of Mary and Abigail. They're relying on you now. You need to take care of them, step up, do the right thing.'

'I'll never deal with this. It will kill my wife. She lives for her son.'

Ben listened to the word 'lives' and its present tense. He didn't choose to correct the older man.

'Look, for the moment, I suggest we place Nigel on that cart and cover him with hay. Give him some dignity. When this is over, you can organise a proper funeral,' Ben said.

Ben and Edward lifted the body, placing it on the wooden platform. They found enough hay to place on top of him, hiding the disfigured face, the blood-splattered clothes, then Edward said his goodbyes.

On the walk back, Edward was reminiscing about Nigel's childhood. Ben listened without interruption to the stories of when Nigel started school, his favourite programmes, his awkwardness around girls and unruly fashion sense. Every couple of minutes, Edward stopped, placing his hands over his face and bawling.

Ben moved across and held him. 'You need to be strong;

you'll have time to mourn. Christ, Edward, I'm so sorry for your loss. Mary needs you, now more than ever.'

'What do I say to her? Do I tell her? I can't say he shot himself. I can't.'

'Maybe you need to say that you didn't find him. That's all I can think of at the moment. She has to get through this, telling her about Nigel will break her in two.'

Edward turned to Ben. 'You're right. It will break her. Thank you for what you're doing. I couldn't go through this alone.'

Ben looked at Edward's tear-soaked face, his bloodshot eyes, the dribbles coming from his nose. Whatever bad things this man had done, however gross his actions as a father, he didn't deserve this.

The phone vibrated in Ben's pocket just as they reached the coach and were climbing the steps.

Ben turned around and went back onto the road. He pressed the answer button, listening with impatience.

'That was quite the outcome, wouldn't you say? I didn't expect that. I knew there'd be blood but not his son's.'

Ben wanted to tear the guy limb from limb, smash him hard in the face and keep going until there was nothing left to hit for what he was putting everyone through. Ben's wife, his daughter, these strangers.

'That poor man. How could you do this to him? How could you put him through such a horrific ordeal?' Ben waited for an answer.

'See, now he feels pain. He feels what it's like to be on the receiving end. For too long, he's had his own way. He's trodden on people, used them, spat them out. Now he knows, he's facing his penance.'

'It's not for you to deal out,' Ben said.

'Then how will he learn? His judgement day would not have come until he'd faced his maker, looked that person in their eyes, spilt out his sins, his wrongdoings, confessed all the terrible things he'd done while he was here. That's not good enough. Who'll be around to see it? None of us would have seen that day, but now we can. He'll understand what it's like to lose someone, to hurt someone, to be on the receiving end and repent. I'm doing him a favour, giving him an option to change before it's too late.'

Ben wanted to stamp on the phone, hurl it as far into the field as possible. He jammed the nail of his right forefinger into his thumb, pressing as hard as he could. The frustration was building fast, edging its way through his body. He wanted to shout, to scream at the top of his voice. He kept quiet, waiting for the caller to talk.

'Listen, Mr Do-Gooder, let me explain something. Every morning, you leave the house for work, maybe you wear a smart suit, polished shoes, your shirt is crisp, pristine, tucked into your trousers. Your tie is clean, the knot tidy, not too big. Your hair is combed with just the right amount of wax. You take care in the way you look, your appearance, how you present yourself. You smile at the people you pass in the street, maybe you wave to a neighbour, wish them a pleasant day, ask how the family are, tell them you'll get together and have that drink you've promised for God knows how long. You feel a sense of pride if you like, being part of the community. Everyone notices Mr Do-Gooder, on his way to work, a nice chap, that's what the people say about you. A genuinely nice guy. He's Mr Do-Gooder. There he goes, what a man.

'Now, let's look at another scenario. The alternative. You get up; you're late for work, you snarl at your wife, leave the house without saying goodbye or telling her you love her. Your jacket is old, worn, the colour fading. Your shirt is dirty, dishevelled, untucked; you're wearing odd socks, a whiff of body odour that people are too frightened to mention. You rush along the road, snapping at people, wound up, wondering why the hell people are staring at you. Your mood is set for the day, dark, dull, sullen. Your neighbour contemplates waving over, they don't like you but all the same, it's a good way to start the day. They watch from across the street, your tight face, gormless expression, ready to pop the next person that gets in your way. Tell me, Mr Do-Gooder, which one are you?'

'What's your point?' Ben asked.

'We bring our own luck, good fortune. Our aura represents who we are, how we think, feel, deal with society. We also bring our misery, choosing to see only the badness in the world. Oh, the latter person I described could be many people you or I know. They are the cretins of this world. The people who charge through life, stamping on the weak, too important for those who suffer at the hands of their ignorance. They are the ones who must be punished, Mr Do-Gooder. They are the ones.'

The phone went dead.

Jack and Gareth.

The cries for help echoed through the basement.

Jack and Gareth had been held in the same room, under the cottage, placed in different corners, their hands tied to the railing above. The room was pitch-black; the only noise from outside was the distant gunshot a few minutes ago, sounding like a firework in the distance. It was the second one they'd heard this evening.

'Help us, someone.' Jack pulled at the restraints around his wrists; they burned, he could feel the cuts, the sharp pain where the rope had dug into his skin.

'No one can hear us,' Gareth said. 'We're going to rot down here.'

'Don't. Please, don't think that way.' Jack was worried about his wife, Lydia. She was alone, vulnerable. 'We need to think;

there has to be a way out.' Again, he tugged hard, ripping his hands down towards the ground.

'What happened to the other guy?' Gareth asked. 'Is he dead?'

Jack hesitated. 'I don't know. You heard the gunshot as well as me. Maybe he managed to wrestle that bastard, shoot him first.'

'I doubt it. I think he's dead.'

'Do you have a family?' Jack asked. He needed to make conversation. They'd been sat in the dark pit for hours; they were cold, hungry and scared for their lives.

'Yes, my mum and dad are still alive. I have a sister who moved to Australia. We're still in touch. She calls every week: her kids love to talk to their Uncle Gareth. What about you?'

Jack could hear in Gareth's voice that he didn't want to talk. The heavy sighs, his broken speech, the way he shifted his body reeked of desperation. He was young; he had a life to live. Like Jack, he didn't want it to end in a dank basement.

'I have a wife. Lydia. She's the most beautiful woman in the world. I'd do anything for her. Life has been a little shitty for both of us recently, and we are getting back on track.' He didn't want to say too much. Jack knew he could let slip at any second what they'd done.

Gareth continued despite himself, 'My best mate, Stephen, and I are going to Thailand soon. We've had it planned for a while. We're going for a few months, see how it goes. We may never come back. That's if we get out of here.' Gareth suddenly focused, conscious of where they both were. He screamed out, startling Jack. 'Help us, somebody; we're in the basement. Please come.' He ripped at the rope, tugging as hard as he could, but the railing was solid and fixed securely to the wall. Then his body went limp.

'Gareth, what do you like to do? In your spare time, I mean?'

Gareth's voice had become slurred, and he'd started to speak with a slight stutter. 'I read, I go to the gym. I'm also at university. I-I live locally, so I don't have to-to stay over. It's one of the benefits.'

'What do you like to read?' Jack pushed, trying to occupy Gareth's mind with a little normality.

'Oh, anything really. Hor-horror is my favourite.' Gareth stopped. He found himself thinking about the dank room where they were held at the mention of horror. 'King is my favourite.'

'I don't read. I wish I had more time. I work for an insurance company in London. Long hours.'

'How do you find working full-time? I'm hoping to go into law.' Gareth was sounding more courageous now and starting to open up a bit.

Jack laughed. 'It's a way of paying the bills. Believe me, it's not all it's cracked up to be, mate.'

Gareth hoisted his body up against the wall, pushing his feet against the floor to straighten himself. He felt weak, tired and his back was sore from lying half slumped on the floor. 'What's your boss like?'

Jack remembered Chloe. What he and Lydia had done. 'I'm the boss now.'

The Coach.

Ben stared at the mobile phone. He hated this small device, a guy's voice on the other end, controlling their every move, pulling the strings, like a puppet master, wreaking mayhem. He needed to somehow deal with the hatred, every time it rang. He climbed the steps and up onto the coach.

Laura was waiting at the front. 'What happened?'

Ben went on to explain the stories the caller was telling him and what he had planned.

Laura wanted to know more about what happened at the barn.

Ben kept his voice to a whisper. 'We were walking out of the barn, and we heard the gun go off.'

'We heard it too. The passengers gasped. I think they know what it was. We can't brush over it,' Laura said.

Ben reached for Laura's arm. 'We can't tell his wife. Edward's not going to say anything until we're away from here.'

Laura hesitated, then nodded in agreement. 'I think you're right. Did you see him?'

'Yes. It's something I'll never forget. He set the trap, knowing blood would be spilt. He's playing fucking mind games with us.'

'Oh, Ben. What are we going to do?'

'I'm thinking of getting everyone off the coach, moving somewhere. We're too vulnerable here. He's watching, but I don't know if it's all the time. He sets traps, plans these sick games. They've been on the coach overnight. Possibly longer.'

'How do you know?' Laura asked.

'Something Nigel, Edward's son, mentioned. He told me the caller turned up at the house, marched them all out at gunpoint and tied them up. The coach was driven and left on a drive overnight.'

Laura covered her face with her hands in disbelief. 'Christ. How the heck can these people keep going?'

Ben was silent for a second as Laura composed herself. 'There has to be a moment when he has his concentration elsewhere. I'm thinking that maybe if he's occupied, we can get these people off the coach, move them someplace safer, we can hide out. He won't expect that. The lights, the engine running, he can see us. He can hear the coach. But they have to keep warm, I understand that. We have no choice. We need to try and escape, Laura.'

'It sounds like a good plan, but how do we get them off without him seeing? Edward and Mary, they're elderly, they can't move that fast. Lydia is a wreck; she's struggling to make conversation. Abigail hasn't said two words since we've been here. It's like she's in a trance. Good luck getting through to her. Stephen's young, he'll make it, but the others... we won't get them out in time.'

Ben looked towards the middle of the coach. His daughter was talking to Stephen. Ben shone the torch near her face as she looked towards him, her eyes gleaming at the sight of him, her hero, the person she admired the most in the world – although she'd never admit it to her mother. Milly joined her parents at the front of the coach.

'How are you holding up, baby?' Ben mouthed.

'Oh, I'm having the time of my life? Who needs the sun and a swimming pool?'

Ben and Laura laughed.

'I need to test the water,' Ben said to Laura.

'How do you mean?'

'There are gaps. Whenever he calls, he goes quiet for a while. I think he moves to where he has the others, checks in, you know? To make sure everything is going to plan. He can't watch us the whole time; he has the others, held somewhere close. It may give us enough time to untie everyone, get them off the coach and somewhere less conspicuous.'

'Ben, it's too dangerous.'

'It's our only hope.'

Jack and Gareth.

'I need to get out of here. I can't stay any longer. I can't deal with confined spaces.' Gareth swung his hips one way and then the other, thrashing like a fish on the end of a line.

'Take deep breaths. You can do this, Gareth. Do you hear me? Deep, slow breathing. I'm here. I'm with you, okay. Let me hear you. Come on. In and out.'

The two men spoke, unable to see each other. They'd been taken off the coach, marched along the road, the caller walking behind them, spouting profanities about sin and how they'd make up for what they'd done. As they reached a barn, the caller had told them to stop. He'd tied Nigel up and left him inside. They heard the door opening across the field as they stood on the path, terrified of being shot. As the caller returned, he instructed them to walk, climb the verge and tramp together across a field. He told them if they looked back or tried to run, he'd kill them both.

As they approached, they saw a line of cottages, illuminated with the outdoor light which hung by the front door of the first cottage to their left. A light at the window upstairs was the only sign of life.

The caller had held the gun at Gareth's face while unlocking the door, and marched the guys inside.

Now, Gareth sucked air, forcing it into his lungs, panting, pushing short breaths out. 'It's no good. I feel like I'm trapped in a lift. I want to go home. I have to get out of here. You don't understand.'

'Gareth, look towards my voice. Tell me about your happy place.'

'Happy place?' Gareth's voice was cracking, damaged from screaming out.

'That's right. Tell me.'

Gareth closed his eyes to aide his imagination; his breathing started to stabilise, slowing down. In his mind, he removed himself from this place, if only temporarily. 'It's a beach.'

'That's right, now imagine you're on the beach. How does it feel? What can you hear?'

Gareth swallowed and continued. 'I'm on a beach. I feel the sun on my skin, warming it. I stand close to the water and listen as the waves gently roll towards where I'm standing. My feet are buried in the sand, and I stand still, listening – Seagulls squawk above as they sweep through the air, swooping overhead, powering through the sky. I look up, and I only see a blanket of light blue, the sun glistens, sat so still.'

Jack smiled in the dark. 'That's your happy place. Somewhere, sometime you'll see again.'

The sudden bang from above brought Gareth out of his trance. 'What was that?'

'I think he's back.'

19

THE COTTAGE

Gareth and Jack listened, knowing they'd heard a noise above them. Someone had come into the cottage. A few minutes ago, they'd heard a door slam. They kept silent, waiting for another indication that somebody had come inside.

'It may have been the wind,' Jack said, wanting to give them hope.

Gareth tried to search the darkness for Jack's shape. 'Thank you for helping me. I'd be broken without you.'

'It's okay. We're here together. We have to look out for one another.'

'Maybe he won't come back. Maybe he's bored,' Gareth said hopefully.

'How long have you and Stephen been friends?'

'Oh, for as long as I can remember. He's a pain in the arse but, you know, he's like a brother.'

'Yeah. Lydia's my soulmate. I couldn't bear to be without her. I'd do anything for that woman,' Jack proclaimed.

'How did you meet?' Gareth was now opening up. He felt a little more relaxed and willed himself to deal with his situation.

'Oh, a good question. She was my neighbour when we were

younger. I lived in North London, and I remember when she and her family moved in. Lydia was friends with my sister; I always had a major crush on her. She'd tell you we were just friends if you asked her but I'm not buying that.' Jack laughed, recalling the early days. 'Anyway, we moved away, much to my disappointment, and I bumped into her years later. I'd never forgotten her. My first crush and the only love of my life. She told me I'd suddenly got hot. I remember how I felt at the time, hearing those words. A mixture of my dreams being dashed and elation all at the same time.'

'Why both?' Gareth asked.

'Oh, you know when you're a kid, you start to get attracted to a person and think of them more and more, you style your hair, wear a little of your father's aftershave, work at your fashion, buy the magazines, and you beg your parents for that trendy jacket or the expensive shoes. That was me, trying to impress Lydia.

'I remember the excitement when she'd come for a sleep-over. My sister was two years older than me, so was Lydia.' Jack sighed. 'That's a gap that's implausible when you're a child, but it didn't stop me having a crush on her. Yes, she was out of my league, two years above me at school and I remember the looks she got as she walked down the corridors from the older boys. But it didn't stop me dreaming. I heard Lydia and my sister discussing boys, someone Lydia wanted to kiss. It broke my heart. I always wanted that boy to be me.

'Anyway, to get back to the story, when I met her years later, I asked her for a drink, and that was that. Her words were, "You've suddenly got hot".'

'That's a great story. She must have–'

Footsteps were coming from above, loud thumps, moving across the ceiling.

'Someone's there. Gareth, stay calm, okay. Do you hear me?'

'I hear you. Look, if we don't, you know, make it, then thank you. Thank you for being so kind.'

'Gareth, we're going to make it okay? Just do as he says, remember the deep breaths. You've got this.'

The person was moving down the steps; heavy footsteps thudded, pounding on wood, getting closer. The handle turned, and the door opened. A switch was pushed, and the light from a weak bulb enabled them to see.

The man stood in the doorway; the hood of his jacket pulled over his head, his face a dim shadow beside the bright light from his hi-vis jacket.

'How's your stay? Are you comfortable? Warm enough? I do hope you'll tell others. Be sure to leave a five-star rating now, won't you?'

'Go to hell,' Jack answered.

'Well now, that's not very polite. I expected a little gratitude, a thank you, maybe a tip left in an envelope at the front desk.' The man in the hi-vis looked at Gareth. 'How very cosy. I trust the both of you are acquainted? You've been together a while, haven't you? You'll be exchanging numbers soon.'

'What do you want?' Jack asked.

The man pushed the door wider, then stepped inside the basement room. 'Are you a gambling man? Do you like the odd flutter?' The question was aimed at Jack.

'Occasionally.'

'Good. Then you'll understand how this game works.'

'What game? I'm not playing any games.'

'Oh, but you are.'

Jack yanked his arms, trying his best to break the railing above. It was no use.

'You'll only end up doing yourself a nasty injury. You don't want that. Now, I understand your wife is on the coach,' the man said.

Jack looked up; he had venom in his eyes; saliva was dripping from his bottom lip. 'Don't fucking mention her. Do you hear? Don't ever talk about my wife.'

'There. That's it – the sweet spot. I knew you'd have one. Now, listen up. We're going to play a little game of swapsies. Your lovely lady must be sick of the coach, so, as a change, you'll walk up and release her, take her place and she'll come to the executive suite. How does that sound?'

Jack paused, allowing the instructions to settle in his mind. 'I won't let her rot in this place. Do what you want to me but leave her out of it. There's not a chance in hell that we'll swap places.'

'Oh, but you must. It's part of the game. See, I've spent some time thinking up these little activities. I'd hate for it to all have been for nothing.'

'Lydia stays. She's safer up there. I'm not having her down here with you, locked in this fucking shithole. She wouldn't cope.' Jack glanced up at the figure in the doorway.

'Then, mister, it's a fail. I had a hunch it would work out that way. We'll have to settle for plan B.'

He slammed the door, leaving the light on.

Gareth was pleased he could now see Jack. He waited a second for the footsteps to move away before speaking. 'That was awesome. The way you stood up for your wife. I've never seen anything like it. That was brave, mate.'

Jack couldn't help wondering what the man in the hi-vis meant by plan B.

The footsteps suddenly stopped. There was a bang like the caller had jumped the couple of steps he'd climbed and landed back outside the room. The door burst open, smashing against the wall. The caller raced into the room, holding a large knife in his right hand. He stood over Jack, cutting viciously at the rope. Jack kicked out, struggling to fend off his assailant.

'Leave him. Please, leave him alone,' Gareth shouted.

The caller brought the knife into the air and stabbed the sharp blade into Jack's leg. Jack winced, wriggling on the floor like jelly dropping from a plate. Then the caller grabbed Jack around the neck, dragged him to his feet and carried him out slumped over his shoulder.

As he left, he turned out the light, leaving Gareth in the dark.

~

Upstairs, the man placed Jack down on the living room floor and went outside to watch the coach through his binoculars.

The family were stood at the front, the husband and wife – such heroes. The daughter was a little further back. The old man at the front had taken his seat. His wife was sat mute, taking in the mayhem around her. The younger woman was sat behind. She didn't speak much from what he could see. He had plans for her later.

He moved to the kitchen sink, first cleaning the blade, running it under the tap so the blood spilt down the plughole. He took a tea towel from the handrail of the cooker, wiped the knife and placed it back in the hip holder under his jacket. He'd need it again, no doubt. Then, he removed his hi-vis jacket and checked for blood. There were marks on the cuffs, smears up the arms and on the collar. He wiped hard with a sponge so the stain spread over the plastic material. Once the jacket was clean, he hung it on the towel rail in the bathroom.

Back in the living room, he wrapped a towel around Jack's leg, stemming the flow of blood. He needed to keep Jack alive for what he had planned later.

Jack winced, holding his leg. He was weak from the blood loss. He tried to sit up while his leg was being strapped and attempted to throw his fists towards the caller's face. It made little impact. Jack was weak, hungry, and the stab wound had made him disorientated. He slumped back and his attacker laughed.

He was pleased with the progress. It was all working out, his plan – the passengers on the coach, the basement, the games he'd created. He picked up his second phone and dialled the number, waiting for the reply. He heard the voice from the coach as he moved back towards the front door; holding the binoculars to his face with the other hand.

'What a great night. I don't think I've ever felt more alive. The power surging through my veins is something money could never buy, a feeling that could never be explained, a wish that could never be granted. I'm running short over here.'

Mr Do-Gooder said, 'Running short? What do you mean?'

'Well, we had three. Nigel, Gareth and Jack. Isn't it unfortunate what happened in the barn? Hey, I must tell you, while you've been busy, Mr Do-Gooder, I've had my own fun down here. I had a task set for Jack. He failed miserably at the first hurdle, choosing to disobey my orders so I had to hurt him. Wow, you should see the mess. Anyway, I have another game. The lady further back – Lydia I think she's called – I want you to untie her, bring her outside. You'll like this one. You're going to help her.'

'How am I going to help her?'

The caller listened as Ben sighed, then he continued speaking, 'Well, here's the plan. I have two boxes hidden in the barn. One of them contains a dead body. Lydia will know what we're talking about. It's something a little close to home, shall we say. She and her husband are used to hiding things. The other box is empty. Now, if Lydia picks the box with the dead body, she can go back to the coach.'

'And if she picks the empty box?'

'The basement is a little dull at the moment. The young lad is all alone. I'll come for Lydia and your daughter.'

The caller pressed the button to end their communication. He watched across the field, seeing the anger in Mr Do-Gooder's face. He was standing alone at the front of the coach, staring at the phone screen. Then he moved along the aisle, holding his daughter, pulling her close.

The caller closed the front door and moved along the living room floor. The place was outdated, the decor old fashioned.

He thought how much he'd like to live here as he opened the closet door to his right. The cottage's two previous tenants were lying slumped on the floor. He'd get rid of them later and clean up. It was a shame that it had to end like this. They'd fallen behind on their rent and avoided his phone calls. When he'd sent final demand letters and hadn't heard anything about the rent he was owed, it was the last straw. The cottage belonged to him, and the tenants were in the way. They were now thieves.

He had feared the blood would run onto the wooden floors.

It appeared to have stopped.

20

THE COACH

'What did he say?' Laura asked. Ben had not used the speakerphone for the last call. It would agitate the passengers if they heard what the caller was planning.

Ben glanced up to see where Milly was and then said softly to Laura, 'I have to find where he's staying. It's close by, along the road somewhere. It has to be. He's got to be near enough to be able to watch, but far enough away so's not to be seen.'

'No, Ben. I won't allow you to go out there looking for him. It's too dangerous. Listen to yourself for crying out loud. Stay here.'

Ben wanted more than ever to follow her instructions. 'Laura, if I stay here and we wait, he'll kill all of us. I have to find where he's holding the others. It's the only way.'

'What about calling the police? We'll ring them. Tell them what's happened. They'll arrive in swarms and take the bastard out.'

'Laura, the phone is monitored. He's already killed the driver, Andrew. He ran, taking his chances and look at how it ended. The caller *listened* on the phone as Nigel blew his head off. The guy may as well have pulled the trigger himself. As soon as a text is sent or a phone call is made, that's it. We may as well sign our death warrant.' Ben hesitated, composing himself for what he had to say. 'He mentioned a game he wants Lydia to play. I have to escort her to the barn.'

'Game. What kind of game?'

'He says there's a dead body in a box. I think he's killed at least one more; he told me he was running low on bodies where he's holding the other passengers. Christ, maybe they're all dead. He's close by, watching us. He's watching from somewhere near.' Ben glanced out of the window, fear washing through his body.

Laura knew her husband was right. There'd be a bloodbath at the first sound of a police siren or the sight of flashing blue lights. The caller would make his escape through the fields while the bodies lay strewn across the seats.

'I have to speak with Lydia. Wait here. If you see anything, I want you to shout,' Ben instructed.

Laura nodded. He was so proud of her and how she was dealing with this. He'd die before anything happened to his wife and daughter.

Ben sat in the seat next to Lydia. 'Hey. I haven't spoken much to you.'

Lydia smiled, but her eyes were dark, empty and lifeless. 'Have you heard from Jack? My husband. How's he doing?'

Ben rubbed his chin, waiting to think of the right thing to say. 'Lydia, we're going to do everything we can to get him back. I think he's being held captive close by. When it's the right time, I'm going to go looking for them, the people he's taken. But right now, I've had an instruction.'

Lydia turned towards the window. 'He's not coming back, is he?'

'I don't want you to think that way. Please don't give up hope.'

Lydia slowly turned her head. 'You're a brave man. I can't thank you and your family enough.'

Ben's face flushed, he looked down to the ground for a second to let the embarrassment pass. 'Thank you, but I'm just doing what's right.'

'I doubt many families would have stayed with us. Stop being so modest.'

There was a shyness about the woman. She spoke with anguish and her aura was one of hopelessness, despondency. She was gentle and completely beautiful, but her body language was closed, like it hurt her to be exposed to the world.

'Lydia, this is going to be difficult. I need you to brace yourself, get ready and come with me.'

Her expression suddenly changed from awkward to startled. 'What's going on?'

'The caller has set up challenges, if you like. He's ordered you off the coach. I'm coming too. We need to walk to the barn, which is further along the path. Lydia, I'll be with you, every step. If we refuse to go, he'll come up here and try to take my daughter.' Ben didn't want to explain the challenge the caller had set for Lydia just yet.

Lydia looked as if she wanted to scream. As he untied the rope which held her to the seat, Ben wondered if she was contemplating going with him. He fished the rope from the back of the seat, untying the knot and she stood, smoothing down her skirt.

She stopped beside Milly on the way out. 'I have to go. You'll be safe; I won't let anything happen to your father. He's a brave man.'

Milly was confused as she hugged Lydia. 'What's going on?' the girl asked.

'There's something I have to do,' she answered bravely. 'But I'll be back soon.'

Ben followed the woman to the front of the coach. He held his wife close, kissing her forehead.

'Make sure you come back in one piece,' Laura demanded.

'I will.' He took the phone from the dashboard and stepped out onto the ground. Lydia followed.

As they moved along the path, the mobile rang in Ben's hand. He lifted the phone to his ear and waited without saying anything.

'Glad she could make it. Now, walk to the barn; you know where it is. I'll call you again when I see you arrive.'

Click. The phone went dead.

They walked, side by side, only the sound of the wind for company, beating against their skin. The lights from the coach illuminated the rough ground ahead, and as they turned left, the road ahead became pitch-black. The cloud cover was still threatening to break, and the tip of the moon was pushing through. Ben worried that any second the caller could jump out from the fields either side and grab him and Lydia. He strained to hear footsteps or a rustle in the grass, pushing himself to prepare. He shone the torch, steering over the bleak wilderness. He couldn't hear anyone approaching.

A short while after, Ben and Lydia approached the barn. Through the open door they could see the light hanging from the ceiling; but the space was completely barren. Ben had flashbacks from earlier; his head started to spin, he felt faint. He needed to gain control. He had to be strong and guide Lydia. He moved along the path, shining the torch and watching around him. Lydia followed.

'I don't get why we're here,' she said.

Ben turned around, looking over the fields, making sure they were alone. He kept his voice low and hushed. 'He has these sick games set out. All you need to do is follow his instructions. Don't do anything else, only what he says, understood? You can do this. I know you can, Lydia.'

Ben pushed the door, letting Lydia inside and then moved next to her. Right on cue, the phone rang.

'Okay, stay calm. I'll talk to him,' Ben instructed, answering the call and putting it on speakerphone.

'Welcome again. You're beginning to like this place – a proper regular. Make yourselves comfortable, relax. We need to make the lady welcome.'

The caller was whispering. Ben was losing his patience. 'What does she have to do?'

'Oh, I sense a little frustration in your temperament. I don't like that. I can't have unruly guests showing disrespect. That won't do at all.'

'I'm sorry if I'm not feeling your hospitality.' Ben was struggling to hear what the caller was saying.

Lydia listened to the voice on the other end of the phone. She peered across the barn from the front door; it was bigger than it looked from outside, as long as it was wide and resembling a warehouse. It smelt like it was used to store manure or some other foul fertiliser. It reminded her of when she was younger, and her father took her horse riding. The smell of the stables was something she never got used to.

The voice spoke, calm, authoritative, and hushed. 'Towards the back of the barn, you'll find two large cardboard boxes. I want Lydia to step forward and pick one. Only one. Remember the rules; I'll go through them again now that she's there with you listening. If Lydia picks the box with the dead body, she can go back to the coach. If she opens the empty box, your daughter and Lydia will join me in the cellar.'

'I'll never let that happen. You can go and fuck yourself. Forget your stupid games, okay. Drop the gun and come out like a man. Show your face, do you hear me?' Ben shouted loud enough for his voice to carry across the barn. His fists were clenched, and he was willing to fight for his life.

Ben thought he heard a car door closing. It was possible the caller was on the move. The mobile Ben held suddenly pinged. A jpeg showed up on the screen. Again, Ben shouted for the caller to come to the barn and show his face.

'I would if I could. But I'm listening. I can't wait to see how it turns out.'

Ben hesitated. He glanced towards Lydia, then back at the screen. 'I know you're close. I'm going to find you, rip the vile heart from your chest and ram it down your throat. You're sick. You'll never get to my daughter. Do you hear me?'

'Why don't you open the picture I've sent?'

Ben fumbled, lifting the phone in front of him and Lydia. It was a photo of the caller, stood outside the coach. Another one came through. A short video recording this time. Ben opened it. Laura was standing at the front, glancing through the window, looking out. Milly was a little further down, waiting, her body was giddy with anticipation, and she was biting the nail of her left thumb.

'Make certain not to lose,' the caller whispered.

21

LYDIA AND JACK

Jack was standing in the kitchen. His wife was at the window, looking out towards the garden.

'I can't dig her back up. Listen to what you're asking. Can you hear yourself?'

Lydia turned sharply. 'Oh, I can hear myself perfectly fine. I said, go out and take Chloe out of the hole.'

'I'm not doing it. There's nowhere else to hide her.'

Lydia unlocked the back door. 'I'll do it myself then.' She raced to the spot where Jack had dug, dropped to her knees and started to scrape the mud back.

Jack stood on the paving slabs. 'I'm warning you, Lydia, you dig any more, and I'm calling the police. I mean it. I swear.'

Lydia looked up; she had mascara smudged under her eyes; her hair was tousled. Any second now, Jack expected fire to exhale from her mouth. 'I'm deadly serious, Lydia. Carry on digging, and I'll make the call.'

Jack's concentration was broken as his mobile rang from the kitchen. He ran towards it. 'Shit. It's Dana.' He reached out his trembling arm and picked up the phone. 'Hey, Dana. You okay?'

'Hi, Jack.'

'Still no word on Chloe?'

'Nothing. I've made so many calls. No one seems to know anything.'

Jack glanced out to the garden. Lydia had finally stopped and was standing, brushing the front of her nightdress and the mud patches from her knees. 'It's certainly baffling. Are you sure she didn't go away for the weekend, maybe a work conference? Or a visit to her parents possibly?'

'I'd know if she had a weekend planned. We talk all the time. Jack, I'm in Woking. I need to call over. Something's bothering me.'

Jack felt his heart skip a beat; the hairs rose on the back of his neck. Dana had driven from her home in London. At least an hour's drive. He was caught on the hop, he opened his mouth but couldn't form the words he'd wanted to say.

'Okay. We're here. See you soon.'

He gave her the address and Dana finished the call without saying goodbye.

'What's up?' Lydia asked.

'Dana's on her way over.'

Lydia and Jack were stood in the kitchen, gobsmacked. He didn't know Dana well enough for her to pop over for a chat and a nice cup of tea. Jack had met Dana a couple of times; they weren't even asked to the wedding.

Jack placed his hand on the worktop. 'You need to go upstairs, Lydia. Let me deal with this. You're not in the best frame of mind.'

Lydia darted a look at her husband. A *what were you think-*

ing? glance that could cut someone in half. 'Call her back. Tell her she can't come over.'

'I can't. She'll know for certain that something is going on. What do I say? "Oh, sorry, Dana, you know what, I forgot it's Saturday. We have plans. A quick shopping trip to town and a bit of lunch. But hey, good luck finding your wife. I'm rooting for you".' Jack needed to get through to Lydia. 'How will that look? My boss is missing, and I'm more concerned about our weekend arrangements. Dana is coming to the house, and there's nothing we can do to stop her.' He paced the floor, feeling like he'd burst at any second. 'When she looks in the garden, she'll know. As soon as Dana steps foot in the house, she'll know something is wrong.'

Lydia was stressing. She placed her hand on the kitchen wall to steady herself, then took a glass from the cabinet, filled it with water and downed the lot. 'I don't think I can cope a second longer. I need to get out of here.'

'Don't. You're letting the situation get the better of you. Take breaths, sit down for a second.' Jack ran a dishcloth under the tap and dabbed the cool material on his wife's forehead. Water dropped onto her nightdress and she furiously wiped the trickles from her face.

'There. That's better, isn't it?' he said.

'How is dousing me with water going to make me feel better?'

'We have to understand her predicament. Dana thinks I was the last person to see her wife. We can't blame her for being suspicious. She's worried about Chloe. I'll meet her at the door; I won't let her inside. I'll listen, answer correctly and she'll be gone before you know it.'

Dana's car pulled onto the drive. His drive, reserved for them. That was the first thing that annoyed him. Someone he didn't really know, helping themselves. It was rude.

The second thing that annoyed him was the reminder that the car was gone. It looked suspicious, a middle-aged couple at home on a Saturday with an empty drive. Not something you usually see these days.

Thirdly, Jack was pissed off that he viewed himself and Lydia as middle-aged.

'Quick, Lydia, upstairs. Don't come down until she's gone. I'll call you when it's safe,' Jack instructed.

Lydia crawled along the hall, keeping as low as possible, her hands flat against the floor. Jack heard the bedroom door click shut at the same time as the doorbell rang.

'Dana, hi. You look well.' He wanted to get on her good side, ease the tension. Settle her down and keep her from spontaneously combusting on their doorstep.

She wore a tight pair of jeans and a plain white blouse. Her hair was up, and her face had a bright red complexion. Jack instantly felt the unease. He pulled the door behind him and moved onto the front step, rising above her. One-nil to him.

Dana smiled; then her face quickly switched to a stern expression. 'I hope you don't mind me parking on the drive?'

'Not at all. My car's at the garage. The dreaded MOT. I always get anxious. You know how it is, like a health check when you smoke forty a day. The car's a piece of shit at the best of times, but hey, it does us.' Jack realised he was rambling to deal with the nerves. He was aware Dana had little interest in his idle chat.

Dana moved closer to Jack, then pushed the front door. 'I assume I'm allowed inside?'

Jack felt his world collapse for a second. He had to pull it together, gain the advantage. He pictured a revolving door at the front of a large office building, people stepping inside, rotating, disorientated and then spat out. He needed to be this door.

He stepped aside, letting Dana into his home, leaving the front door open, a subtle hint that she wasn't welcome for long.

Jack moved past Dana, brushing against her, then opened the door to the living room at the front of the house. 'Here, come in and sit down. Can I get you anything? Tea? A coffee maybe?'

She waved her hand in the air to indicate she didn't want a drink.

'Okay, then,' Jack said awkwardly.

Dana sat in the middle of the long sofa which stretched along the wall. Jack, who preferred his guests to sit at one end of the sofa while he took the other, had to choose the armchair that was too big for the living room, and it gave the impression of swallowing anyone who sat in it. He contemplated asking her to move to the end of the sofa, but he wasn't courageous enough.

Dana looked around the living room taking in the pictures on top of the cabinet. She edged forward on the sofa. 'Actually, I'll have a glass of water.'

Jack struggled to get up, pushing his hands on the sides of the armchair for support like someone pushing to get out of a car when the airbags are engaged. 'Of course.'

'I may need to use the loo, if it's not a problem.'

Jack was peeved. Their toilet was at the back of the kitchen, a small box room with a downstairs shower and a corner basin. There was no way he could let Dana into the kitchen. She'd see the garden, the disturbed grass and the mound of mud. The toilet was old and the base was loose. He could use this problem as an excuse. He'd have to steer her to the bathroom upstairs.

'Upstairs. First door on the left.'

Dana moved across to the photographs as he left the room.

I need to be quick, don't let the tap run for long, cold water will only make her stay longer.

Jack turned on the tap, staring through the window at the hole he'd dug. *She can't see it. How suspicious would it look? We'd be bang to rights.*

He heard the living room door open and, though he saw her turn slightly on her way upstairs, she did not look into the kitchen.

He waited, hearing her move around above. Sweat ran down the middle of his face. He scrubbed his skin with a towel and then fanned it in front of his face to cool his body temperature. A few minutes later, Dana returned to the living room.

Jack needed to keep Dana in the living room, give her the water, tell her how sorry he was that Chloe had cold feet, how she'd probably left her partner for a better life. *Hey, shit happens, Dana Goodwin, you need to deal with it. Move on. Plenty more where she came from.* As the glass filled, the water seemed to trickle, like an egg timer. Jack glanced to the side, making certain he was alone. He turned, half expecting Dana to be stood behind him, looking out over the garden, seeing an arm pushing through the mud.

Jack knew Chloe wasn't in the hole, but maybe somehow she'd be there now, waiting for Dana, her body rising, stepping out of her grave and making her way to the woman she loved.

Jack turned off the tap and went back to the living room. Dana was stood by the cabinet, holding a picture of Jack and Lydia on a weekend break, eating at a fancy restaurant on the lanes of Brighton.

Dana took the drink, lifting the glass to her lips and taking a small slug. 'There's something on my mind, Jack.' The woman returned to the sofa and sat down.

'Go on. What is it?' Jack sat on the edge of the armchair: the task of getting up again was too much.

'I woke this morning; the bed was empty, the house quiet. I made my way downstairs; at the same time checking my mobile for messages. There was nothing. It's as if Chloe has vanished into thin air, puff, and she's gone. No one has seen her; no one seems able to help. Don't you think that's a little strange, Jack? I think it's strange. Wouldn't you? If your wife – what's her name again?'

'Lydia,' Jack answered.

'Lydia. Wouldn't you find it strange if Lydia just left? No note, no clue as to her whereabouts, just gone. Like that. Wouldn't you think it strange, Jack?'

'I think it's certainly odd behaviour,' Jack said, his voice breaking slightly as he gulped the saliva from his mouth.

'*Odd.* I like that. It's odd behaviour isn't it, Jack. Odd that my wife just left. Odd that no one knows where she's gone. Odd that she hasn't called and fucking odd that I should find a bracelet with the name Lydia etched along the face.' Dana dipped into her handbag and lifted the jewellery out.

Jack watched it dangling in the air, swirling in a circle. The light caught it and temporarily blinded him.

Dana continued. 'It was in the hall. I missed it at first. It was under the closet door. You can imagine the shock as I picked it up, saw your wife's name. It's the same one she's wearing in the picture on the cabinet. Funny that.'

'Yeah, odd, I'd say,' Jack answered.

'Odd. You're so right, Jack. It is odd. So, I now have a couple of options. A couple of questions I'd like to pose for you to mull over. One, you come clean, tell me where she is. I'm a big girl and can deal with most things thrown at me. If it's simply that Chloe and Lydia have driven off into the moonlight, hand in hand, confessing their undying love for each other – it would explain the missing car from your drive, by the way – then I will deal with it, Jack. I will take it on the chin, move on and learn from the experience. Hey, you never know, maybe we'll get together too. What a twist that would be. Secondly, I call the police and have them investigate it, give them this address and have them call over, check you and Lydia out, search for any skeletons in the closet. By the way, where is Lydia?'

The living room door flung open. Lydia was holding a brass figure above her head. She charged towards where Dana was sitting.

22

BEN AND LYDIA

Ben stared at the screen of the mobile, listening to the voice. He and Lydia had moved outside. They needed fresh air to clear their heads and prepare for the task ahead. He'd seen the caller moments ago, standing by the coach. He'd sent a video. Laura and Milly were alive but Ben had a problem. He'd foolishly watched for the caller as they walked along the path towards the barn and didn't realise the caller would drive around the road. He was pissed off at how he'd missed it and been so naive.

What the heck was he thinking? The caller had him. If he left the barn and moved towards the coach, he risked the lives of everyone on board. If he stayed and helped Lydia, he also risked their lives. Ben had to get Lydia through this. He was tempted to flee and race back to the coach, but he was aware of the outcome. The caller would see him coming and most certainly get to his family before Ben could. He felt annoyed, agitated that he could put his family in this vulnerable position.

'I want Lydia to step forward and open a box. I'll be listening. Don't turn the phone off.'

'You do anything to my family, and I'll spend the rest of my days hunting you down. I won't rest until I've found you. That's a promise,' Ben warned.

'Well, you better hope that Lydia finds the body then.'

'Regardless, if anything happens to them, my life will be dedicated to finding you.'

Again, the caller was calm, his tone harmonious. 'Oh, you do know how to spoil the anticipation. You're a real party pooper, you know that?'

Ben moved the phone away from his ear.

'I'm going to keep listening.' Then the caller went silent.

Ben lifted the phone out, holding it, stretched in front of him, doing as the caller asked. He watched from the door as Lydia stepped across the floor of the barn. It was roughly eighty foot in length and she walked slowly, like a child creeping towards the kitchen in the middle of the night. The cardboard boxes were wide, roughly the width of a washing machine, and about six feet tall. They were placed together against the back wall.

As Lydia walked, listening to Ben behind her, she prepared herself for whatever was lurking under the lid. She had to open one of the boxes. That was the instruction. Then, she could go back to the coach, to safety, with Ben by her side.

'You can do this. Take your time,' Ben called. 'Open a box, slowly; I'm sorry you're in this situation. Just do your best.'

'I'm trying to get this straight in my head. I need to find the one with the body in it. That's the task, right?'

'That's it, Lydia. You have a fifty-fifty chance. Don't think too much, all I can say is keep calm. I'm here with you.'

Lydia reached the two boxes. She felt her heart quicken; her cheeks reddened with the prospect of what she'd find, her lips quivered. She paused, settling herself. Lydia scanned the boxes, searching for a sign that one of them contained a dead body. But she saw no indication. The boxes were strong and robust. It was impossible for her to tell. It was a chance guess.

Ben was stood at the door, watching as she walked to each side of the boxes. Even if Lydia opened the box containing the dead body, would the caller walk away from the coach? Leave Milly alone?

Even if Lydia picked the correct box and there was a dead body inside, Ben doubted it would end there. The other alternative was Lydia opened the empty box. The caller calmly informs them that Lydia has lost the game, that she and Milly would be taken to the basement. Ben would never let that happen. He'd die before the caller got his daughter.

Lydia reached out, touching a cardboard box, her arm was trembling. 'I think it's this one,' she said. She had her hand on the box on the left.

'What makes you say that?' Ben asked. He realised it was a stupid question.

'I don't know. I think it's bulging but I can't be sure. It looks different. Like something could be inside,' she answered.

Ben glanced towards the box on the right, pointing his arm. 'What about that one?'

Lydia crouched slightly. 'I don't know. The one on the left looks more likely to be hiding a body. Something is telling me the box on the right is empty.'

'Take your time, Lydia.'

Ben pictured her opening the box, it being empty and the caller FaceTiming, holding Milly under his arm and charging towards the car. He thought about switching the phone off, taking a peek in both boxes, he'd never do it in time. The caller would know something happened. He'd get suspicious and take Milly for the fun of it.

'Are you okay, Lydia?' Ben asked.

'Yes. I'm going with the box on the left. It's the one I said from the beginning.'

'Okay. Take your time. When you're ready, open the box gently.'

'I don't think I can.'

'Lydia, concentrate, I'm right here with you.'

She removed her hand from the top of the box and turned around. 'I can't do it. What if–?'

'I'm here. Whatever the outcome, I'm here with you. We can deal with it. Focus, Lydia. When you're ready, open the box.'

She turned, facing the boxes, then back to Ben, watching at the front of the barn. His face still, void.

'Okay. I'm going with the box on the left. Here goes.' She'd made her choice. There was no turning back. Lydia clasped both sides of the box; her fingers twitched, her body awash with fatigue. She was dizzy with the adrenaline that surged through her skin, causing an itching sensation. She slowly opened the box, lifting the edge of the cardboard.

Lydia pulled the box, bringing it towards her, tipping it and moving it left and right with complete ease. 'I think it's empty, Ben. It's too light,' she called out.

'Keep going. Look inside. Can you see anything?'

Lydia called out; her voice was strained, 'Nothing. Only bubble wrap and filler. Hundreds of polystyrene shapes. That's it.'

Ben was steadying himself. If the box was empty, he'd race like the clappers with Lydia towards the coach. The caller would never get Milly while Ben was still able to breathe.

Lydia furiously pulled out the packaging, grabbing handfuls of the stuff and throwing them to the floor. 'It's empty, Ben. I've chosen the wrong one. I'm so sorry.'

Ben felt the pounding of his heart through his shirt; he pictured his daughter, how brave she was, talking to the passengers, making them feel at ease. She'd often said that Ben was her hero; well, the feeling was mutual. He and Laura couldn't be any more proud of the woman she'd become. Now, the caller was listening on the phone, standing next to the coach, ready to grab Milly the second Lydia emptied the rest of the contents. He backed further away. Ben had to get to his daughter.

Lydia was on her tiptoes, her body leaning slightly over the edge of the box on the left-hand side, digging her hands further towards the bottom. She pulled the top of the box to her chest, tipping it downwards. She dipped her left hand inside, frantically shovelling everything out. Half the contents were now on the floor. 'Wait. I can feel something.' Her hands were three quarters of the way inside the box.

She turned to Ben, the box now lying on its side. 'There's something here. I can make out the shape.'

Ben was gripped with anticipation, his eyes glued to where Lydia was standing.

She was on her knees, crawling inside the cardboard container. Small pieces of polystyrene scattered everywhere. Ben could see her body from the waist down and she was struggling to get to whatever it was that she'd felt.

Lydia screamed, a muffled cry from inside the box. She manoeuvred her body backwards and out of the large cardboard container. She was holding something in her right hand. Her eyes were closed. As Lydia stood, she screamed, looking at the long clumps of hair in her hand. The heavy, bulky item felt like a basketball and weighed much the same. She held the object high in the air, turning it towards her.

Lydia was holding the decapitated head of the coach driver.

She cried out, then turned and retched over the ground, dropping the head to the floor. Her legs buckled, and she fell onto her knees.

Ben raced to where Lydia was kneeling. He shone the torch

on the head which had landed hard on the ground and rolled slightly on its side. He stared at the bushy, wild hair, the overgrown beard. Some of the head had been blown away from the temple upwards. The caller had obviously watched Stephen and Ben lifting Andrew and placing him in the field. Then, he'd gone in and cut the remains of the driver's head from the body. Part of the facial hair had been stripped away, possibly with a knife.

Underneath, three letters ran along Andrew's chin, etched with a black marker. The word *WIN*.

'I'm sorry, Lydia. I'm sorry you had to see this. We need to get out of here. Come on.'

Lydia was crying; her top was soaked in bile. She started rocking. 'No. No. Why is he doing this? Why?'

'Lydia, you need to stand up. We have to go. The passengers are in danger.' Ben placed his hand on Lydia's, slowly lifting her to her feet, moving his arms around her waist for support.

'I want Jack. I can't go on without him.' Again, she yelled, throwing her head onto Ben's shoulder. She stayed like that until she had no more energy to cry.

As they reached the front door and stepped outside of the barn, they heard the caller's voice. He'd been quiet for so long.

'Well done. You should be extremely proud, Lydia. I understand you picked the correct box. I heard everything.'

Ben lifted the phone to his mouth. 'I'm coming for you. I'm going to find you. Believe me. I'm going to fucking find you.'

The caller continued to talk; it seemed Ben's threats had little effect. 'What about the other box? I've left a little something for Lydia. Something I'm sure she'll appreciate. I want her to open it.'

'She's not opening anything. We're done here.'

'Let me remind you, Mr Do-Gooder, I'm a few feet from your daughter.'

Another jpeg came through, a picture of Laura and Milly in much the same position.

'You lay a hand on them, and you're finished. Do you understand?' Ben threatened.

'Let Lydia open the box then, see the gift I've left for her.'

Lydia gripped Ben's shirt. 'I'll open it.' She made her way along the floor of the barn. She purposely avoided looking at Andrew. She'd never forget the horror of crawling inside the box and pulling out his head. The image would be etched in her mind until she drew her last breath.

Again, Lydia placed her arms on top of the box on the right. As she stood, preparing herself to open the flaps, a hand pushed out from the inside. Like a jack-in-the-box, bursting its way out.

The box toppled over and there was a loud thump as it hit the ground. Ben saw it first. The boots, the khaki trousers, the hi-vis jacket. The caller came out from the box with a sawn-off shotgun.

He'd made sure not to speak while they were inside the barn, keeping his voice to a whisper while they were outside. He'd watched them through a small peephole, hidden by the box filler.

He'd sent pictures, a video, making out he was standing by the coach. Now, Ben realised he'd taken them earlier.

The caller grabbed Lydia around the neck and pointed the shotgun directly at Ben.

23

BEN AND LYDIA

'Let her go. She's done nothing to you.'

Ben stared down the length of the gun, too frightened to charge towards the caller.

His life suddenly flashed in front of him, the life he had with Laura and Milly. He saw his daughter as a little girl, holding Ben's hand. He was steering her into a room, Milly blindfolded. He lifted the scarf from around her eyes and listened to the voices shouting, 'Happy birthday'. Another snippet of a recent holiday, Ben and Milly were out by the pool and the weather was amazing. He ran up to the apartment, begging Laura to come down and then lifted her over his shoulder, racing to the water and the two of them dropping into the pool. Milly was laughing; people began to clap.

He imagined her leaving for school, grabbing her lunchbox, her hair tousled, Ben instructing Milly to pull her skirt down, take the make-up off. Milly laughed while Laura made coffee, saying she imagined he'd still be protective when she started work, him barking orders from the sitting room. They'd leave the house together, late as usual, Ben dashing to the car, instructing Milly to rush while she gazed at her phone, her shoelaces undone and oblivious to his despair. The car journey would involve loud music, the smell of perfume, quick, one-word answers from his daughter. Ben wouldn't have it any other way.

Now, Ben focused on the caller in his hi-vis jacket. He was certain he was going to shoot, then move out of the barn with Lydia. The caller stared back at him, finger wrapped around the trigger. It wasn't the time for heroics. Ben had so much to lose. He wanted to get to Lydia, wrestle the gun from the caller but he couldn't take the chance.

'Move to the side,' the man in the hi-vis ordered. 'I promise I'll blast you as I stand here.'

Ben watched the fear on Lydia's face. 'I'll find you. Do you hear me, Lydia? I'll find you.'

Lydia was clawing at the guy's hand, pulling hard and making little progress. His arm was tight around her throat.

'I won't tell you again. Move to the side.'

Ben reluctantly stood back. Lydia's legs dragged along the floor as the caller walked. A minute later, the two of them went out of the front door.

Ben stood for a moment, trying to digest the madness that had unfolded.

A few hours ago he and his family were on their way to Barcelona. Now, he was in a barn in the middle of nowhere, staring at a decapitated head and seconds ago, a guy had a shotgun pointed at his face. He waited, struggling to believe how his life had changed so drastically.

He feared for the lives of his wife, his daughter, his life, the passengers relying on him.

He had to find where Lydia was being taken, where the others were being held. Ben hoped they were still alive, waiting to be rescued.

He walked along the floor, kicking hay into the air, contemplating his next move. He had to go up to the coach, make sure everyone was still alive.

He pondered Edward, a loose cannon, trying to escape earlier and wondering if he'd told his wife what had happened to their son, Nigel. Ben hoped not.

He thought about Stephen; earlier he was running along the path, shouting that he had to go and get help.

He thought about Andrew, the driver, and what the caller had done to him. Ben imagined how he'd stood over the body, a few feet from the coach, and removed the head. How he'd cut into it, detaching it from the body.

Ben stepped out onto the path from the barn to the road. He looked into the distance, listening for bushes being trampled, heavy boots treading on grass, Lydia, crying out, begging for mercy, her legs dragging along the earth.

His surroundings were tranquil, lifeless. If anyone passed this place, they'd never believe what was happening here.

He thought about the caller. He'd never felt fear like he had moments ago, watching him, waiting to see if he pulled the trigger. It was so easy – the toss of a coin, the pull of a finger on the trigger and BANG. The life he'd built, the friendships, the links to his family, all gone, just like that. It could have been taken away in one split second.

They say when you face death, images flash in your mind, the people closest to you, visions so real. Ben had those. He'd never been closer to death than this evening. Tonight, Ben had to make sure he wasn't put in that position again.

He walked out to the end of the path, onto the road and ran towards the coach.

The Cottage.

Lydia lay in the boot of Ben's car. The caller had removed the suitcases and dumped them in a ditch. She shouted out, thumping the sides with her fists. She heard the driver's door close, and the car rolled forward.

She was struggling to breathe; the air was sparse. The smell of oil sunk into her lungs, and she felt like her insides were on fire. 'Let me out. I beg you; I can't stay in here. Let me out.'

Lydia felt as if the sides of the boot were closing in towards her, about to clamp her face. Her heart was throbbing; she kept seeing the gory head of Andrew, the dead coach driver. How could the man in the hi-vis do this? How could someone be so cruel, tormenting her? Lydia was hysterical. She turned her body in the tight space, kicking at the sides, stamping, begging to get out.

The caller had the radio on, playing low. She knew that no one could hear her.

After a few minutes, the car stopped. The radio went off, and the driver's door opened and slammed shut.

She waited, anticipating the caller's next move. Lydia placed her ear to the side of the car, unsure if the guy had left or was standing outside the boot of the car. She opened her mouth, controlling the sound of her breaths, too frightened to make a noise. A minute passed. Lydia was certain he'd gone. She swung her body backwards, rolling on her shoulders and kicked the roof. It didn't budge. Again, she kicked, hearing a snap as the heel of her shoe broke. She shouted at the top of her voice. 'Let me out. I can't stay in here. You don't understand. I can't stay in closed spaces. I'll die. Let me the fuck out. Can you hear me? Please.' Lydia broke down; she placed her face on the cold carpet underneath. 'I have to get out.'

Suddenly, she heard a clunk from the top of the car. The boot had been unlocked.

She pushed her hands upwards, now able to peer through the crack. She waited, imagining the caller grabbing her, placing her over his shoulders and taking her to a field to shoot her, leaving her dead body for the wildlife to pick at.

She pushed the hatch, opening it slightly, then sat up, grabbing the edge of the car for support.

'Hello.' She expected an answer, a simple instruction. 'Is anyone there?' Lydia shoved her hands against the boot hatch, opening it wider and manoeuvred head first out of the car, placing her hands on the ground as the rest of her body followed.

Lydia got to her feet and brushed the earth from her clothes. She was standing alone; the driver's seat was empty, the engine was turned off, and the lights were on, shining across the field. Lydia moved to the car door, opening it and checking to see if the keys were in the ignition. No such luck.

She thumped the dashboard in frustration and slammed the vehicle door. Then in the distance she saw a small light gleaming through a window. She stared across the field, facing it, wondering if she could go and get help.

While Lydia had laid in the boot, she was certain the car had moved further away from the coach. The caller had driven slowly. She'd estimated that the journey was three to four minutes. It would take too long to walk back to the coach, and she was not sure of the right direction. The lighted window was a better bet.

She thought about Jack. He had to be close.

Lydia was going to find him.

She was going to get help.

The Coach.

Ben was elated to see Laura and Milly tending to the passengers, still alive, still here. Laura saw him first and shouted to Milly. She joined her mother at the door.

He climbed the steps, and his wife and daughter mobbed

him like he was a celebrity. The three huddled, and the women could smell the cold, fresh air on Ben's clothes.

'Thank God,' Laura said. She poked her head out of the door, looking where Ben had walked moments ago. 'Where's Lydia?'

Ben explained what had happened, leaving out the part where they'd found Andrew's head. He didn't want to stress them out more than was needed. 'He had a shotgun pointing in my face. There was nothing I could do. He walked out with her,' Ben stated.

Laura held Ben's face, moving her hand along the line of his jaw. 'Ben, you can't go out again. Do you hear me?'

'I had no choice. You know what would have happened if we disobeyed his instructions. He's taken her, Laura. He's holding her someplace close. She's not a well woman. You've seen her. Lydia can't cope. I have to find the house.'

'Dad, Mum's right. You can't go looking for her.'

Ben felt helpless. Their car had been taken. Lydia had been kidnapped, and he couldn't call for help. It was like he'd been dropped in a maze with no exit. 'How are you both coping? Not what you expected on the way to the airport I'm guessing?'

The three of them smiled nervously. It felt good to relieve a little of the tension.

'I have a plan. But you're both going to need to let me go,' Ben said.

Laura tightened her grip on him. 'Oh, God. Why do I not like the sound of this?'

'Dad, please. I don't want you to go out there again. Maybe someone will drive past. See we're stranded and come and help us,' Milly said hopefully.

'Baby, look out there. It's so bleak, barren. I haven't seen a light for hours. No one is coming for us. I need to do something about it, but I'm going to need your help. Trust me, okay?' Ben placed his hands on his daughter's face and kissed her forehead. 'Okay?' He could smell the familiar scent of coconut oil from his daughter's skin.

She smiled, her quivering lips extended across her face. 'Okay.'

'I'm going to keep walking, past the barn. The road leads around in a full circle. I think the place where he's holding the others is along that stretch of road. He's not going to expect anyone to go there. He's busy at the moment with Lydia. I need to find the house, weigh up my options and then decide what to do. In the meantime, I want you both to untie the passengers, but make sure they stay seated.'

Milly and Laura both gasped.

'If he gets a sniff that they're free from the ropes, he's going to start shooting. Please, tell them to stay in their seats. I can't stress too much the importance of this. When the time is right, we're going to move them off the coach.' Ben reached forward and turned on the full lights to aide his way along the road. 'I'm going to find the house.'

24

STEPHEN AND GARETH

Stephen, having lost the man who had been chasing him after he set fire to the car, came out of the woods to the road on the other side and looked frantically for Gareth. The road was clear both sides. He placed his hands on his hips, gasping for breath – he'd run through the woods to escape his pursuer. He swallowed to rid the taste of smoke in his mouth, wondering if he would ever be able to stop thinking about the car with a body in the boot that he'd torched.

He raced along the ground, looking behind him, into the woods, searching for the man who'd been watching. The forest was empty.

As he rounded the next bend, he saw a car heading towards him. Stephen stood to the side of the road, unsure if it was Gareth. He crouched, his breathing started to slow, the sweat which masked his face had begun to dry.

Then Stephen saw the familiar number plate and jumped out onto the road. Gareth swerved, hit the brakes and unwound the window, staring shocked at his gasping friend. 'Sorry, mate, I fell asleep.'

Stephen opened the passenger door. 'Someone saw me.'

'Who?' demanded Gareth.

'I don't know. I set the car alight and he was standing there. I ran, and he followed me.'

Gareth looked across the woodland as Stephen closed the door and placed the seat belt around his body. 'You're sure someone was there?'

'Yes. I wouldn't make it up.'

'I'm not saying that, but you have been seeing a lot of crazy shit.'

'So you're saying I made it up?'

From the corner of his eye, Stephen saw a figure standing at the side of the road. He slowly turned his head, seeing a woman in a white nightdress, her body ablaze, her face melting as she stood with her arms out as if pleading for help. He jumped. 'Shit. Drive!' he shouted.

Gareth turned to his friend. 'What's wrong?'

Stephen pointed. 'Look.'

'At what?'

'You can't see her?'

'I can't see anyone, Stephen. It's just us.'

Stephen bent forward, placing his head in his hands. 'I can't deal with this. I need help.'

'You're tired, mate. That's all. You need to rest.'

Stephen looked back. The figure was gone.

'Come on. Let's get out of here.' Gareth turned the car around and drove away from the woods.

They were oblivious to the car following them.

On the drive back to Stephen's flat, Gareth had something on his mind. He'd remembered the road where he'd dumped his own

Volkswagen. He had to go back and get it. 'I have to go somewhere first,' he told Stephen.

'Where?'

'I'm going to get my car back. I know where it is. I remember.'

Stephen looked across at his friend. 'Do you think that's a wise move?' Stephen had flashbacks, remembering the body in the boot of the car that Gareth had stolen off the drive. He couldn't work out whether his mind was playing tricks again. But he was certain it was dangerous going back.

Gareth was insistent. 'The tax runs out soon. Someone will call the police about an abandoned car. They'll put one of those "police aware" signs on the window, and it'll get clamped. It will come back to bite me on the arse. I'll have fines, they'll pile up. I have to get it.'

Stephen pushed back on the seat: the frustration of the last twenty-four hours had taken its toll. He was uneasy going to the place where Gareth had stolen the car, but he knew Gareth couldn't get there alone. 'I'll drop you off and drive this car back, mate,' he said.

'I'm sure this is the road.' Gareth indicated left, and turned the steering wheel gently, guiding the car into the side road. 'Yes, I can see it further up. Look.' Gareth tapped the brakes and rolled past the car on the left.

'Shit. That's going to cost you.' The bumper was hanging off the back of the vehicle; one of the corners was touching the road.

They parked Stephen's car and got out. The day had turned bitter cold, and a stiff breeze hit them as they stood on the pavement. Stephen placed his hands in his pockets, his body was fighting the fatigue, and he struggled to stop the trembling. They walked together to Gareth's car.

Gareth saw the empty drive on his right; he suddenly got a

flashback to last night, parking his car, getting out, racing along the road, grabbing at the door handles of the parked vehicles. 'This is where I stole the car.' He looked at the large detached house with the white-painted brick and the glistening marble-style paving slabs. He glanced at the mailbox.

Stephen grabbed his arm. 'Keep walking.'

Gareth pulled away and stopped. 'I need to say something. I need to knock and let them know what happened.'

'You're not serious? Say what exactly? Oh, hey, thanks for that last night. I'm so glad you left the keys in the ignition. I don't know what I would have done if the lecturer I'm planning to blackmail had caught me. By the way, you'll find your car in the woods. Well, what's left of it.'

Gareth knew his friend was right. There was no way they'd greet him with a welcoming smile, an offer of tea and biscuits. He had to forget about the car. As they passed the house, Gareth looked inside the large, doubled-glazed front window. The curtains were open. Two people were chatting; a man was sitting at the far end of the room, the woman was closer to the window.

'Gareth, come on. Let's get the car.'

But Gareth was glued to the spot on the pavement, watching the couple through the windows which were slightly open. Suddenly there were raised voices and an atmosphere of hostility. He imagined the conversation, the husband in turmoil, looking for their car. His wife, sat close, telling him to calm down. *It will show up. Worse things happen. It's just a car for crying out loud.*

'We need to get out of here,' Stephen instructed.

Gareth was transfixed, wanting so badly to knock on the door and apologise. But his guilt turned to horror as the living room door was flung open. Another woman entered, holding a large object in her hands. She raced towards the woman near the window, raised the object and hammered it down on her head. She lifted it again, struggling to hold it, then dropped it on the woman's head a second time.

Gareth stood in complete shock. It felt like his jaw had pounded against the ground. His legs went weak, and his world started furiously spinning until he could not focus his eyes.

'Are we going or what?' Stephen asked, oblivious to what Gareth had just witnessed.

Stephen felt the surge of electricity pulsating through his neck a few seconds before Gareth. They fell to the ground, and hoods were placed over their heads.

25

THE CALLER

'It's nearly that time, Evelyn. I've been looking forward to it. If I'm truthful, I've been counting the days, a virtual calendar in my mind, nothing on paper but I visualise the date, hear the page flipping over, as the next day arrives. I'm sure you have too – time to bring the world to rights, rid the trash. I've got a good feeling, Evelyn.'

Henry Mitchell stood in front of the bathroom mirror. He gazed at his reflection, feeling every day of his fifty-three years. He still had a thick head of black hair; grey strands were starting to show, the odd wisp. He usually plucked them out, kept on top of them, but today they were determined to work their way through faster than he could deal with them.

He reached for the cup on the stained sink. It contained a couple of toothbrushes, an electric hair trimmer, a nail file and other items which aided in the process of ageing. He worked his fingers into the cup, seeking the small tweezers which had worked their way down the back. Henry brought the tweezers to the side of his head. 'Bang. You're gone.' He lifted his head back, turning to the left. 'You think I don't see you?' He grabbed the small strand and yanked hard. 'There you go. That's beautiful.

It's taken ten years off me already.' He raised his voice. 'Evelyn, two this morning. That won't do now, will it?'

Dropping the long strands into the toilet, he yanked the handle. Water poured into the bowl like a cascade, and the cistern screeched as it began filling. 'Another job on my list.'

He stared at his face in the mirror, the rugged complexion. Lines had developed under his eyes, deep, furrowed marks which had spread. He stood back and considered a quick shave. Henry eyed the five o'clock shadow. The hassle was too much, and besides, Evelyn preferred the rougher appearance.

When they'd first met, he shaved daily. Sideburns were fashionable, but they were uncomfortable and his curled at the ends. The longer he'd left between running the blade along his face, the more Evelyn preferred it.

Out in the upstairs hallway Henry listened, unsure whether Evelyn was awake. He remembered talking to her and her answering, but he couldn't remember when. A half hour ago possibly. Maybe more. He wanted to call out, see if she fancied breakfast but didn't have it in him to wake her.

He whispered, 'Evelyn. You awake?' Henry waited for an answer and considered creeping across the landing, tapping the door before he entered. *Must knock before invading anyone's privacy. Them's the rules. It's called etiquette.*

He decided to let her rest. He'd make coffee, toast, lightly buttered, a couple of cheese singles. Evelyn loved those. In the early days, she'd preferred Marmite and went through a phrase of peanut butter. To Henry, it was more an American delicacy, but she loved the stuff. He often caught her dipping her finger in the jar, swirling it in the thick gloop and bringing it to her mouth. He'd tasted it, but Henry wasn't a fan.

In the kitchen, Henry removed the bread from the freezer. Why had Evelyn insisted on chilling it? Something about it lasting longer. To Henry, it was a hassle he didn't need, waiting the extra time to brown the toast was something of a chore. He filled the kettle then flicked the switch and waited for the hiss of the water as it started to bubble, churning over, the steam rising, pushing against the kitchen cupboard.

Henry opened the bread, his hands cold, splitting the tag, then removed it from the packaging, forcing his fingers between the slices which had stuck together. He placed them in the toaster, pushing the lever, turning the knob to full. She liked her toast well done.

He stared into the garden to the woods beyond. Though they lived on the edge of town their position on an incline meant the views were amazing. He and Evelyn loved to take walks as the sun set, listening to the animals, busy in their habitat. They were guests in this beautiful environment.

The toaster clicked, making Henry jump. It got him every time. He grinned to himself, wallowing in the burnt smell, listening to the kettle which was almost at boiling point, the clunk of the switch as it came to a finish.

There was something about the smell of burning bread. He fixated on some smells, like filling the car up with petrol. Some people lit candles, or kept crystals in a bowl by the toilet. Not him, he preferred the rugged fragrances that were tough and resilient.

His wife loved when he'd spend time repairing their coach, the smell of his overalls did something to her. It turned her into a sex crazy beast, unable to control her emotions. Henry went along with it. He'd do anything for his wife.

He placed two cups on the worktop, a teabag in one, a spoonful of instant coffee in the other, then he slowly poured the water. He preferred tea himself, or on the odd occasion he would drink real coffee, not the shit in a tin. To him it was artificial, it didn't taste right, like an overcooked steak or a corked bottle of wine. But Evelyn liked her coffee instant, and that's what she'd have.

Henry cocked his head, thinking he may have heard a stir upstairs. He moved away from the kitchen, into the hall. *She couldn't be up, no way.*

He stood in the hall for what seemed like minutes, pondering, thinking about his life. How he loved that woman. Today was a special day. He'd gone out last night and bought the cake and two packets of birthday candles from the corner shop. He needed everything to be perfect.

He moved along the hall and opened the front door, looking out at the long path to the road, and round to his car on the right, with his coach parked just behind it, along the drive that led to the back of the house.

Recently, the topiary had overgrown. The football boot, the small castle and the elephant with its trunk in the air would need attention. He'd have to trim them, make them tidy. He had the time now. He hadn't taken the coach out for so long. Work had dried up; he'd been replaced by someone younger, able to cope with the long hours. And for much of the year he got a good income from the three country cottages he let out to tenants and tourists.

He closed the front door gently, hoping not to wake Evelyn. He had to prepare the cake, plant the candles in the sponge and light them, all sixty-one. He kept as quiet as possible as he finished making the drinks, with a light dust of sugar in both, then placed the cups and the toast on a tray. He walked along the hall and climbed the stairs.

Evelyn's bedroom door was still open. Henry knew he should set the tray down and let her come for her breakfast. He hated entering the room unannounced. He left the tray by the bedroom door, then returned to the kitchen.

Gently, he removed the sponge from the fridge. It was plain, no writing or icing or any fancy shit – just the sponge with a layer of jam in the middle. He reached for the lighter in the middle drawer and planted the candles. He placed them around the edge of the cake first, then a second row further in, finishing with a couple in the middle.

He thought about spelling her name across the cake, but she'd laugh at his efforts. Henry loved it when Evelyn laughed. It meant she was happy, content, a joyous moment he was sharing with his wife.

Quickly, he lit the candles, scorching his thumb more than once. He ran it under the cold tap. The candles were short, although he'd asked in the corner shop for longer ones, they'd given him stumps. He'd need to talk to Mr Burton.

Not today, today was Evelyn's day.

Once the candles were lit, Henry smiled, straightened his back and walked out of the kitchen, through the hall and up the stairs. He paused in the landing, now sombre at seeing the tray untouched by the bedroom door. Henry knew he shouldn't just walk in; it was rude. He hated rudeness. But today, well, today was different.

Holding the cake plate firmly he started singing *Happy Birthday* followed by a rendition of 'sixty-one today, sixty-one today'.

He walked into the bedroom and placed the cake on the side table. Then Henry picked up the tray from the hall and returned. He placed it beside the cake and then sat on the bed, looking at his wife. She'd be so pleased with the effort he'd made. Henry reached forward, touching Evelyn's shoulder, gently turning the board slightly on its side and placing a piece of copper pipe underneath it to support her. Of course, Evelyn couldn't see the cake, the candles, the coffee or toast lightly buttered and done just how she liked it. Henry stared at the corpse. Bacteria which had helped her digest food had long since eaten her body.

He'd attended her funeral and they'd dressed Evelyn in her favourite white nightdress. He returned that night and got her back out. Henry had cut a piece of boarding, a little wider and longer than her frame and held her in place with wire. Then, he dropped the seats and placed Evelyn's body along the back of the car. He was so pleased to have her back.

He'd sat on the bed, day after day, watching as her body had swelled and released putrid substances. The chemicals and gases were something Henry struggled deeply with. The fumes made it difficult to breathe, but he was determined not to let it stop him from being with his wife.

He'd instructed the undertakers not to embalm her body. He didn't want Evelyn's blood drained and unnatural chemicals pumped into her. He wanted her back in the house, the same way she'd left.

The flies had enraged Henry. He stood in the room as more and more of the bastards gathered, working their way into Evelyn's nose, her mouth and all the other orifices. He swatted at them, but they seemed to keep coming, more of them, laying eggs inside his beautiful wife's body. Then the maggots, hundreds of them, thousands. He scooped them with his hands and watched them wriggling on the floor. It got to a stage where he couldn't control it, watching them feed on her beautiful skin until most of it had disappeared. How he hated the food chain.

After a number of weeks, her blood cells began to haemorrhage iron, which turned her body a deep black colour. Her skin tissue was now a watery mush, and her nightdress had started to decompose, due to the chemicals her corpse had produced. Her face was dry, hollow looking but to Henry, Evelyn's beauty was everlasting.

During the last year, Henry had sat in this room, every day, talking, hoping she could still hear what he was saying.

He placed the black wig over her head and removed a clean nightdress from the drawer, draping it over the one she wore, like a blanket, and made her look just how she appeared the night she died. As the candles burned on her sixty-first birthday and Henry sat perched on the end of her bed, his hand on her body, he swore he saw his wife smile.

He sat for over an hour, talking to Evelyn. Telling her about his morning, the trip to town yesterday, the candles which would burn too quickly and how he'd have words with Mr Burton. He told her how he missed her voice, soft, caring, compassionate. She seemed happy here. Henry couldn't contemplate having his wife rot in a hole out in some cemetery, that wouldn't do at all. It was implausible.

He touched her leg. 'Don't you worry, love. People are going to pay. That's a promise. People will realise the consequences of their sins.' Henry stood and turned to his wife. 'Happy birthday, my beautiful lady.'

Downstairs, Henry removed the box from the bottom drawer in the kitchen.

He lifted the lid, removing the paper cuttings. He didn't want to read too much; it upset him. He took the top newspaper clipping, seeing the headline, 'Woman killed in a hit-and-run'. There was a picture of Evelyn and Henry, his arm around her, looking into each other's eyes. The press had got the photo from a recent charity dinner that Evelyn had organised for homeless people. Henry scanned over the report.

Evelyn Mitchell was tragically killed on her sixtieth birthday after returning from a hike with her husband, Henry. The two were walking along the road at Bourne Woods in Farnham when a car lost control, hitting Evelyn and killing her instantly.

It's thought the car was driven by a young man, possibly in

his early twenties who continued to drive without stopping. A witness said they saw someone driving erratically, close to where the incident happened a short while after and gave a brief description of the young man.

Surrey police are urging anyone who may have seen the incident or know of this man's whereabouts to contact them immediately.

Evelyn is survived by her husband of twenty-seven years. The family has not issued a statement.

Henry Mitchell could have struck sooner, the night after it happened. A week later, a month. But he needed time to grieve. To deal with what had happened. He believed Evelyn spoke to him. He thought he heard her at night, walking the floors of the house, calling for him. As long as she stayed here, up in her bedroom, she wasn't really gone.

The days after the accident were the hardest. The smell, the decay. He thought many times about bringing Evelyn over to the woodland and digging, but in the end, it would mean his wife was gone forever. Henry couldn't cope with that happening. He couldn't deal with not looking at her.

Tonight, Henry Mitchell would get his revenge. It was time. Evelyn died on her birthday so it made perfect sense to strike on this very date. There was no other gift for his wife, no other present that could top what Henry Mitchell was planning. He had to make her happy, to please her. It had to be done now. The birthday of all birthdays.

Avenging her death.

Henry checked the kitchen clock, watching the second hand as it pushed around in a circle. It was getting late. He'd made Evelyn's day special. He didn't want anything tarnishing or spoiling the occasion. Henry wanted the two of them to have an intimate celebration. But now, he needed to do this, for his wife.

Henry had ordered an extra large woman's white nightdress

online. He stood in the kitchen, numb with anticipation as he opened the box. He pulled it out, removing the wrapping, flapping it in the air with both hands to shake out the creases. The material was cold, soft. He removed his boots, jeans, his jumper and placed them neatly on the chair at the table. Then, he slid into the nightdress, adjusting the shoulder straps. He looked in the mirror, admiring the likeness, then walked up the stairs to Evelyn's room.

The candles had long burnt out, the coffee and toast untouched. Henry leant forward, removing the long black hair which he'd cut from her head in the early days, and placed the wig he'd made on top of his head.

He looked at his wife's corpse. 'I'm ready.'

As he left the room, he was sure his wife whispered, 'Thank you.'

Henry stood, hidden in Bourne Woods. He was unsure of the time, but it was after 11pm. He could see his house a little further up; the coach parked on the drive, his car parked close to where he stood. He waited, worrying if he'd left it too late. This stretch of road was quiet, and not many vehicles came through. He stood, looking down at the nightdress, his legs bare, his body shivering and his fair skin coated in pimples from the cold. While he stood, hidden in the trees, Henry thought about how wrong it could all go. He had questions. So many *what ifs*.

He glanced towards the house, stamping his bare feet on the ground, flinging his hands outwards and back around his body. The cold was too much. Henry thought about going back to the house, switching the heating on. Their home looked so inviting from where he stood. A hot bath, soak his bones and lie there for hours. No bath bombs, no extravagant oils or false smells. Just hot water.

His thoughts were interrupted by the sound of an engine in the distance. Henry squeezed his fists together; his legs were giddy, the excitement building as the car approached where he stood.

This is it, he thought. *This is my moment now.* Henry was standing on the side of the road, waiting, ready to pounce: his and Evelyn's day had come. His vengeance for the wrongdoing of others.

The lights approached, enlarging, the brightness blinding him. Henry placed his hands on his forehead, shielding his eyes. The driver was speeding, racing through the countryside without a care for anyone else, selfishly rushing to get home.

This is it, Henry thought. *It's only the beginning. This is for you, Evelyn. Happy birthday, my love.*

As the car slowed around the bend, Henry jumped out and stood on the road.

The driver swerved, grappling with the steering wheel.

Henry leapt into the bushes. From behind the trees he saw the car, the doors open, two young lads standing out on the road. Then they got back into the car, and the driver pulled away.

That was all Henry Mitchell needed. He jumped into his car and followed the hit-and-run driver.

Henry kept enough of a gap so as not to look conspicuous, knowing his plans could be scuppered if he was spotted. He stayed with the car, pressing the pedals with his bare feet, following it through town, keeping his distance. He pictured Evelyn, lying on the bed, a mass of bones, ribs. Her skin, wasting away.

Henry was struggling to stem his anger and come to terms with the guy driving away. Once he could get himself under control, the punishment would follow.

The hit-and-run driver parked up and the passenger got out. Henry made a note of the address; then he continued to follow the car. After a time, the driver pulled over. He was grappling with his conscience, with what he'd done, distressed, crying in the front seat. Eventually, he reached home, and Henry got out, staying close behind. He saw the young lad opening the communal doors and going into the first flat on the left.

Henry had all he needed. He left immediately, now he knew where the lad lived.

The following morning, Henry drove to where the passenger had got out. After a short wait the guy got in his car and drove to the local university. Henry sat in the car park. He had all the time in the world. Later that day, the passenger came out of the main building, bewildered, disorientated. He got into his car and sat there, pounding the dashboard. Henry watched, like a stakeout, seeing the guy fall apart. The young lad fell asleep in the car for maybe two or three hours.

Henry had wanted to take him there and then but he risked being seen. There were so many students, possible cameras. It was too conspicuous. When the young lad woke, he looked across at the man making his way to his jeep. Henry guessed he was a lecturer, well dressed, long grey hair, smart looking. The old man pulled out of the car park, and the young lad followed.

Henry joined the chain. He witnessed the lecturer's lewd act, feeling repulsed, disgusted that someone could do this. She was young enough to be his daughter. Henry watched through binoculars, peering at the wedding band on the lecturer's ring finger.

He saw the young lad take photos, and how the flash revealed him to the lecturer. The older man pulled up his trousers and ran to his car.

Henry waited until they'd left, then followed. He tailed Gareth and the lecturer all night and eventually followed the old man home.

The following day, Henry saw thick smoke rising above the forest as he drove back from town. When he investigated he found the hit-and-run driver was standing by a car, watching it burn. Henry followed him, watching the young lad running through the woods. He followed on foot, then returned to his car. As he drove towards the other side of the woods, he saw his friend pick him up. Again, Henry followed them.

He had to time it right, intending on using the stun gun, injuring them both on the side of the road. Then he'd place them on the coach, tie them to the seats, blindfold them and hold them there until the games could begin.

As he pressed the stun gun to both their necks and watched them drop to the floor, he happened to glance through the window of the house he was outside. He hadn't expected to witness a murder.

He had just aimed to punish the guys for driving away from the scene of the hit-and-run.

But now... he was going to have a field day with this lot.

26

THE COTTAGE

Lydia, still sore from her time in the car boot, stood on the road, watching the lit window in the distance.

She needed to get to Jack; he'd make everything all right. She was going to find him, untie her husband and make off.

She felt bad for Ben and his family, they'd done so much for her, looked after her and the other passengers. They'd made her comfortable, reassured her and given her the confidence to continue. She'd never forget that. But Lydia couldn't be here. She couldn't cope with this. She'd free Jack, then cross the fields and make their escape.

Lydia was certain the caller was more interested in the larger group, held on the coach. He dropped her off, opened the boot and was now headed back to the others.

The alternative scenario was one that Lydia didn't want to consider. The caller had played games, set traps, like a hunter stalking prey. It was possible he'd let her out of the boot to fuel his appetite.

She went for the former scenario. It was much easier to digest.

As she walked, hobbling from the broken heel, she pictured

her husband. How he'd shielded her from the outside world, the hatred, bitterness, everything that came with situations Lydia had gotten herself into. He was her protector; he'd never let anything happen to her. Now, she was going to do the same, repay the kindness her husband showed.

She thought about Chloe, buried in the garden, how Jack had made it better by taking control of the situation.

She recalled that Saturday afternoon, when Dana came over, asking questions and threatening to go to the police. Lydia wasn't a violent person, she would run at the first sign of trouble, but Jack was helpless, caught in the headlights. Lydia had had to hit Dana, to take her out of the equation. She remembered the sound, how the crack filled the room, and Dana, her eyes wild and startled as Lydia ran at her.

Jack was cross at first. He screamed, charging to where Lydia stood, taking the brass figure from her, wiping the blood. He shook her, his hands placed on her shoulders, rocking her body back and forth, shouting, asking why she'd do this.

Lydia had no answer. She didn't know why she'd hit Dana that afternoon, except that she was an obstacle in the way of their happiness.

Dana knew what had happened; the bracelet placed Lydia at the house. Dana was playing games. That's why she had to go.

Lydia had to kill her.

It was the only way.

Their world tumbled even deeper out of control when the door knocked.

The caller had seen everything.

She walked, guided by the light in the window shimmering across the fields, until she saw a sign of life. Now she was closer, she could see the light was in the upstairs window of a cottage. She didn't have a plan. She hoped to go inside, find her husband and run.

There were other cottages further along. If Jack wasn't here, she'd check the others. He had to be in one of them. He had to be here somewhere.

She stood outside the driveway and removed her shoes. It was too much of a struggle to walk in them with the broken heel. She stepped onto the grass, feeling relief as her feet sunk into the wet soil. She moved closer, taking the place in, wondering where the caller may be holding her husband.

She thought about the barn, how he'd grabbed her around the throat, dumped her in the boot of the car and driven. Why had he gone and left the boot open knowing she'd get out. It was like he wanted her to escape. He'd chosen to let her go, knowing she'd run. That was the reason he'd pulled up on the road and let her out. He was playing games.

No, she told herself. *He is making his way to the coach. He doesn't care what I do. He's let me go, and now he's a long way from here.* She needed to be quick; this was her chance. Grab Jack and run.

The cottage was detached, just a small shell of a house, nothing fancy. From the outside, it looked like a movie set, like a large cardboard cut-out. There were two floors. A lantern hung on the wall to the left of the door, lighting the front garden. Lydia noticed how neat the grass was and the bushes had been recently trimmed. There were other cottages, three more further down the path but nothing suggested they were occupied.

She was distracted by the light suddenly going off upstairs. Lydia backed away and moved to the arch-shaped hedge beside her. She dropped to her knees, keeping hidden. The light came back on, and a few seconds later, a shadow appeared. Lydia saw a woman with long hair, wearing a nightdress. She came forward and seemed to look out of the window.

'Oh, thank God. Help me. Call the police. My husband's been taken, and we need help.' Lydia was ecstatic, waving her arms and jumping up and down on the grass. The figure tilted their head.

She called out, louder this time. 'Ring the police. My husband's been kidnapped. Help me.'

The figure stepped back from the window. The light went out, and a few seconds later, the front door opened.

'Oh, thank you. You don't know how happy I am to see someone out here.'

Lydia moved towards the front door, peering behind to make sure she was alone. She smiled, intending to call the police as soon as she stood inside the cottage.

This was it.

They were safe now.

She pushed the front door slightly wider. As she stepped into the downstairs hallway, she saw the house was in complete darkness. 'Hello. Thank you so much for opening the door.'

The smell hit her instantly – a moist, pungent odour like wet clothes. Lydia concluded it was damp. The woman she'd seen at the window seemed elderly, she probably lived here alone and struggled with the upkeep of the place. She wondered how anyone could live out here; the seclusion would drive her mad. She moved her hand to the wall, frantically searching for a light switch. 'Hello. Are you there? Please don't be scared. I'm not going to hurt you.'

Come on. There must be something on the wall to light this place. How can this woman live like this? The middle of nowhere in the pitch dark?

Her hand brushed across a square plate, protruding from the wall. She found the switch and clicked it downwards. Nothing happened. Lydia tried again, pressing one way then the other. She fumbled in the darkness, patting the pockets of her skirt, needing her phone torch and remembering the caller had taken their phones. She needed a light, something to help her see.

Lydia closed the front door and stepped further inside, swinging her arms, jabbing forwards, her hands trying to feel through the bleakness of the hallway.

'Are you there? I'm not going to harm you. I just need to borrow your phone. See, my husband was taken earlier, we were on a coach. It's a long story. Anyway, if I could call someone to help us, they can find him.' Lydia listened; she expected to hear something. The shuffle of the woman in one of the rooms, maybe her footsteps on the floorboards as the woman hid. Lydia felt a pang of guilt. This poor woman was probably living alone and not used to visitors. She was so sweet and trusting to open the door for her, realising her distress. Lydia needed to find her, let her know she wasn't threatening. All she wanted was a phone; then she'd be out of her hair.

'Don't be frightened. I'm not going to hurt you,' Lydia called out.

She stood for a moment, then walked forward, her arms in front, her eyes wide, preparing, tensing and ready if she banged into something.

Lydia reached the end of the hallway, then turned around. She wanted to open the front door, let the light hanging on the wall outside show her where she was going. She couldn't chance it. The caller had taken off earlier; if she left the front door open, he could get inside. She couldn't take that chance. It was much safer this way.

Lydia reached her arms out, pawing for a handle or a switch. She felt the cold brass handle then turned it slowly and pulled the door towards her. Again, she fiddled on the wall, dabbing her hand to find the light switch.

Click.

Click.

The bulb failed to illuminate the room.

For Christ's sake. This is ridiculous. 'Hello. I need help. Can you hear me?' Lydia was losing her patience. She'd seen the woman at the window, shouted to her for help. She'd opened the front door to let her in and had now gone.

She pawed her way around the kitchen, arms extended, feeling her way along the large room. She had to find something. Anything to aid the safe return of her husband. She suddenly had a weird feeling about this place, trying to understand how this woman could see Lydia calling for help, come down and open the door, then hide. Why open the door? Why leave the place in complete darkness? This was her idea of abnormality. The old woman. Out here. Alone.

Lydia needed to hear life, people walking past her house, the sound of communication. Although she rarely left her home these days and trusted only Jack, she felt safe in the knowledge people were there. It was a comfort.

Lydia turned suddenly. She finally heard something – a noise coming from the front of the cottage. Like a shuffle of feet being dragged gently along the floor. Lydia's heart quickened, now galloping in her chest. She stood frozen to the spot in the kitchen, unable to see. She felt the presence of someone ahead, standing by the front door. She could sense the shape, standing there, watching. The woman was fumbling about, like she was searching for something in a cupboard.

'Can you help me?' Lydia whispered into the darkness, waiting for an answer. 'Hello. Are you there? Really, there's no need to be frightened.' Lydia waited, peering towards the front door. She tried to see if the figure was moving, listening for the old lady making her way towards her. She couldn't tell. She waited, closing her fists into small balls, sensing the sticky sweat coating her hands.

The lights came on, causing Lydia to jump. The loud clunk penetrated through her body.

At last, she could see. The old woman stood still.

'Hi. I'm so sorry to intrude. I just need to use your phone, and I'll be on my way. Thank you for opening the door,' Lydia said. She stared, then slowly edged towards the woman. 'I need your phone. Can you please help me? My husband–'

Lydia saw her face. The rugged complexion, the rough, weathered skin. The frame, tall, solid, strong-looking. She recognised the person now – the same person who'd taken her and Jack, who had held them on the coach. The same person she'd seen in the barn. Lydia backed away, grabbing the kitchen door and slamming it hard. The lights went off. The cottage was again a mass of blackness.

She screamed, pulling at her hair with both hands, then fell to the ground. 'Leave me alone. Please, I want to go home. Leave me the fuck alone.' She crawled on her hands and knees, banging against the leg of a table. Lydia needed to get out. Her heart was rushing uncontrollably, like it would burst at any second.

She made for the corner of the room and crouched by the wall. She waited, her eyes struggling to find the kitchen door. She watched the blackness across the room, needing a way out. She wanted to hide forever, to sink into a hole in the kitchen and never be found.

She was too frightened to function and terrified of what she'd seen in the hallway. The only sound now was the sharp pants thrusting from her mouth. Her lips were dry; she needed water.

Lydia stood, hearing Jack's voice in her head. He'd know what to do, how to cope. His deep, calming voice was all she needed to make things better. She took deep breaths, feeling as if her head had been separated from her body, her windpipe blocked.

Lydia pawed along the kitchen worktop and found the sink. She turned the tap on the right, letting it gently run, then reached forward, cupping her hands under the stream. She threw the water onto her face, gulping, swallowing as much as her body could manage. It felt so good, it had a calming effect on her sweltering body. She was distracted by a creak, a low groan from the other end of the room.

The door was opening.

Lydia moved along to the wall, then sunk onto the ground. The noise stopped. She was certain the caller was in the kitchen. She waited, mustering all the strength she had and crawled to the middle of the kitchen, hiding under the table. The footsteps moved slowly across the kitchen floor. She could hear the person, gaining, getting closer. Lydia placed her hands on her mouth, forcing the air from her lungs. The noise was now beside her. Lydia's body began to give up. She tried to stem the noises coming from inside, the shriek that her body gave as the person in the kitchen stopped beside where she was hiding.

She gripped the leg of the table, squeezing it to cope. She hesitated, counting backwards from ten, then charged at the kitchen door on her hands and knees, shouting for help. She grabbed the door handle, pulled herself up and managed to get into the hallway and close the door behind her.

'Help. Somebody help me!' Lydia fell at the front door; her legs were gone, weak, flimsy. She stood, then looked back towards the kitchen. The door was opening behind her; she could hear the handle being turned. Lydia pawed over the wood, trying to find the lock.

The person was moving towards where she was standing.

Lydia had to make a decision. Stay by the front door and risk the caller getting her or run upstairs.

She turned, seeing the shadow moving towards her, then threw her body forwards and pelted up the steps. Lydia reached the top of the house. She heard the caller coming, climbing the stairs. She had to hide. She ran, her arms fixed in front of her body, brushing through the air as she raced along the upstairs hall. She found a door which faced her, twisted the handle and entered. She slammed it behind her and held her body against it. She listened, hearing the pounding of the steps suddenly stop, the house went quiet. Lydia was unsure if the caller had come upstairs. She cupped her ear to the door, again, holding her breath. She could see nothing, only a blanket of darkness.

A minute later, Lydia heard the footsteps, moving away from her. She turned her head, trying to focus on her surroundings. She pushed her body upwards, clasping her hips and let out long, slow breaths. Finally, she heard the steps a good distance away. She hoped he'd given up. She knew this is where Jack was being held. She'd wait until the caller left, then she'd find her husband.

She leaned against the door and laughed. Her body was finally returning to normal, calming down, her heart rate slowed, the numb feeling dissipated. She waited against the door, her body aching, her mind had turned to mush. She wiped her face: the sweat trickling down her cheeks was irritating her as she began to cool. She waited, sat pressed against the door, then got to her feet.

The lights came on – the room where she stood immediately brightened.

Lydia screamed at the top of her voice as she looked towards the bed, seeing the corpse, lying right beside her. She looked above and saw a banner reading 'Birthday Girl' in red felt letters.

The sound of footsteps charged up the stairs and along the hall.

Henry Mitchell had moved his wife's body from the house to the cottage.

He wanted Evelyn there. To witness everything.

27

THE COACH

Ben was standing at the door of the coach. He'd asked Laura and Milly to untie the passengers while he was gone. Now, he needed to find Lydia and the others. Ben was sure they were being held somewhere close. He planned to surprise the caller and do what he could to stop him. As he went to step off the coach, the phone rang.

Ben didn't want to answer. He was tired of the games. He knew there would be another instruction, but if he didn't play along, the caller would most probably kill everyone for the sake of it.

The caller had taken Lydia, Jack and Gareth. He'd listened on the phone to Nigel shooting himself. He wasn't going to stop. They hadn't seen another vehicle in all the time they'd been here. Ben needed to act now.

The phone continued to ring. Edward was shifting in his seat. 'Don't answer it. The bastard's a maniac. Leave it bloody ring.'

Ben stepped towards it, pressing the answer button.

'It's been a while, Mr Do-Gooder. How is everyone faring?'

'If you mean "are they still alive?" then yes. They're fighters. You're not going to break us.'

'I'm glad to hear it. Where would the fun be if you all bowed out and submitted? Now, I hope you're back on the coach.'

Ben realised the caller couldn't see them. 'Where else would I be?'

'Good. I have someone who wants to talk to you.'

Ben heard the screams in the background and something dragging along the floor. The caller groaned as if lifting a heavy object.

A woman's voice came on. 'Ben, please help me. I'm at the–'

There was a slap, then the thud of something heavy landing on the floor. He guessed it was Lydia.

The caller said, 'I want you to go to the barn. I have something waiting there. You're going to untie the one Edward has been... shall we say, "playing around with". We can't leave her out, that would be rude. She's sat there, barely speaking, Miss Innocent. Well, she needs to account for the way she's behaved. What she did to that poor lad. She played her part in what happened at the barn. I want you to take her with you. She's going to witness something simply horrific. It's the least she deserves.'

A shiver darted along Ben's back.

The caller continued, 'When you get to the barn, we'll play a game. It will be such fun. Let's look at her behaviour. As I placed the family on the coach, I held her back. I told her I knew what she and Edward were doing. I asked her to tell me everything before tying her with the others on the coach.'

The caller's breathing quickened, as if the thought of the interrogation excited him. 'I understand she played around with the old guy, the married one. They had a baby. Did you know that? It's amazing when you hold a gun to someone's head, what you can find out.

'Anyway, as far as I see it, they terminated it – the baby. It was an inconvenience. Evelyn and me, we tried for so long without success, and here you have these two parasites, doing what they did. Well, it's payback.'

Then the caller gave a few more instructions, telling Ben he would call when he saw him and Abigail at the barn.

Ben knew this wouldn't stop. The games were just the beginning. It was getting late. Tomorrow, there was the possibility of cars passing. The coach may be found. But would the caller kill everyone before morning?

All he could do was follow the caller's instructions for now, then work out how to save the lives of the passengers.

He went to Abigail and told her what the caller had said. Then he led her off the coach. As they walked to the end of the path, she started to speak and Ben listened. She'd been mostly silent while she'd sat on the coach. 'I don't know what you must think of me? It's true, what the caller said happened, I mean.'

Ben searched for the correct way to phrase his thoughts. 'It's between you and Edward. I'm not going to judge you.'

'He's a philanderer. Edward takes what he thinks is his. The night he came over to my place, I had no intention of sleeping with him. I think, on the other hand, that he called over to seduce me, taking what he wanted. As soon as he walked through my front door, he had nothing else on his mind but making love to me. I'm not going to deny that I found him attractive. Christ, who wouldn't? He's a powerful man. He promised he'd take care of me. Give Nigel and me anything we wanted. Only he wanted something in return.'

Ben felt awkward hearing the sordid secrets she was spilling out. He couldn't understand how she and Edward could do this to the innocent parties involved. But he wasn't going to give an opinion out loud. He needed to get to the barn, do what they had to do and then he'd try and find where the caller was holding the others.

As they approached the barn, Abigail was still talking. Ben's mind had drifted, worrying about what they'd find when they got there. Suddenly, Abigail stopped walking and turned to face him. 'Where's Nigel?'

It was a question that hit like a blow to the head. What did he say? How did he answer? Knowing what had happened. Ben quickly changed the subject. 'That's where we have to go.' He helped Abigail up the grass verge and through the sharp barbed wire. They walked along the field.

'Why does he want us here?' she asked.

'He likes to play these games.' Ben stared hard at the door of the barn. 'I want you to wait here. I'm going to check inside first. Wait by the door. If you see anything, run.'

'Ben, I'm scared. What does he want?'

'Just do as I say. If you see him coming, run through the field. Don't stop until you reach the coach, okay.'

'Okay.' There was fear in her voice.

Ben slowly opened the barn door. The boxes were still at the far end, lying on the floor. Andrew's head had been removed from the floor. The cart on which Edward and Ben had placed Nigel was now empty.

He walked slowly across the floor, shining the torch over the ground towards the corners of the barn. The place was deserted.

He had a terrifying thought that maybe the caller was under one of the boxes, hiding on the floor. Ben moved to the far side of the room and lifted them slightly off the ground. They were empty. He turned, listening for any movement. *Why had they been asked to come here? It wasn't the way he played. Usually, the phone would ring. Earlier, Nigel was waiting with the gun he'd been given; the boxes were ready for him and Lydia. Now, there was nothing.* He suddenly thought about Abigail, standing at the barn door. Was this his way of taking her? Getting them down here to add to his collection of hostages.

Ben raced across the ground, calling her name. 'Abigail, are you there?'

'Yes. What's going on?'

'The barn is empty. I don't know what he's playing at.' Ben waited, looking across the fields. *The caller had brought them both to the barn. He'd intended on setting something up. A sick task for his entertainment. He hadn't called. Maybe something had happened. Jack, Lydia. Gareth. Could they have tied him up? Got the better of him?*

Ben glanced at the phone, waiting for a call. It was silent. He turned to Abigail. 'I think we should go back.'

A noise came from inside the barn, like a radio crackling, switching between stations – white noise.

Ben stepped inside, and Abigail followed. He turned, keeping his voice low. 'Stay beside me. Whatever happens.'

A glow came from the left corner. A monitor, hanging on the wall. Ben hadn't noticed it when he came in a few minutes ago. He'd been shining the torch in the other direction. He heard a voice. Ben knew who it was.

'Welcome. Both of you. I want to show you something. It's taken a little time to plan this, so I want you both to watch – concentrate on what is happening. In a moment, once I can work out how to operate this thing so you can see me properly, you'll witness retribution in its finest form. I explained to you earlier, people being punished for their wrongdoing. Well, this is no different. It took a while to devise a game where both Lydia and Jack could be placed in a similar situation to one they created themselves. I thought long and hard about this one. I think you're going to like it. In fact, it's going to make for great viewing.'

The caller was humming to himself as he tapped buttons,

filling in the silent gaps, forcing the situation under his control, making sure his visitors didn't lose concentration. 'Okay, I think we're ready to roll.'

Ben and Abigail moved closer to the monitor.

The screen was still unfocused, a blurry mess of flickering lines and irritating sounds were pushing through the speaker. Suddenly, they saw something. The screen became split. Ben struggled to see what was happening. He stepped nearer, looking up onto the wall, aware the caller could come into the barn at any second. The monitor showed a live feed. Two people, lying face down in a hole. The lights that shone on them made it easier to see what was happening.

The voice came through again. 'So, here you have it. I think it's very apt to the recent events of both these participants, don't you? Let me explain what's happening. I'd hate for you not to get it. Lydia is in one hole, her husband in the other. Very much like graves. I've filled the bottom with cement; they're lying face down, placed inside sleeping bags which means their movement is limited, their hands are tied behind their backs. The hole is narrow. If they turn over, they lose. The graves I've dug contain water, roughly a foot deep and almost covering their heads. They have to last for one hour without drowning. Can you imagine the pressure it would put on their necks, holding their heads up for that long. It doesn't bear thinking about.

'They've been instructed to ring the bell when they've had enough. It's a small cord which is linked to where I'm sitting. I've placed the cords by their mouths so they can pull on it with their teeth. It's amazing technology, Bluetooth they call it. If they ring it too soon, I'll kill them both. Keep watching. It should be fun. They're doing well. I hope I have your attention.'

Abigail spoke first. The tension in the barn was one of desperation. 'I can't believe what he's doing. That poor couple. It's sick.'

They could see the screen. Lydia was frantically wriggling her body, her head was tired, and her face was dropping into the water for longer periods. Jack was on the right of the screen and seemed to be coping better. They could hear as he spat out the liquid.

'They have to be close,' Ben said. He kept his voice low. 'We'll find them. It's obviously a field, he's dug two large pits, and the place is well lit. He has a florescent light set up. It can't be too far from where he lives. He needs power. He's probably run a cable from his house. He has the monitor, watching when they ring the bell. He said it was rigged to where he's sat. We find where he lives, and we find Lydia and Jack.'

'How do we do that?' Abigail asked.

'This guy thinks he's God himself. He's convinced that it's his duty to hand out punishment. That he's within his rights to do this. He thinks it's his responsibility.'

They heard Lydia scream. They watched as she ripped her head left and right. She was frantically trying to keep from burying her head in the water.

Ben looked at Abigail. 'I'd say when the hour's up, he's going to shoot them regardless of the outcome. Lydia looks like she's about to ring the bell. We need to find them.' He dropped the phone onto the floor. 'I'm certain the caller thinks we'll stay in the barn, so I'm leaving the phone. If he's tracking it, he'll think we're here.'

They walked across the floor of the barn and out onto the road. Ben continually looked around, expecting the caller to spring out at any second. He was certain he'd hear the rustle of bushes, the footsteps, the heavy breaths as the caller approached. They'd have to run, hide and stay hidden.

Ben could see the lights of the coach in the distance. He pointed in the opposite direction. 'That's where we need to go, Abigail.' Ben began running through the fields, Abigail was close behind. The ground was soft under their feet, and it made it hard to move.

They got to the verge, leading onto the road. Ben waited, offering his hand and helping Abigail down. He glanced around, turning his body full circle and then started to jog away from the coach.

They ran side by side, both panting heavily, searching in the distance for lights. The area was a mass of darkness, only the stones under their feet to tell them they were on the path and the minuscule light from the torch shining on the ground. He kept it low, not wanting their visit announced. They were silent, preserving their energy. The air was chilly as it smacked against their faces, and the breeze swept hard from the surrounding fields and open space.

Ben was unsure whether to cross into a field. It seemed to go on for miles either side.

They ran into the darkness, Abigail dropping slightly behind. Ben stopped, clasping his hands on his waist, struggling to fill his lungs. 'Are you okay?'

She joined him a few seconds later. 'Just about. Christ, I didn't realise how unfit I am.'

'I think we need to keep moving along the path. The house must be here somewhere,' Ben said.

They waited a minute, then continued together, side by side, urging each other to keep going. To push. A mile along the path, they saw a light in the distance: the upstairs front bedroom, a dim glow radiating onto the field. They stopped. Ben walked to the side of the field, placing his hands on the fence. It was low, with barbed wire running along the top. He pulled it apart, allowing Abigail into the field, then he squeezed his body through, being careful not to rip his skin.

'Okay,' said Ben, 'I have a feeling Lydia and Jack are close.

We need to find them quickly and get them out. I have a plan. But it's dangerous.'

'I'm all ears.'

'I'll explain when we get there, okay?'

They kept walking, trampling in the mud underneath. Their feet were wet, cold and sticking further into the ground which slowed them up.

As they approached the cottage, they saw two lights, placed around twenty yards apart from each other.

Ben pointed. 'That's where he's dug the holes.'

'What are you thinking, Ben?'

He paused for a second, trying to work out the plan in his head. It could go so wrong, but they had little choice. They kept moving, getting closer to the lights and watching the glow at the top window. As they neared, Ben saw more cottages to the right. The lights were off, and there was no sign of activity. It had to be the right place.

He explained what he wanted Abigail to do. To wait by the front door, keep hidden. The light from the bedroom window above them would allow Ben to see her. She'd wait, then knock the door on his signal. 'Can you do that?'

'I don't know, Ben. It's so fucking dangerous.'

'Yes, it is. If you can't do it, just say. I'll have to think of something else.'

Abigail took a deep breath, pursing her lips together and blew hard. 'Let's do it.'

They split. Ben moved towards the lights in the field; Abigail made her way to the cottage.

He watched as she crouched on the drive, waiting with anticipation, keeping hidden from view, ready for his signal.

He waited a few seconds to make sure she was coping with the task, then moved to where Lydia and Jack were held. He stopped around fifty yards from the pits. Ben could see the small cameras on the same stands as the neon lights. He braced himself, mustering all the strength he had left. He moved closer, now able to hear the low whimpering sounds as they gulped air and spat water from their mouths. Lydia was crying; Jack had started calling for help.

He glanced towards Abigail and lifted his arm, beckoning her to get ready. Abigail stayed crouched behind a bush in the front garden. Ben hoped they had the right place. He needed to be fast. He glanced quickly towards the pits where Lydia and Jack were, then waved frantically.

Abigail stood. Then keeping as low as possible, she went to the front door.

Ben saw her turn towards him. He lifted his arm as if to say, *You got this.*

She found the door knocker, then hammered it as hard as she could. A figure came to the window.

Right. Compose yourself. You can do this. I have to jump into the holes and untie Lydia and Jack. The caller is away from the monitor. It's time.

Ben approached the holes and looked inside. He was standing directly in front of the cameras.

'Who's there?' Jack asked. His head was turned to the side. Ben saw the dirt on his cheek; he was struggling to hold his head out of the water.

'My name is Ben. I'm going to untie you. We haven't got long.'

'Oh, thank God,' Jack responded.

Lydia's head was down, and she wasn't moving now.

'Lydia, can you hear me?'

She didn't respond.

Ben sat on the side of the pit, then lowered his legs into the hole. He crouched, reaching his arms into the cold water, moving them around. 'Lydia, it's Ben. Can you hear me?'

Still no response. Ben turned her body on its side. There was no movement from Lydia. Her face was still and her lips had gone a dark purple colour. He lifted her body from the waist and pulled her upwards. She was light, and Ben managed to manoeuvre her easily. He laid her on the bank, untying the cord around her hands and ankles, cutting it with a key from his pocket.

Then he removed the wet sleeping bag. Ben placed his hand on Lydia's shoulders and moved her. 'Lydia, come on. You're not going to die out here. Can you hear me?' Pressing his fingers into her neck he felt a weak pulse. He tipped her head back and checked her airways.

Suddenly, she coughed, her eyes opened wide, she struggled to focus, confused. She turned to the side and vomited.

'Thank God. Wait here. I have to get to Jack. Don't move.'

Ben jumped into the other shallow grave. Jack was much heavier, and he struggled to turn him onto his side. There was minimal room. He found the plastic cords holding his hands and feet, cutting them with his keys. Then, he reached under the water and felt for the zip of the sleeping bag, quickly ripping it open.

Ben was thankful that Jack was able to crawl out of the hole without being lifted.

Jack sat beside Lydia, and they held each other tight. Lydia burst into tears, holding her husband's face, repeating over and over again how much she loved him.

Ben knew that whatever they'd done it wasn't the caller's responsibility to hand out retribution. He couldn't call the shots. After a few moments, Ben interrupted. 'Hey, sorry to break up the party but I need you both to go back to the coach. Those people need us.'

Lydia glanced at her husband. He could see she had different ideas.

Jack stood, brushing himself down, suddenly wincing. 'That bastard stabbed me,' he said. He was covered in mud and looked like he'd been attacked by a plasterer's trowel. He wiped the dirt from his clothes. 'I can't thank you enough. You've saved our lives.'

'You can thank me by going back to the coach. The passengers are terrified. My wife and daughter are there. If you run now, he's going to kill us. He has guns, and he isn't afraid to use them. Have you seen anyone else?'

'Yes. Gareth. He's in the basement. I was with him until the maniac placed Lydia and myself down here. With this leg wound I don't think I'll be running away soon.'

Ben hesitated, struggling to ask the next question. 'How's Gareth doing?'

'Well, he's alive. For how long I'm not sure.'

Lydia started to cry. 'Why's he doing this? The cottage. It's terrifying. I thought I was going to die. He strapped me to a chair in the kitchen and left me there. Why the hell is he doing this to us?'

Jack held Lydia, telling her how brave she was.

'I need you both to go now. Don't let me down. Go back to the coach, help the others. I'm going to try and get everyone out of here when the time is right.'

Jack extended his hand, shaking Ben's, and the couple moved away across the field. Jack was struggling to move as he hobbled across the grass.

Ben turned, pulled down both cameras and crushed them under his shoes, then he moved towards the cottage, looking for Abigail.

What the hell is she doing? As Ben moved closer, he could see the person at the window more clearly. The long hair, the white nightdress. *It's the wrong house*, Ben realised. He thought about the cameras, filming him. The caller had seen everything and any second now he would appear and kill them both. He tried to work out how long he'd been at the graves. Minutes. Had the old lady been watching Abigail all this time from the window?

'Abigail, it's the wrong house,' Ben shouted.

The window opened. The old lady peered out. Ben could hear her from where he stood, though her voice was frail, weak. 'Can I help you, dear?'

The plan was scuppered. Any minute now, the caller would be there.

'I'm sorry to have bothered you at this time of night,' Abigail said.

The old lady leaned over the window frame from the first floor. 'It's not a problem. How can I help?'

'It's okay. We're looking for someone. I really do apologise if I woke you.'

'It's okay, dear. Don't think anything of it. It's quite all right. Who is it you're looking for?'

Abigail was trying to move away subtly. 'Oh, a friend of mine. I was sure they lived here. As I've said, I'm so sorry if I startled you. Please accept my apologies.'

The old lady made no attempt to end the conversation. She pushed her body further, now halfway over the ledge. 'Wait there. I'll come down. I can help you look, young lady.'

Ben was waving to Abigail, calling as low as possible. 'Abigail, move away. We don't have the time.'

'It's quite all right. You don't need to come down, honestly. I'll find the place. Thank you anyway. You're very kind,' Abigail stated.

'The other cottages are empty dear. They're holiday homes. Wait there. I'll be down in a second.'

As the lady pulled herself back inside, Ben watched in horror as her wig dropped to the ground below. He knew who it was. The person lifted a sawn-off shotgun.

'Abigail, run. Get the fuck away from there.'

She turned, facing Ben. 'What's the problem? I think she's coming down, bless her.'

'Abigail, run. You need to get away from the cottage.'

'What's wrong with you, Ben?' Suddenly, she saw the wig on the ground and realised something was wrong. She screamed, attempting to get away. Her legs went, and she tripped, falling onto the gravel. She pressed her hands in front, managing to get into a push-up position, then got to her feet.

Though the front door was still shut, they could hear the caller's feet pounding on the stairs.

'Quick, Abigail. You need to get out of there.'

She moved backwards as the door opened. Abigail was too frightened to run. She screamed. 'Help! Someone help!'

The caller grabbed her, his right arm around her neck, the shotgun in his left hand. He lifted Abigail off the ground, wrestling her, turning his body around to get a better grip. Her legs were dangling in the air, kicking out. She let out another scream, weaker this time. Her voice was muffled. She was choking.

Ben watched in horror as her kicks slowed and she stopped struggling. He raced towards them. *I've got to get her out of there,* he thought.

All of a sudden, Abigail kicked her legs out, like a child on a swing pushing to go higher. She hammered them back into the guy's knees. His legs buckled and he dropped to the ground, writhing in agony.

Abigail composed herself and charged towards Ben, emitting gurgling sounds from her throat. The caller got to his feet and fired a shot into the sky.

Ben and Abigail raced through the field, their ears ringing from the loud explosion, running in the direction of the coach. They dropped to the ground and crawled through the long grass. The caller was only a few feet from where they were. They had to keep hidden or they risked being shot.

They could hear him, muttering to himself, charging one way and then the other, using the gun to clear his path.

'Keep down. Whatever happens, we need to stay hidden. If he finds us, he'll shoot. That's a certainty,' Ben whispered.

'I'm so scared, Ben. How are we going to get away from here?'

'We've untied the other passengers. We need to get back, get them off the coach,' Ben said.

'Then what? Bring them where? He'll find us.'

'I haven't worked that bit out yet.'

Ben stayed in front, crawling like an animal. Abigail followed close behind. Their hands were stung by the nettles, grazed by small stones buried in the earth. They were moving slowly. Ben stopped, then pushed his body up off the ground.

The light from the upstairs window was now in the distance. The sounds of the caller's angry search were further away. He reached his hand out and helped Abigail to her feet.

'He's probably at the graves. He'll see we got them out. We need to run. If we stay in the grass, we won't get back to the coach for hours. Once he sees that Lydia and Jack are gone, he's going to head for the passengers. He didn't bank on us ruining his plans. We need to run. Are you ready?'

'I'll do my best, Ben.'

'Let's go.'

They raced through the fields together, guided by the lights of the coach in the distance.

28

THE COACH

Ben and Abigail stood by the door of the coach. They were panting and exhausted. They bent over, catching their breath. They looked behind, knowing the caller would find them.

Ben opened the door and climbed the steps. Abigail followed. Laura leapt on Ben, overwhelmed to see him back safely. 'I can't do this anymore,' she said. 'We need to get out of here, Ben.' He could see the stress on her face – the worry lines which had developed in the last few hours.

'How's everyone coping? Did you untie them?' Ben had a hundred questions.

'Yes. It's been a struggle keeping them in their seats. Edward has attempted to leave on more than one occasion.'

Ben looked along the aisle. The troubled expressions added to the mounting pressure. 'Where are Lydia and Jack?'

'They're not here. I thought they were with you.'

Ben was peeved that they hadn't returned. 'Is Milly okay?' Ben glanced at his daughter.

'Yes. She's scared though. What would you expect.' Laura made a statement rather than a question.

'We need to go now. He's on his way. He has a gun, and he'll use it.'

'Oh Christ, Ben. Go where exactly?'

He hesitated, then said firmly, 'I say we walk along the road, keep concealed. We can't go to the barn. He's holed up at one of the cottages across the fields further back. There's no one else there. I think they're holiday homes.'

'Wow. Can you imagine living next to him for the summer?'

Ben smiled. 'Not an ideal break, to be fair.'

Ben moved along the coach, checking one last time to make sure everyone was alive. Milly was talking to people, reassuring them. Ben was so proud of her.

'How are you holding up, baby?' he called.

She smiled, then broke down. Ben went to her and rested his hands on her shoulders. He pulled her close and let his daughter cry into his chest. After a minute, she lifted her head. Her brown eyes were filled with tears and she wiped a finger under them. She laughed to relieve the stress of the night's events. 'I knew I should have stayed at home with Zac.'

'What? And miss out on all this pre-holiday fun?' Ben said sarcastically.

He returned to the front of the coach. He took a deep breath, needing to deliver the sense of urgency. 'Okay, listen. Can I have everyone's attention?'

The place instantly fell silent.

'We need to leave the coach now,' Ben announced. He imagined everyone clapping like when a plane lands safely at a holiday destination somewhere hot, and a voice coming over the public address system: *We'd like to thank you for travelling with us today. I understand you may have been a little unsettled with the situation earlier, but hey, it was an adventure, wasn't it? Please take all your luggage with you and have a safe, onward journey. The weather looks great, but he may still be out there. I'm calling from the back of a limo. You're on your own now.*

Edward was the first to speak. 'Not before time. We'll make our own way. Mary and me. Oh, and Abigail.'

Mary quietly questioned her husband. Her expression was one of embarrassment. Ben would never have put them together if he met them at a party. The difference in personalities was inconceivable. 'What about Nigel? I need to see my son,' Mary called out.

The doors of the coach opened and everyone looked towards the front. Someone was climbing the steps. Ben was searching for a weapon to use in defence.

'Are we ready or what?' Lydia's voice was weak.

Ben felt the tension release. 'Yes. How's Jack doing?'

'He can't walk. His leg is bleeding and he needs medical attention.'

'I need everyone off the coach. Now,' Ben shouted. People started to leave their seats. Milly and Laura stood helping everyone off the coach. Milly held Mary's arm and guided her down the steps, then reached for Edward.

'I'm quite capable of walking myself thank you, missy,' Edward snarled.

Milly looked towards her father with a cynical eye-roll. Edward was a problem.

Once everyone was off the coach and on the path, Ben did a quick headcount of the startled faces as he walked quickly down the line.

He passed Edward, Mary, Abigail, Lydia, Jack and Stephen. Then he glanced towards his wife and daughter.

'Okay, that's all of us – nine in total. Let's keep it that way. As you know, there's a guy with an array of guns and ammunition. He's out to kill us. I'm not going to deny the situation is serious, or make light of what could happen. If we stay on the coach, we'll be dead within minutes. That's the immensity of what we are all dealing with here. As you know, he's still holding Gareth, possibly in the basement of the cottage.'

'What about my son?' Mary asked. 'I'm not leaving without him.'

Ben hesitated. He couldn't tell her what had happened. Not here. 'I'm sorry, Mary. We need to hide. That's the only way we're going to survive. Please understand. He's going to kill us.'

Mary broke down, she turned towards Edward and sobbed into his jacket. 'What's happened to my boy?'

Edward placed his hands around the back of his wife's neck, then looked at Ben. He wanted to tell her what had happened to their son. He didn't have the heart to do it at the moment.

After a minute, Mary pulled her head away from Edward's jacket. Her eyes were red, mascara had smudged onto her cheeks, and she sniffed hard. 'He won't be able to cope. I know my boy. He's such a delicate person. He's gone through so much. Please, let me go to him. I don't care what happens to me. He's still so young. He has his life to live. I don't care what happens to me.'

Ben swung his head to the left. He was the first to see it. 'I don't want to alarm you all, but we need to get out of here.'

'Let's just get our bearings. We need to work out where we're going,' Edward insisted. He turned to Mary. 'Take deep breaths, love. In and out. I'm here. I won't let anything happen to you.'

'Er, we need to go now,' Ben said again, putting his point with significant authority. He pointed across the fields. Everyone turned in the direction Ben was pointing.

A light was moving quickly towards them, swaying left and right.

'Does anyone have a phone on them?' Ben asked. He already knew the answer, but needed to ask.

'No. He took everyone's phone when he put us on the coach.

Placed them in a bag. That was one of his first moves when he left us overnight. He tied us and blindfolded everyone,' Jack said.

Ben turned to his family. 'Milly. Laura?'

They shook their heads.

'I left my phone in the car. So did Mum.'

'Shit. The phone he called me on is in the barn.' Ben was silent for a second. 'I can make it.'

'No, Dad. He's coming for us. You said we need to stay together. You're not risking your life by going back.'

'She's right, Ben. We'll move along the path, out to the road. Surely we'll find someone to help us,' Laura said.

'Fine. That sounds like the best thing to do. Okay, everyone, it won't be long until he gets here. Let's go.' Ben led the way, shining the torch along the path and keeping his arm as low as possible so's not to be seen. The others followed in a train; everyone keeping close to one another.

As they left the coach and headed along the road, Ben glanced back, seeing the light.

It was getting closer.

29

THE CALLER

Henry had grabbed Abigail at the front door of her house. He'd had so much planned for her. He'd wanted to tie her in the basement and let her rot. Starve her to death and watch as the insects fed on her.

He was enraged by the story of her adultery. He despised people who couldn't commit to one person. Even in death, he couldn't let go of his wife, Evelyn.

When he'd opened the door of his cottage this evening, he hadn't been ready for her strength. Christ, she'd kicked him so bloody hard. He had to let her go as he fell to the ground, and she'd bolted with Mr Do-Gooder.

He'd moved across the field, peering into the empty graves. It had taken hours to dig the pits, now Mr Do-Gooder had spoiled the fun.

He thought back to how he had caught the lecturer. Henry had followed him on Friday evening, while the lecturer had pursued the hit-and-run passenger – he'd discovered he was called Gareth – out of the car park. He'd kept behind both vehicles, driving discreetly so neither saw him. Henry was disgusted at what he'd seen the lecturer doing with the young woman.

Eventually, after he'd lost Gareth, he decided to follow the lecturer. Pursuing the jeep took him to a particular street, where the lecturer stopped and banged on a door.

Another young woman answered. She was shocked but seemed pleased to see him at her front door. She looked over the lecturer's shoulder to make sure they were alone, but Henry made sure she didn't see him waiting, watching in his car. She kissed the old man hard on the lips, then closed the front door.

Henry had got out of the car, and spied on them through the living room window. He waited patiently, seeing the filthy act, hands everywhere. The lecturer then dressed, and left. All over in minutes. Henry followed him, wondering if there would be any more stops to visit young women.

The lecturer pulled up outside a detached house on a remote road. The place was perfect – electronic gates, but no security cameras or outside lights. And anyone could just walk up the path to the front door. Henry would have little concern about anyone seeing him return for the lecturer.

Once Henry knew where the lecturer lived, he had returned home, satisfied.

Now, he recalled when he'd used the stun gun on Stephen and Gareth. He'd placed cloth hoods over their heads, tied them up and dumped them behind the bushes on the house's front lawn. It had taken a matter of minutes.

Then he'd dealt with Lydia and Jack. They were still standing, frozen with horror in their front room, staring at the woman's bashed-in head and at the gore-covered brass figure.

He knocked on the open front door, waiting for an answer. He remembered the fear on Jack's face as he stood in the hallway, asking what Henry had wanted.

Once he'd used the stun gun on Jack and Lydia, he pulled Stephen and Gareth into the house. Henry tied Lydia and Jack the same way, with hoods over their heads. He ripped small holes so they could breathe and tied them all securely to radiator pipes with strong rope. Their hands and legs were also secured together with rope so they couldn't move.

He left, taking the house keys with him and returned later when it was dark with his shotgun, in case anyone disobeyed orders. He knew it was a risk being seen, so he had to be quick. He laid Jack and Lydia in the back seat of his car and put Stephen and Gareth in the large boot.

Then he drove them to his house, placing the four of them on the coach which was parked on the drive.

Phase one of his plan was now dealt with. The added excitement of the murdering couple was a real bonus. Henry had walked into the garden, he'd seen the earth disturbed. *So they've killed that woman and plan to bury her out the back.*

Henry revelled in the anticipation and couldn't wait to tell Evelyn what he'd done. What a birthday present, a gift. She would be so very pleased.

Henry woke early Sunday morning and went out to the coach. The smell, as he stood in the aisle, was rank. The passengers (that's how Henry saw them), had desecrated the seats with the fear they'd felt overnight. Henry knew it could happen, but it didn't stem his rage. He walked along the coach, removing the hoods, finding Stephen, and hit him in the face with the butt of his gun. Then he swung the barrel, catching Jack in the side of the face. He gave them water and fed them small pieces of fruit.

Then he moved the car onto the road and got into the driver's seat of the coach. Once he'd pulled off the drive, he moved the car back.

He couldn't get it out of his mind, what he'd seen, how the lecturer had behaved in the car park.

As he pulled up to the gates, he saw the jeep. There was another car in the drive, parked alongside it. Henry grabbed the gun and calmly walked up the path. He didn't worry about the coach, the passengers tied to the seats. He'd driven for years, motorways, towns, villages, desolate roads. He'd never been stopped by the police. Not once.

Edward and Mary answered the door together. As Henry pointed the gun at Edward's forehead, the old man reached out, trying to grapple the end with his hands and steer it away from his face. Henry turned the sawn-off shotgun to his wife, ramming the barrel into her mouth, and promised to pull the trigger if he tried anything.

He quickly marched them out the front door, telling them he'd kill them if they didn't get on the coach. As he led them out, he whispered in Edward's ear that he had the photos so Edward knew he had to do precisely as Henry had ordered.

Henry placed Edward and Mary on the coach and tied them to the seats, Nigel came running out with a pan, ready to defend his parents. Abigail was standing at the door, frantically shouting for help. Henry had seen her before, the other night, up against the wall with the lecturer. Edward was a despicable human being.

Henry calmly stepped off the coach, pointing the gun towards Nigel's chest. A couple of minutes later, they'd joined the others on the coach.

He'd waited so long for this evening to happen. He'd planned everything perfectly.

The ball had to start rolling on Evelyn's birthday. It was only right. Now, he'd take matters into his own hands. It was personal. These people were going to pay. It made the bitter pill easier to swallow, what had happened to Evelyn, how their lives had been destroyed that evening in Bourne Woods. People were going to pay.

Now, Henry stood for a moment letting the frustration rise through his body. It charged out of his mouth like a possessed soul, a cloud of deviance, a scream that rose into the night air.

Ben was good. He'd tricked Henry, getting Abigail to go to the front door while he untied the others. A very smart move. He'd followed them, looking in the long grass and scrub, listening for their movement. Henry knew they'd make their way back to the coach.

He ran back to the cottage, making sure no one had got inside. Gareth was in the basement, tied to a railing. But the others were more important now. He'd return later and deal with him.

Henry went upstairs, opening the door and seeing his wife. He knelt beside her, pulling the wooden board towards him, tilting it slightly. 'Are you comfortable, my love? It won't be long now. I'll get them. You wait. I have to be quick. I'm going to the coach. I can't let any of them leave. You understand that, right? We agreed, Evelyn. We came to the same conclusion. All of them must pay. You understand that, don't you? It's why I brought you here so you can watch. Once, it's done, we'll go back to the house, and you can rest in your bedroom. You'll like that, won't you, my love? You've been resting so much lately. I don't mind though, that's what you like to do. All I ever want is for you to be happy. That's the only thing that matters, my love.'

He glanced at the remains of her face. She seemed to smile as if giving Henry her blessing.

'You don't look well today, my love. Are you eating enough? Maybe I'll get you water. Hold on. I'll be back in a second.'

Henry went to the kitchen, filled a glass, then returned.

'Okay. Don't drink it all now; you know how sometimes you suffer from indigestion?' Henry lifted the glass to her jaw. He tilted it, touching the top of her head and slowly poured. The water leaked over her white nightdress and onto the bed. Henry looked down. 'Have you wet yourself again, Evelyn? It's happening so much now. I'm so sorry. It's not a condition to be embarrassed about, okay? We all do it from time to time. I'll get something from the chemist to help you. How does that sound?' Henry placed his hands on her body.

He looked at her hands, the bony fingers. The skin was melting away. She still wore her wedding band. 'When this is finished, Evelyn, we'll dance. We can return to the things we love. I know you laugh at my clumsiness. I often stand on your feet. I don't mean to; you always say I have a touch like an elephant. But you, you can dance. You do it effortlessly. Like a swan gliding across a pond. You have finesse, elegance. When the passengers have paid for what they've done, I'll get you a red dress. I can drape it over your body. It's always been your favourite colour. It brings out your face. Your eyes. Well, you don't have eyes anymore, but what does that matter, my love?'

Henry stood, then kissed Evelyn on her forehead.

He walked out of the room and down the stairs, muttering, 'These fuckers are going to pay.'

30

THE CHASE

They'd been moving for over half an hour. Ben leading, his family and the passengers close behind. Jack was struggling to walk with the injury he'd sustained and leant heavily on Lydia.

Mary was still demanding answers from Edward as to where her son was.

They hadn't seen the light since they'd reached the end of the road and taken the turning which led away from the coach, the barn and the row of cottages. Ben checked his watch. It had gone midnight.

He doubted they'd see a car until they'd made it to the main road. He couldn't recall, but he feared it was miles from where they were. He listened to the noises coming from behind. Everyone was struggling. It was cold. The passengers were tired, hungry. They were aided by the torch, but the light was becoming weak, and they had no more batteries. Ben kept the beam as low and as obscure as possible.

The caller was out there, and it would only be a matter of time before he caught up with them. They had to find help as quickly as possible.

Mary stopped suddenly. She was panting hard. Abigail went to help her, linking her arm.

'I can manage myself. I'm not completely useless,' Mary insisted.

Edward dropped back, helping his wife while Abigail took the hint and moved out of their way. He sniped, 'How much longer do you insist on walking out here? This is bloody ludicrous. We should have stayed on the coach. At least it was a little warmer.'

Ben was at the front. He stopped and turned back to address Edward. 'We need to keep walking until we find help.'

'That could be hours. We'll end up walking all bloody night.'

Ben took a deep breath. 'We don't have a choice. You know what will happen if he reaches us.'

Edward turned to his wife. He held her arm, steadying her. 'Can you continue?' he asked gently.

She forced a smile. Her eyes were blank, her face weary. She looked as if she wanted to drop to her knees and give up, lie on the road and stay put until the morning. 'I'm so tired, but we need to keep moving. I understand that. It's the only way we'll get out of here. Ben is right. He's trying to help us.'

'Are you sure you can continue, Mary?'

The older woman's legs buckled. She held on to her husband's arms.

Ben moved towards her. 'Has anyone got water?'

Lydia reached into a bumbag which she managed to grab from the coach. She held the water to Mary's lips. She sipped a quarter of the small bottle, then gave it back to Lydia, thanking her.

Once she'd regained her composure and was able to stand by herself, Edward addressed the rest of the passengers. 'We're going back to the coach. Who's with me?'

The rest of the group kept their heads down. They stayed

silent. 'Right. It looks like we're on our own. Good luck to the lot of you. Have a nice life.' Edward grabbed Mary and steered her back to where they'd just walked.

'Edward, please don't. It's safer to keep going. I'm begging you to come with us,' Ben said.

Mary was like a death row prisoner being led to her execution. She didn't have the courage to go against her husband.

Edward let go of his wife's frail body and turned on Ben. 'You don't call the shots. I know what I'm doing. If you want to be a hero, then it's your funeral. We're going back.'

Amid sighs from the others, Ben said, 'The caller will go to the coach. That will be his first stop. For crying out loud, he could be a few feet away. You're playing into his arms. Please. Don't go back.'

'We'll take our chances,' Edward confirmed as he and Mary set off back to the coach.

Ben turned to Abigail. 'Are you coming with us?'

She smiled, then placed her hand on his face. 'If you make it out of here and get help, make sure you send them for us. You're a hero. Thanks for everything.' Then she followed Edward and Mary. She tried to hold Mary's hand, but the older woman pushed her arm away.

The three of them walked along the path and into the darkness. Soon they were out of sight.

The six that remained, huddled close. Ben could sense the fear from the others. He was struggling to keep the momentum going. They worried for their lives and had been through so much. He walked beside Laura and Milly.

'Dad, I'm proud of you,' Milly said.

He reached his arm to the side, holding Milly's hand. 'I'm proud of you too. You're incredible. I watched how you were, with the passengers, how you looked after them. Lots of other girls your age would have cracked under the pressure, but not you.'

Laura was standing just behind. 'I'll second that. I think it's definitely our good deed for the day, don't you think?'

The three of them laughed. Ben said, 'How are you holding up, Lydia?'

'That cottage. I'll never forget the things I saw in there.' Lydia went on to describe the corpse and how the caller had kept a dead person in the upstairs bedroom.

An ice-cold chill rose through Ben's body. 'I'm sorry you had to deal with it. We're going to get out of here, okay?'

Lydia smiled. 'Okay.'

Suddenly a scream ripped across the fields. They all stood, alert.

'What the hell?' Stephen said.

'Someone please, help. Help me.'

It went quiet.

'It's Mary. Shit. I have to go back.'

'Ben, you'll die if you go back. Please. Stay here.' Laura grabbed his hands and held them tight, bringing them to her chest.

'Dad, I'm scared.'

They stood on the road as Ben shone the torch to where they'd heard the scream. He saw tarmac, the uneven, rough path, with wild grass growing in patches. He moved the light along the ground and into the distance. They couldn't see anyone. Ben shone the light into the fields either side then quickly moved the light away realising it could draw attention to where they were hiding. Everyone kept silent as the torch explored their surroundings.

Ben wanted to shout, but what? *Run? Get away? Come back to us?* He risked the lives of the others if he called out. Edward was too stubborn to listen. He thought he knew better.

The rain had started, and the wind blew water into their faces making it difficult to focus. Ben looked into the bleak distance. It was like they were completely alone, only a blanket of darkness as they stood together.

'What do we do?' Laura asked.

'Maybe he'll go away. Perhaps he never got to them. Mary may have fallen. There could be a multiple of explanations for her crying out. All the same, I should go back,' Ben insisted.

'And do what? He's a madman, Ben. He'll kill you. You know he will.' Laura was determined to keep him there. This was stupidity, and she was determined not to let her husband go.

'Mary needs our help. If I walk along the road, maybe I can see what's happened. I can–'

Another scream exploded beside where they stood.

'No. Please. No.' The voice was a woman's, maybe fifty yards away.

Milly pulled at her father's arm, her body tense, agitated.

Three shots were fired.

The screams ceased.

'Run! He's shot them. We have to run,' Ben hissed.

A light appeared not far from where they stood.

Ben let Stephen, Milly and Laura sprint past him along the road. He helped Lydia with Jack, each taking one arm, and followed close behind, shining the torch on the ground. They kept running, trying to get as far away from the shots as possible.

There was, Ben decided, little point going back. The three shots were a testament to what the caller had done. He knew if he went back now, he wouldn't walk away alive. He had to protect his family and the other passengers. He thought about their car, left in the field near the cottage. Maybe he could go there, get the car and drive. It might be the only way to escape.

Lydia stopped suddenly. Her feet were cut from walking barefoot after discarding her shoes because the broken heel made it too difficult to walk. She reached forward, panting heavily. The others stopped beside her, trying to recover.

'Can you go on?' Ben asked.

'Give me a minute,' Lydia confirmed. 'I'll be okay. I need to get my breath back.'

Jack placed his hand on her back, rubbing it as if he was trying to push oxygen through her body.

'Look,' said Laura suddenly. 'He's getting closer.'

'Is everyone all right?' Ben asked. He shone the torch among the group.

'Okay. Let's go.' Again, Ben let everyone move past. He kept behind the pack, making sure they didn't lose anyone. Stephen was now helping Jack. After a few minutes, people stopped, too exhausted to go on. They'd been moving for over an hour. There was no sign of life. The fields seemed to go on for miles. They were cold, stressed, and their bodies were giving up.

Laura moved to her husband. 'They have to rest. Look at them. They can't do this for much longer.'

Ben pushed out a sigh from deep within his body. 'I understand. But he's gaining on us. Any minute now there'll be another six dead bodies.' He looked around the group, watching the sullen faces, rosy cheeks, the purple lips. They were shivering, pushed close to one another. 'I have an idea. The car is back near the cottage. Lydia told me where she got out of the boot. I say you all hide in the field here. If you keep as quiet as possible, I think he'll pass by. He has no reason to stop and look in this particular spot. I'm thinking he'll keep going. I can get the car and drive along the road.'

Laura was taking in what Ben suggested.

Ben insisted, 'It's the only way, Laura. We'll be out here for hours otherwise. Either that, or he'll catch us. He's not far behind. He'll be on us in a matter of minutes.'

She looked into the dark space, and then at the people around her. 'Okay. Let's do it.'

Ben turned to the others. 'Right. We have an idea. We can't keep going. It's too cold. People are tired, I understand. I want you all to move into the field. As quickly as you can. Keep hidden. I'm going to go back and try and get the car. It's our only option.' He turned the torch on their faces, seeing their eyes. The fearful expressions. He looked at Lydia, Jack, Stephen, Laura. 'Where's Milly?' Ben spun around, shouting her name.

'She was here a second ago,' Laura confirmed.

'Milly. Milly. Where are you? Milly.'

Their daughter was gone.

31

BEN AND LAURA

'Everyone, into the field now.' Ben ordered the passengers to hide. His wife completely lost it. She was running along the road, screaming for their daughter. 'Milly, where are you? Ben, she's gone. He's taken her. He's going to kill her. He's going to fucking kill her.'

'We'll help look,' Stephen said, his voice urgent. 'You stayed with us when you could have left. We owe you our lives. It's the least we can do.'

'Hide,' insisted Ben. 'Please. We'll find her. Take Lydia and Jack and go into the field. It will only slow us down. I'm going to find my daughter; then I'll get the car. Stay here.'

Laura and Ben sprinted along the road, bawling Milly's name. They didn't care if the caller jumped out on them. They had to get to Milly. Ben feared hearing another gunshot, knowing his daughter could die at any moment.

'Ben, has he got her? Has he got our daughter?' Laura was struggling to breathe.

'We'll get her back,' he answered. 'I promise.'

Their first stop was the coach. As they ran, they looked for

Edward, Mary and Abigail. There was no sign of their bodies, though; the caller had probably hidden them.

At the coach, Ben stopped Laura boarding. 'Wait here. I'll have a look.'

'Ben, be careful.'

He came back a minute later. 'It's empty. He must have taken her to the barn. If she's not there, we'll try the cottage. It's along the path, about a mile from here.'

'Well then, let's go and get her back,' Laura said.

'It's not safe. He's armed, extremely dangerous and he doesn't give a shit who he kills.'

Laura glared at Ben. 'There's nothing more deadly than a woman who's had her daughter taken.'

He smiled. 'That's the spirit.'

They jogged together, side by side, adrenalin keeping them going. The rain had eased up, and their bodies had warmed slightly. His wife was wiping the tears from her eyes. 'I'll kill him if he lays a finger on Milly.'

'You'll have to get in line,' Ben answered.

They saw the light in the barn as they ran along the road.

'That's the place.' Ben pointed to his left. They slowed, and Ben helped Laura up onto the verge and into the field.

As they reached the door, Ben whispered, 'Wait at the door. I'll take a look.'

Ben stepped inside. He saw the monitor, heard white noise, saw the large cardboard boxes towards the back. There was no sign of the phone. He silently checked the place over, then he called his daughter's name. 'Milly, are you in here?' Ben didn't expect an answer. 'Milly, baby, are you here?' There was no reply: just stillness.

The barn was empty.

He re-joined Laura. 'She's not in there.'

'Ben, I can't do this. I can't cope anymore.' Laura fell to her knees, then clutched the front of her head with her hands. She screamed, pulling clumps of her hair.

Ben knelt down and held his wife. 'We'll get her back. I promise. But we need to be strong. Come on, Laura. You are an amazingly brave woman. I love you so much. You can do this, okay? I know you can. Be the rock for Milly. We're tougher than this bastard. We're better than him.'

Laura wiped her face and then stood up, summoning the strength she needed. 'Okay. Where do we need to go?'

'That's it. You can do this. His cottage is across the fields. He's probably taken Milly there. It's where he took Lydia and Jack. I think Gareth may be there too.'

They embraced, holding each other tightly. Laura got the strength she needed from her husband before they set out again.

Ben shone the torch through the fields as they walked. They were too exhausted to move any faster. He thought about his daughter, the passengers. So much had happened tonight. He felt so awash with emotion that he wanted to lie on the grass and scream at the top of his voice. He couldn't tell Laura how he felt, but he was fearful for Milly's life. The caller was playing another game, taking Milly. It was punishment for Ben and his family helping the passengers. He began to doubt that anyone would leave this place alive.

He suddenly remembered the car. Maybe their phones were still locked inside. Lydia had told him the caller had parked on the road: she'd got out and walked towards the cottage looking for Jack. Another part of the caller's torturous game. Letting Lydia think she could walk free as she climbed from the boot. He remembered her saying she'd left the vehicle and walked towards a light. The car was parked close to the cottage.

They needed to find the car: time was running out.

~

Moving across the field was difficult, the ground being much wetter with the rain. Every step felt like a mammoth task. Their shoes seemed as heavy as concrete slabs with the mud they'd collected. They pulled their feet out of holes and the ground squelched underneath. But they kept going into the darkness, occasionally stopping to rest.

Laura pushed her body to its limits, fighting to keep going, thinking of her daughter, picturing her beautiful face, her calming voice. She suddenly blurted out, 'If only she'd stayed with Zac.'

Ben didn't have a reply. He felt guilty, putting his family in danger. Yes, it was heroic, helping the others. The three of them had acted incredibly bravely and gone way above and beyond to help these people. He knew many would have backed away as soon as they saw the passengers tied to their seats. Ben guessed he could just have easily got his family into the car, hit reverse and they'd be drinking champagne on the balcony in Barcelona now.

He fought to rid the thoughts from his head. He knew it was too late to start the regrets. If Ben was truthful, he'd have done it all again in a flash.

'There. That's the cottage.' Ben pointed towards the light in the distance.

A small flicker glowed across the field, like a lighthouse, warning them to stay away and steer clear. Ben could feel a knot in his stomach and his insides were dancing, as the adrenalin had turned to fear. He clasped Laura's hand. Although it was cold, he could feel the heat from her body.

They walked in silence towards the light, watching it grow. Ben gripped his wife's hand tightly. 'Whatever happens, you run. Do you hear?'

'I'm not leaving you, Ben.'

'I'm deadly serious. I'll do everything I can to get Milly. If she comes out, if something happens to me, the both of you run, away from here.'

They stopped for a moment. Laura grabbed her husband, then kissed him, tracing the outline of his face with her fingers. She cried, suddenly her emotions were spilling out as she stood in the field. 'I love you so much, Ben. These people were lucky to have you come along. You did everything you could. You're the bravest man I've ever met. Remember that.'

He kissed her on the forehead. 'Let's get our daughter back.'

32

THE COTTAGE

The front door was slightly ajar. Ben and Laura had crossed the field, watching the window above, worried that a security light may come on, alerting the caller of their presence.

The building was old. There was ivy crawling along the front, working its way to the top of the cottage, sprawled like a spreading disease. The two windows at the front were small, and the frames a dull grey colour. They allowed a view into the living room but the curtains were pulled tightly together. To the right was a small parking space leading to the back of the cottage. The grass was overgrown and wild.

Ben glanced behind, searching for a light in the distance. He listened for footsteps or a wet squishing sound coming from the field behind them. When he was sure no one was there, he pushed the front door slightly. Blue paint crumbled in his hands and dropped to the floor. The door creaked. The sound grated through his body and Ben hesitated.

He could hear Laura's fatigue, her body filled with anticipation as she caught her breath. She stood close to him. He reached forward, pushing the door again. The creak resembled the groan of a coffin lid closing on the body that lay inside.

Ben stepped into the hallway. He shone the torch through to the kitchen. Shadows became visible, hollow and empty. Laura stepped inside, brushing against the door and making more noise than she intended. They moved together, taking small steps, working their way through the downstairs hallway. They stopped by the living room door. Ben counted to three, then gripped the handle and swung it open.

He steered the torch towards the plain white sofa, the telly on a flimsy stand, the dull grey walls covered with damp patches.

Ben closed the door, and they moved towards the kitchen. He shone the torch through the glazed panels on the kitchen door. Once he was sure it was empty, he opened it and they stepped inside.

White cupboards adorned the back wall; the butler sink was old and stained, the floors had lino that had started to fold and crease.

'She's not here,' Ben said. 'I think we should look upstairs.'

Laura nodded, silently closing the kitchen door.

Suddenly they heard the screams, coming from underneath.

'It's Gareth,' Ben said. He shone the torch over the living room and found a large open hatch through which the top of the stairs was visible. They walked over, hearing the young lad shouting for help. The hairs stood on Laura's arms as she listened to his pleas.

Ben stood over the steps, ready to tackle the caller if he jumped out. They quickly glanced at each other without talking, knowing what Ben had to do. He shone the torch, looking below, then started the slow descent. As the steps creaked, Gareth shouted, 'Who's there? Is someone there?'

Ben hesitated, standing at the middle of the steps. 'My name is Ben. I'm going to get you out. Are you alone?'

'Yes, I'm here alone. Please get me out of here.'

Ben moved to the bottom of the stairs and pushed the door.

Gareth was lying on the floor, arms tied to the railing above his head. Ben shone the torch over his face and he blinked. 'We need to be quick. He may come back any second.' Ben crouched, undoing the knot around Gareth's wrists and lifted him to his feet. He held Gareth as he cried, a mixture of dread and elation together.

On the way back up, Ben explained what had happened and introduced him to Laura.

'How are the others?' Gareth asked.

'They're doing okay, considering what you've all been through. Our daughter has been taken. We have to find her,' Laura told him.

Gareth was stretching, helping the blood to flow around his aching body. 'I'll help,' he said. 'We can tackle him together.'

Ben already liked the spirit the young lad had shown. He went first up the stairs, grasping the torch and placing the light on either side of the walls.

The ball of light jumped and flickered above their heads. The smell of the cottage reminded Laura of an old treehouse her father had built when she was a child: damp, rotting timber, sodden from years of being exposed to the weather.

Ben reached the top of the house, looking at the door at the end of the hall. He was sure it was the same room where they'd seen the light from outside. He moved forward, hearing Laura tiptoeing behind. 'Wait here. If he's inside, run, okay?'

Laura looked as if she'd faint at any second. Ben reached for the door handle, then pushed it hard.

As he stepped into the room, he saw the corpse on the bed. 'What the hell?' Then he remembered what Lydia had said about this room.

'What, Ben? Is Milly here? Please, Ben. Is she okay?'

Ben was speechless. He tried to get the words out, but it felt as though his tongue was trapped. He glanced at the wall covered in newspaper cuttings. He moved closer, reading the headlines.

Laura and Gareth stepped into the room. Suddenly she screamed, a gut-wrenching cry as she saw the body lying on the bed. She'd never felt so terrified. She looked to where Ben was standing. 'Ben, what the hell is happening here? It's disgusting.'

He shone the torch over the articles, reading what had happened.

Police are still no closer to finding the hit-and-run driver who killed local man's wife.

Evelyn Mitchell was out hiking with her husband when a young lad ploughed his car into her, killing her instantly. The vehicle was thought to have been speeding along the country roads through Bourne Woods when the tragic accident occurred. It's reported the driver initially stopped, but then sped off leaving the body on the road.

Evelyn died on her sixtieth birthday and leaves behind her husband, Henry Mitchell.

He has not yet issued a statement to the press.

The couple had no children and spent most of their time organising charity events for the local homeless.

Police are asking for anyone with information to come forward. All calls will be treated with the strictest of confidence.

Ben looked at other articles, relaying pretty much the same story. 'It's why he's doing this. That's the reason.' Laura gripped his arm as he continued, 'His wife was tragically killed. They never caught the guy driving the car, so he's avenging the attack. He dresses like her, the wig, the nightdress. That way, he thinks she's still alive. It's the reason he had the passengers on the coach. That's why he's doing this. He's taken Milly to get revenge on us, for helping the others and jeopardising his plans. It's all about people and their mistakes, that's what drives him to do these things. It fuels the anger. Avenging what happened to his wife.'

Gareth said, 'It's what happened to us. To Stephen and me. Last Thursday night, we were driving through Bourne Woods. We saw the old lady, wearing a white nightdress, the long black hair.' Gareth pointed to the woman lying on the bed. 'He's emulating what happened to his wife. Dressing as her, recreating the night she died. It's her birthday. It probably makes it more significant to him.'

'Quick, we need to find Milly,' Ben shouted.

Ben glanced at the body on the way out. The caller had run after him and Abigail, chasing them through the fields and had returned here to drape the nightdress over his wife and place the wig on her head. Always fixated on the way she looked and how he remembered her.

Ben and Laura checked the other rooms, then raced down the stairs and out of the cottage.

'Where's Gareth?' Laura asked as they stood outside.

'Gareth, we need to go. Come on.' Ben listened at the front door. He waited to hear the lad's steps coming down the stairs. 'Gareth, we're going to find the car. Come on.'

'We can't wait, Ben.' Laura started running along the path, hoping it led to the road.

Ben looked along the row of cottages, then ran with Laura. 'I say we try and find the car. You can drive out and get help,' Ben suggested. 'It's somewhere between here and the barn. There's only one road that leads around in a circle. I'm hoping that's where Milly is being held. Come on.'

Ben jogged as Laura fought to keep up with him. They ran side by side, puffing heavily, the chilly air pushing against their faces. Laura had a dreadful feeling that the next time she saw her daughter she'd have a bullet in her head. She steered the thoughts away, trying her best not to let the visions of Milly lying slumped in a field affect her. She had to keep strong for her daughter and Ben. She wondered where it would end, and how.

Laura had listened to the caller talking to Ben, going on about retribution, the passengers and how they'd done wrong. The caller's wife had been killed in a hit-and-run; now he was avenging the terrible tragedy on the same date she died. One year later.

In a way, she found herself feeling sorry for the arsehole. How would anyone cope, losing a partner, a loved one, knowing the person who'd killed them escaped justice? The caller would keep going, keep justifying his actions by wreaking his vengeance. She feared the worse. If he murdered Milly to get back at Ben for helping the passengers, he'd kill her too. None of them would escape. None of them would leave tonight.

'Wait a second. I need to catch my breath.' Laura stopped and placed her hands on her hips.

'Take a rest, Laura. There's another couple of miles or so of the road until it leads back to the coach. The car must be here somewhere. Lydia told me she got out of the boot and walked to the cottage. It can't be far.'

'What if it's gone? What if he's taken Milly? Driven some-place miles from here?'

'He won't. He's going to try and find the others. He has beef with all of them. He won't stop until he's killed everyone. He's playing a game, Laura. That's the way he's wired. He has some-thing for us. Something he's planning with Milly.'

They swung around as two lights flicked on and off in the distance.

'What was that?' Laura asked.

'I don't know. It looked like car lights. I couldn't see. It happened too quick,' Ben answered.

Laura pointed. 'It came from over there.' They stared along the road in silence. 'Do you think it's someone coming to help?' she asked optimistically.

Ben kept quiet. He took a couple of steps, looking ahead. He lifted the torch, pointing it into the fields to his left. 'I'm not sure what it was. Come on, let's move. Keep watching.'

'Ben, I'm so scared. I don't know how this is going to finish. I don't know if I can keep going.'

Ben stepped towards Laura and held her, stroking her short black hair and placing her head gently on his chest. 'You are such an incredible woman. I know you can keep going. There's not much of the road left. We can do this.'

Laura screeched, 'There it is again.'

Ben turned, seeing the lights in the distance going off. After a few seconds, they flashed again. On-off, in succession. 'It's him,' Ben said.

They moved towards the lights, keeping low. Ben held Laura's hand, feeling it tense, trembling and damp. The place was drenched in blackness, and Ben kept the torch low to the ground as they crouched, determined to remain hidden. They walked slowly, almost creeping, heading to where they'd seen the lights. They were exhausted and their bodies spasmed and jolted with anticipation.

Suddenly, they heard a muffled whimper.

They stood still as Ben shone the torch. He and Laura gasped as they saw Milly, tied to a telegraph pole, thick rope wrapped around her waist, a cloth pulled hard against her mouth.

'Milly!' Laura shouted. She charged towards her daughter as Ben shouted for her to stop.

Suddenly, the lights came on again, appearing from nowhere. They heard the car start, the loud screech of tyres spinning and gripping the road as Ben's car accelerated, racing towards where Milly was tied. The caller was in the driver's seat.

'No! Laura, watch out,' Ben bellowed.

The car stopped a couple of inches from where Milly was held. The window wound down, and the caller shouted above the screams. 'Take one more step, and I'll cut her in half.'

The car was almost pressed against Milly's waist.

'What is it you want from us? We're not a part of this. Let us go. We'll walk now, and you'll never see us again. I promise. Or is it me? Do you want me? I'll gladly swap places with my daughter. Let her go,' Ben insisted.

'You don't get it, Mr Do-Gooder. You don't understand what this is about.'

'Oh, I get it, all right. You're sick. You lost your wife, and you're still hunting the guy who was driving the car. I saw her in the bedroom of the cottage. Where will this end?'

'I'd planned this day for so long. When I saw your car, steering you along this patch of desolate road, it was like the final piece. It had all come together. Christ, I'd worried that I'd picked a spot that was too quiet. I stood on that stretch of road for hours. I began to regret not doing it somewhere busier, more populated. But then I realised it was too risky. You and your family, coming when you did, was simply perfect. But you couldn't help but get involved. Disobeying my clear instructions. I wanted you to help, to guide these people in the tasks I'd set. You couldn't do it, could you? You had to go against everything I'd done. Do you realise how long I've waited? How many times I'd counted the days, the minutes in my mind as I sat with my wife? This was her gift, my contribution for what happened on her birthday. You fucked it up for us. Don't you see?'

The caller opened the car door and pointed a gun at Ben and Laura. He stepped forward then removed the gag around Milly's mouth.

Milly spat. She was struggling to breathe.

'Let her go. I'm begging you,' Ben shouted.

The caller continued, 'I waited so long for this night. A few evenings ago. The hit-and-run. Those two boys out driving in Bourne Woods. What would happen, Mr Do-Gooder? How would justice be served? I'll tell you, a year, maybe two, a small cell with a telly and access to the outside for walks and exercise. When the justice system had announced they'd served their time, they'd let them go, back out into society to mix with normal people. To slip under the radar, to go forth, be fruitful and multiply. A nice house, a car, a decent paying job, friends, nights out, evenings in front of the telly, holidays. My Evelyn, she won't have any of that.'

'It was you,' said Ben. 'Last Thursday night. Dressed as your wife. You don't get it. You are not her. It's you who is deluded. Those two lads didn't kill anyone. They didn't kill Evelyn. Surely you see it. You can't dress as her and continue to relive the night she died. It won't bring her back. None of this will bring her back.'

The caller started screaming and banging the side of his head with his free hand.

'Let my daughter go,' said Laura.

The caller pulled himself together. 'I'm afraid it's a little late for that. Your apologies are meaningless. You have ruined everything. The night it happened, we were out walking. We'd been trekking along Bourne Woods. It was her birthday. I had the evening planned. A bottle of wine chilling in the fridge. The table set out, a casserole in the slow cooker, soft music in the background. We were going to go away the following morning; a cabin somewhere secluded in Wales. I remember walking back with her. I'd never felt so complete. She made me; I, her. We completed each other. Evelyn was my life, my world, every thought I had, every word I spoke, was about her. But, you see, she hasn't gone, not really. I picked her up off the road that night; I placed her in the back seat of the car. She wasn't moving. She wasn't breathing. Her body was twisted, mangled, like she'd contorted herself into a magician's box – her final trick.'

He drew in a shaky breath. 'I called the police. I waited for news, days passed and I'd heard nothing. I was told the investigation was still ongoing, they're following leads, making inquiries. All meaningless while the two culprits were out there, unpunished. I attended Evelyn's funeral. And then I brought her home. So you see, she's with me now and nothing those bastards have done can take that from me.

'Evelyn is very much with me, she's a part of me. It was her birthday a couple of days ago. I carefully planned and executed a way to bring my own retribution. Evelyn and I were counting down to this weekend. We couldn't wait to avenge what had happened.'

Laura found herself pleading with the caller. 'Please don't do this. Look at her. She's our daughter.'

The caller was now facing Milly, but he couldn't see what Ben could see. The rope was wrapped around her waist and tied at the front. Milly was slowly working it loose, managing to move it away from her body. As he got into the car, he stared at her face, looking straight into her eyes. Milly kept expressionless, staring and focused.

The car revved and smoke poured from the exhaust, the wheels started spinning, and the car reversed. Henry Mitchell sat still for a moment, in the driver's seat. 'This is for you, Evelyn. I love you, baby. I love you so much.'

The car raced forward. Milly wriggled loose from the rope and hurled her body out of the way.

The caller smashed the car into the pole.

Milly darted along the path, away from the car.

The vehicle reversed, the front bumper ripping from the

pole. The caller turned the steering wheel and now the vehicle was facing where Milly was running. Ben tried desperately to open the car door, but the vehicle was moving too fast. He screamed for Milly to get off the road and into the fields. Milly was trying to get away, jogging along the path, too frightened to look behind.

Ben and Laura watched as the front of the car clipped their daughter's leg, and she fell to the ground. Milly landed on her back and crawled on her hands and knees, forcing herself to get away.

The car stopped, the engine revving loudly. They could see Henry in the driver's seat, giddy, laughing to himself.

'No. Don't do it. Please. I'm begging you.' Ben was charging towards the car.

As the caller went to reverse over Milly's body, a woman appeared to run across the fields towards them, now visible in the lights as she moved towards the car. Henry cried out, turned off the engine and got out of the car, his gun by his side. He yelled across the fields, his excitement evident. He started to jump up and down elated, and then he raced towards the figure.

The person wore a white nightdress and had long, scrawny black hair.

The caller ran with his free arm stretched, towards the woman. 'It can't be! Evelyn, you'll catch your death out here. Oh my goodness, quick, I'll get you inside.' Henry Mitchell ran towards his wife. He was ecstatic, waving his arm in the air, enthused.

Ben and Laura were running towards their daughter as Henry raced away and across the field.

As they reached Milly, they dropped to the ground, holding their daughter. She whispered, 'I'm okay. Take us out of here, Dad. We need to get out of here.'

'Thank God you're alive.' Ben placed his hands under his

daughter's waist and slowly lifted. They walked their daughter to the back seat, closed the door and then he and Laura got into the front.

Suddenly, they heard a gunshot. Then another. The woman in the nightdress slumped to the floor. Henry was screaming, shouting that he should have killed him in the basement while he had the chance.

'Gareth,' said Ben. 'It's Gareth. He came to help us.'

Maybe taking matters into his own hands was Gareth's way of showing remorse for what he thought had happened in Bourne Woods that night.

Now, Gareth would never know the truth.

33

DRIVE

Ben struggled to get the car into drive. His hands were shaking as he grappled with the steering wheel. The windscreen and side windows were cracked, the bonnet dented and there were bloodstains and pieces of glass on the seats.

Laura shouted from the passenger seat, 'Quick, Ben, get us out of here.'

He rammed the gearstick into first, edging the car forward. The wheels were spinning, kicking mud onto the windscreen. 'I can't see anything. The window is too smudged with mud.'

'Go, Ben. Just bloody drive.' Laura reached behind, placing her hands on Milly's shoulder who was sat on the back seat. 'I love you. We're going to get away from here. Are you okay?'

Milly smiled; she couldn't find the words to explain how she felt. She was just happy to be back with her family.

'I have to clean the windscreen. I can't see out,' Ben shouted.

'I'll do it.' Laura grabbed a scraper from the footwell.

'Laura, no. He's out there.'

But she opened the door and flung herself round to the front of the car. She wiped the mud, stretching her body over the bonnet.

Ben put on the windscreen wipers, flicking the switch to push water onto the screen.

Laura saw her husband's face. He was looking beyond her and into the distance. He was mouthing to her as she stood. Laura watched the shape of his lips, the lines which appeared on his forehead, his elevated eyebrows.

'He's behind you, Laura. He's coming behind you.'

Laura screamed out; fear caused her to drop to the ground. She scrambled, turning her head in the direction her husband was looking. She saw the caller, maybe twenty yards from where she stood. He was racing towards the car.

Ben was shouting hysterically. 'Get in the car, Laura. He's coming.' He opened the door. Henry was standing, pointing the shotgun towards Laura.

A gunshot rang across the fields.

'No. Please. No.' Ben was already at the front of the car, lifting his wife. Her body was limp. Henry charged towards them as he placed Laura onto the front seat. There was so much blood. It looked like her leg was shattered. 'We have to get her to a hospital.'

Milly was sitting up, shouting at her father. 'Is she dead? Dad, please answer. Is she dead?'

A bullet hit the side of the car. Milly held her ears, screaming for her father to go. The windscreen wipers cleared the glass.

As they pulled away, Henry fired more shots.

Ben drove away from the coach, the barn and the cottage. He steered the car, avoiding the bumps on the road, jabbing the brakes as they reached a large pothole. He listened as something under the seat crashed against the pedals. Ben reached down, feeling along the floor as he drove. He grabbed Milly's phone which had been under the seat and tossed it to his daughter.

'Call the police. The passengers are still hiding: we need to get help.'

Milly dialled 999 and explained what had happened to them tonight, finishing with a description of where to find the cottage. When she hung up, Milly reached forward, rubbing her mother's face. 'Is she going to live, Dad? Please tell me she's going to be okay?'

Ben looked across as he drove, desperately trying to find a way out and onto a main road. He glanced at his wife's leg; it looked like she'd been shot below the knee. Her eyes were closed, and she was bleeding heavily. 'I hope so, baby. We'll find a hospital. They'll patch her up.'

When it was safe, he pulled the car over and wrapped Laura's leg with an old jumper from the boot to stem the blood flow. The suitcases had been removed. The caller had emptied the boot when he'd taken Lydia. They'd get them back when the police arrived. Now, he had to get Laura to a hospital.

He knew it would be a long time before she was able to walk again.

Ben followed the satnav, racing along the winding roads, the full lights glaring onto the path ahead. 'Are you okay, Milly?' He was worried about his daughter. She'd been through so much. She'd come out of it relatively unscathed. Ben knew it could have been so much worse.

'I'm hanging in there.'

'I'm so sorry you had to witness it, everything that went on.'

Milly placed her hand on her father's back. 'We did the right thing.'

They reached the main road, following the instructions from the satnav. There was a hospital about twenty minutes' drive from where they were. As Ben and Milly saw other vehicles, they gasped, feeling overwhelmed to be back in civilisation.

Ben drove holding his wife's hand, praying she'd be all right.

He'd never been more proud of his family. The police were probably there now. Milly had told them where to find the others. The caller was too far away from them. He wondered whether they'd stayed hidden, or if they'd kept walking, desperate to get away. Ben hoped they'd listened to him.

As he drove with Milly in the back, his wife unconscious next to him, he turned the heat up and switched on the radio.

Chris Rea sang, 'The Road To Hell'. Ben had a feeling that it was the place they'd just left.

34

SIX MONTHS LATER

'You look beautiful. The both of you.' Ben's wife sat in front of the bedroom mirror, wearing a black dress and applying a final touch of foundation. She looked breathtaking. Milly wore a suit, again black, with a skirt that her father thought was a little on the short side. He wore a tuxedo, his hair styled forward and his face cleanly shaven.

'Okay, we're going to be late. Are you both ready?' Ben asked.

'Yes. Good to go. It's a fuss over nothing though. You and Milly should be the ones getting the honour. I didn't do much.' Laura reached her arms forward, clasping them around her husband's neck.

'On three.' Ben lifted his wife and carried her down the stairs.

As soon as the surgeons had seen Laura's leg and how badly it was shattered from the bullet, they knew there was little hope in saving it. A severe infection and destroyed nerves that caused constant pain left them with no choice but to amputate half of her leg.

She refused a false one, saying it would be too hard to get used to. She had crutches, but they blistered her hands. Laura rarely went out since the accident. She'd gone into a deep depression, refusing to see people or have visitors. She'd put on weight and was overcome with anxiety most days. She rarely left her bedroom.

Ben had begged her to get help and talk to a professional. He'd wanted to get her on a course of antidepressants and was certain Laura was suffering from PTSD.

Laura had waved it off, stating she just needed time to recover from that horrible night.

Ben was there for her, nursing her back to health. It was a struggle, especially for Laura. She didn't want to learn to stand, to walk, to move. It was all too much for her, but Ben and Milly were there every step of the way.

The story of what happened that night had been major headlines across Europe. The police filled in the details. Edward, Mary and Abigail had been found lying in a ditch. The three of them had been shot dead. Nigel was found near the barn. Next to him, police found the head and body of Andrew Wilson.

Gareth's body had been recovered in the forest – though there was no mention of the wig and the nightdress.

Jack, Lydia and Stephen had heard the sirens and raced towards the noise from the field where they were hiding.

Police found the stranded coach with the slashed tyres. Then they had searched the cottage and found Henry Mitchell's tenants in a closet, both of them murdered with deep knife cuts across their necks.

They found no sign of Henry, the birthday banner, the newspaper clippings pinned to the bedroom wall upstairs; or Evelyn's body. He'd parked his car at the back of the cottage and made off. Police found fresh tyre tracks confirming this.

They'd searched the house in Bourne Woods and found it

empty. Despite a colossal hunt and a massive search, Henry Mitchell was still on the run with Evelyn.

Today, Ben, Laura and Milly were to receive medals for bravery. They stood together, lined up in a grand room of Buckingham Palace. Although Ben had thought that most people would have acted the same way and helped the passengers, he accepted the medal. As he watched his wife and daughter being honoured, he'd never felt more proud. Laura and Milly were incredibly brave.

When they got home, they spoke about what they'd experienced, about the palace and how they needed to put the past behind them.

They rarely spoke of Henry, Evelyn or what happened that dreadful night. It was a nightmare they'd rather forget.

It was late when Laura said she was tired. It had been a long day, and her body was exhausted.

Ben reached down, placing his hands under her waist. They'd have to get a stairlift. He worried about taking her up and down the stairs, thinking they could so easily fall. He struggled to the living room door, his arms shaking and weak as he lifted Laura slowly up the stairs, one step at a time.

Ben gently placed his wife onto the bed. 'I love you so much. You were amazing today. You know that, Laura. You're my hero.'

'I love you, Ben. You're a wonderful man. Don't ever forget that.' She smiled.

'You're not so bad yourself.' They laughed together, and Ben felt optimistic for the future.

He was proud it had been them who had arrived when the passengers were on the coach.

35

EVELYN'S BIRTHDAY

Henry Mitchell opened the front door of the squat where they were hiding. 'Evelyn, I'm home. Don't get up, sweetheart. I have something for you.' He noticed the final demand letters, lying on the floor. They'd have to move soon.

He made his way to the kitchen and flicked on the light. He stood alone, taking in the peaceful surroundings. 'Wow, it's good to be here. Right, so, let me think, I have the cake, I'll boil the kettle, light the candles and then bring everything up on a tray.' He laid it all on the kitchen table, then he climbed the steps to the top of the house. Henry opened the door while balancing the tray. As he walked into the bedroom, he smiled.

'Look at you, Evelyn. You beautiful lady. Happy birthday. Sixty-two today, sixty-two today. It's so exciting – another year. You still look the same. So, I have your coffee and a cake I picked up in town. It's your favourite – sponge with a strawberry topping. Oh, and I made sure they gave me longer candles this time. We can't have them burning too quickly now, can we? That just won't do.

'You know what happens soon? It's almost that time, Evelyn.

I have to go to work again. People need to pay. You know it's how it has to be, Evelyn. But let's enjoy your special day first. I'll sit on the bed beside you, my love.' Henry held his hands out and placed them gently on Evelyn's body. Then he took a fresh white nightdress from the drawer, slowly draping it over her decayed body and adjusted the wig on top of her head. 'Happy birthday, my darling Evelyn.'

He stood up. 'I'm going out, but I'll be back later. I'm so excited. Remember, this is all for you.'

Henry undressed, then placed a nightdress over his head and pulled it down over his body. He placed the wig on his own head, took a quick look in the mirror and then left the squat where they'd been hiding.

It was only a matter of time before the police caught up with him. He and Evelyn could never return to the house in Bourne Woods. It was getting hard moving around and Evelyn was most certainly tired of the upheaval.

He drove the twenty-five miles to Bourne Woods. Although he'd thought about doing it somewhere else, in the end, it had to be this place.

Henry stood on the side of the road, keeping hidden. He glanced at his watch; it was late. He worried that maybe it was too late.

Ben heard the pounding against his car first. He swung the steering wheel and brought the car to a halt. Although he'd expected to see the figure and was driven by his determination, it was still shocking as it played out. He looked in the rear-view mirror and stared at the figure standing in the shadows. Ben felt sick as he saw the long black hair and the white nightdress. It brought back the horrific memories of that night. Then he stamped on the accelerator and reversed. As the body lay on the road, he pulled forward, rolling the vehicle over it. He reversed over it a second and third time, just to make sure.

As he drove away, he wallowed in the triumph.

Ben knew that Henry Mitchell had paid dearly for the sins he'd committed.

When Ben had first found the cottage with Laura while they'd searched for Milly, he'd seen the corpse lying in the bedroom and the birthday banner pinned to the wall.

It had been those newspaper articles that set him thinking, and he'd put two and two together. Striking on his wife's birthday made the revenge that little bit more sweet for Henry. Ben had spoken to the police about his concerns, worried Henry Mitchell would kill again. When they ignored him and the case went cold, he had to do something. Ben went to Bourne Woods a week before Evelyn's birthday and he'd driven up and down the road, hoping that Henry would strike again. He had a feeling the man wasn't going to stop. He'd driven for hours, out there, alone, waiting for the figure to jump onto the road. He'd come back the next night, and the next, determined not to give up.

Tonight, the exact date of Evelyn Mitchell's birthday, he returned again. Ben drove, patiently waiting. It was late when he saw the figure, the black wig, the long, white nightdress.

Ben drove home, keeping to the speed limit, making sure not to look conspicuous. There'd be blood on the tyres, the bonnet. The last thing he needed was to be pulled over, explaining how the blood had got there. He'd have to find a car wash on the way home.

Ben found out that just after Evelyn had died someone had returned with a shovel, digging until they'd reached the coffin and then removing her from her place of burial. He knew who had done it. He'd seen her at the cottage. Even in death, Henry Mitchell couldn't bear to be without his wife. He had to admit; it certainly was a love story.

Now, as Ben drove, he thought about the passengers. Stephen kept in regular contact. The latest picture was of him and his older brother, somewhere in Phuket. Stephen and Gareth had planned the holiday of a lifetime, but it was great to see Stephen with his brother. He was glad to see Stephen's smile.

Lydia and Jack had been arrested and were imprisoned for the murders of Chloe and Dana. Lydia was unable to live with the guilt and despite Jack's pleas to keep it quiet, they knew they'd never get away with what they'd done. Ben had read that they'd walked into a local police station and confessed to everything. Ben hoped that Lydia was able to cope.

He had read about the funerals of the other passengers. Edward, Mary, Nigel, Abigail, Gareth and Andrew. He had wanted to attend, but looking after his wife took precedence.

Ben said a prayer for each one. He'd felt guilty for what had happened, but Edward was too stubborn to listen. There was only so much Ben could do for them. He hoped if they met their maker, Edward and Abigail could be forgiven for the way they'd behaved.

On the drive home, Ben stopped off at the car wash, cleansing the last memories of Henry Mitchell.

He parked on the drive and stepped out of the car, then looked towards the front door.

He'd have to tell Laura. She'd find out. Ben didn't know how she'd take it but he was going to tell her.

He opened the front door as relief washed over him, knowing he'd never have to worry about Henry Mitchell again.

He climbed the stairs, keeping as silent as possible. As he entered the bedroom, he looked at the corpse of his wife in the bed.

He still couldn't understand why she'd taken her own life on the night she'd received the medal of honour. Laura had gone to bed early, swallowed pills and drank nearly a bottle of spirits.

Ben struggled to come to terms with what had happened.

When he'd found her body, lying in the bed, something broke inside him. His brain temporarily stopped functioning and he completely broke down.

Milly had been his rock. They were devastated, but they'd get through it. They had to look after each other.

She nursed him, made him see a doctor and booked appointments to talk to a professional. Ben was diagnosed with psychosis, a medical condition they said was probably brought on by stress and anxiety. He was given a course of antipsychotic medication. Milly waited until her father was able to function again. Ben was confused and suffered hallucinations but he convinced Milly he was feeling much better. The PTSD he suffered made the delusions more powerful. Ben was non-compliant to the medication and some days were better than others. He drank copious amounts of alcohol and took painkillers to conceal the hurt which as a result, added to his condition and the mental torment which he suffered.

At times, he believed he was Henry Mitchell.

The night Milly had left for university, he went to Laura's grave and dug her up.

He couldn't accept that his wife was dead and in his mind he saw her, thumping against the lid of the casket, screaming to get out.

He needed Laura back.

During the first days, when he'd brought her back here, Ben had sat on the bed, just like when she'd been in hospital.

Her body had started to swell and release putrid substances. The chemicals and gases emitted was something Ben struggled deeply with. The fumes made it difficult to breathe, but he was determined not to let it stop him from being with his wife. He sat on the bed, talking for hours, day after day, hoping she could still hear what he was saying.

Milly would be disgusted, but Ben hoped that somehow he could keep the bedroom door locked when she returned from university. If Milly found her mother, Ben hoped she could come to terms with what he'd done and somehow forgive him. After all, that's a lesson they've all learned.

Ben couldn't let Laura go.

Just like Henry and Evelyn, Ben was unable to deal with the thought of Laura being gone.

Ben left the bedroom and closed the door behind him. He walked along the upstairs hallway, needing a drink to help him relax. His head was working overtime with the events of the last hour, and he needed a quick relief before going to sleep.

He moved down the stairs and walked into the kitchen.

The radio was on as Ben made his way towards the fridge and grabbed a bottle of beer.

He listened as the local news bulletin started.

Ben heard the newsreader's deep voice as he started to talk.

'Police in Farnham are appealing for information this evening on the whereabouts of an elderly patient missing from Bourne Woods Care Home. Ethel Braithwaite, who suffers with dementia, was last seen at around 9pm when a nurse brought her water and found she was missing from her bed. Ethel is seventy-four, and the police are concerned for her safety.

'Ethel has long black hair and is wearing a white nightdress and brown slippers. She is considered extremely vulnerable. Police have asked anyone driving through Bourne Woods to take extra precautions and to call them if they see her. Police and locals are worried for her safety and want to find her as quickly as possible.

'On to other news now–'

Ben stood in the kitchen open-mouthed. He stared at the radio.

The beer bottle he was holding dropped to the tiled floor and smashed.

THE END

ACKNOWLEDGEMENTS

I have a few people to thank for helping me on my journey with Stranded.

Firstly, everyone who has bought the book, who has talked about it, shared my posts on social media and recommended it to a friend. You really don't know how much I appreciate it and the messages I get, which I will always, always respond to, brighten my day. So thank you all for that. I'm so incredibly lucky and proud to have so many wonderful reader friends, and for that, I am really grateful. You are amazing people, and an author's work is nothing without the love from readers and book bloggers. You are incredibly supportive, and I wouldn't be writing without your unbelievable support. We love book bloggers. You are amazing.

I'd like to give a special mention to Emma Louise Bunting, my pun partner and a great friend who picked the name, Stranded.

Thanks also to Sara Crean-Muir for your invaluable knowledge and expert insight into mental health. You are an amazing lady.

Thanks to Anthony Polden for all your help and input on the

coach industry. You have been so incredibly helpful, and as promised, a signed copy of Stranded is coming your way.

To Wendy Clarke, founder of The Fiction Cafe Book Club for the incredible work you do, how your support has changed the lives of so many. Thanks for everything. Our world would be missing something without these wonderful people and admin. In alphabetical order, Ellie Bell, Emma Louise Bunting, Emma Louise Smith, Jennifer Gilmour, Katy Dawson, Melanie Thomas, Michaela Balfour, Pam Chantrell and of course, Wendy Clarke.

Also, a big shout out to The Reading Corner Book Lounge on Facebook.

Danny Nicole and the admin are amazing.

Thanks to Mark Fearn, his page is so worth following. Book Mark. His reviews are always honest, and he posts the odd joke too.

I've also started a podcast with best selling author Keri Beevis. We have interviews with your favourite authors, ghost stories, unsolved mysteries, creepypastas and horror film reviews. You can find it by searching, Stu and Keri's reviews, news and interviews. We are bringing a new episode every Saturday. We'd love it if you could subscribe to the show.

Thanks also to Bloodhound Books for giving me the opportunity to tell my scary tales and to the most incredible editor I know, Clare Law.

That's it for now.

I'll have a few new books coming next year. 2021.

Find out the details on my website where you can also subscribe to my mailing list: stuartjamesthrillers.com

Facebook and Instagram: Stuart James Author.

Twitter: @StuartJames73

Printed in Great Britain
by Amazon